C000056291

MERCS

CRIMSON WORLDS
Successors I

Jay Allan

www.crimsonworlds.com

MERCS

ISBN: 978-0692354803

There is no avoiding war; it can only be postponed to the advantage of others.

\- Niccolo Machiavelli

Chapter 1

Outskirts of Petersburg
Planet Karelia, Gamma Hyrdus II
Earthdate: 2317 AD (32 Years After the Fall)

The sky was deep red, the last rays of late afternoon sun casting an eerie glow over the nightmare below. Pillars of black, acrid smoke rose from the clusters of dying buildings, like great shadowy towers reaching into the darkening sky. Many of the structures had been flattened in the fighting, others were still enduring their death agonies from the raging fires. The city was in flames, the fortunes of war turned harshly against her. The battle was all but over, lost by those who had lived there. But still, the dying continued.

Darius Cain stared across the narrow plain into the raging hell of Petersburg. He stood, motionless, his impassive face hidden behind the sealed helm of his battle armor. His life support system pumped fresh, clean air into his suit, but he imagined the stench outside, the smells of death and destruction that had followed man throughout his bloodsoaked history. Cain knew he was the ultimate incarnation of that violent history, the very manifestation of Mars, the god of war, standing on a small hill outside his command post, watching his soldiers win yet another crushing victory.

He stared at the columns in the distance, maneuvering

around the outskirts of the city in perfect formations, positioning themselves to cut off any enemy units retreating from the capital. The operation was running smoothly, almost as if they were on a parade ground and not a battlefield. He felt pride—in his soldiers, in his officers—in the job he had done turning a sea of outcasts into the best military outfit in Occupied Space.

Cain saw the ruin before him too, and he understood the almost incalculable human suffering he was watching. He knew his soldiers had done this, brought devastation and despair to this world, yet he felt nothing but cold satisfaction at a job well done. That is all he allowed himself to feel. Anything else would be weakness. And Darius Cain despised weakness.

There was no hatred in him for the people now fleeing for their lives, leaving all they had behind to the fires, seeking only to escape alive from the apocalypse that had come to claim them. Indeed, his soldiers would ignore the refugees as much as possible, targeting only their surviving military forces—and anyone who got in the way.

Yet there was no pity either, except perhaps a passing thought that would have no effect on his actions. The people now running before his relentless attack would blame his soldiers, curse the Black Eagles for their bitter fate, but Cain knew this day was one they had brought upon themselves. He had neither provoked nor escalated the conflict culminating in this battle. He had not continued it through constant rounds of petty escalation and provocation. This world's leaders had done that. They had placed their pride above the safety of their people, cast aside their duties in a reckless pursuit of power. No, Cain and his people had no responsibility for what had led to war. They were merely the instrument of its resolution.

Cain's profession was war, and he viewed it as such. He didn't lust for power, nor to see pliant populations bend their knees to him. But it was hard to excel at something if you allowed pointless guilt and lingering doubt to affect your judgment. And Darius Cain excelled at war. He was widely regarded as its greatest living practitioner, and he and his veterans had never tasted defeat.

Yesterday had begun normally for the people of Petersburg, he knew, filled with work and play, the mostly mundane joys and sorrows of a typical day. But the new dawn had brought horror unimagined upon them, as his ships brushed past Karelia's minimal orbital defenses, and his soldiers landed all around the capital city. His Black Eagles, hardened veterans all, equipped with the very best weapons and armor, sliced through the defenders almost immediately, capturing all their major objectives in a few hours. After that, it had just been a question of mopping up.

Cain knew there were thousands of enemy soldiers dead—and a good number of civilians too. It was unfortunate, but this was war, and it had its costs. He wasn't a bloodthirsty or sadistic man, but neither was he empathetic or merciful. He was cold, rational, driven. A professional in every way. He didn't crave battle, but when he saw it done, he saw it done well. And he didn't work for just anyone. Darius Cain wasn't an indiscriminate butcher, willing to simply kill for money. He took contracts only from employers who had legitimate grievances against their enemies. He didn't act as judge or jury, trying to discern good from evil. He merely demanded a reasonable dispute, one that would have led to war even in the absence of his irresistible legions. Analyzing deeper than that would be a waste of time. Cain didn't believe much in good, at least not in matters involving large groups of people. In most human interactions, he saw only varying degrees of evil. His view of mankind and the universe had made him what he was, and he'd never seen anything to dissuade him from his beliefs.

He knew the dirty truth of human history—that virtually all disputes were ultimately resolved through organized violence, whether warfare between nations or states turning their weapons loose on their own citizens. It was a reality historians refused to confront, but one proven by the facts nevertheless. He and his people actually saved lives, ending conflicts far more quickly than local conscript armies could hope to match. A surgical strike by the Eagles was brutal and violent, but it was almost always quick and decisive as well. In the end, years-long wars, bogged down in endless trench warfare and accompanied by famine and pestilence, were far worse than one of his lightning assaults.

It was a logic few people could understand, the inevitability of conflict, but he believed in it completely. Diplomacy had a poor record for creating permanent peace, and appeasement usually led to greater bloodshed when war finally came. Once he and the Eagles took a job, they didn't question the motives or rationale further. They simply ended the dispute, decisively and finally, shedding only as much blood as was necessary.

Once an operation began, he was indifferent to the destruction around him, to the untold suffering of the terrified masses running through the streets, fleeing the doom that had come upon them. Cain didn't subscribe to man-made standards of ethics and morality; he viewed them as constructs created to control people, the tools of those who would make themselves masters over men. Politicians, monarchs, religious leaders—throughout history they had been slavemasters and tyrants far more frequently than shepherds, and Darius Cain had never met the man he would call master.

Cain's religion was cold hard realism. This was the way things were, the way they had always been, and it served no point to whimper about the harshness of the universe. Idly wishing that things were different, that men were less wretched creatures, that they truly cherished peace and freedom as they so loudly proclaimed to, was a game for children—and the weak minded who knelt down before their overlords.

No man ruled over Darius Cain, nor would one ever. He would never be conquered, he had sworn that to himself long ago. He might be defeated one day, but he would die in

defiance, weapons in hand, defending his free will with his
last strength. Darius William Cain would never draw a single
breath as a slave. Not ever.

When he was younger, Cain had often tried to understand
people, to comprehend what caused most of them to behave
as sheep, to yield up their good sense and cast aside self-
preservation, to follow leaders blindly. But he'd long stopped
such fruitless efforts. This was all mankind was capable of, and
history offered ample proof to support that assertion.

The destruction on Karelia was the work of his soldiers,
but it wasn't they who had condemned this city. Indeed, the
Eagles were not the root cause of this devastation, nor even
could they have prevented it. If Cain had refused the contract,
one of the other companies would have taken it—and then
these people would have experienced the true horror that war
could become. The Eagles were professionals, an elite and
highly disciplined army, trained to a razor's edge by their iron-
willed leader.

Most of the other mercenary forces were barely disguised
packs of pirates—savages and brigands who too often enjoyed
inflicting horrors on the defeated. They were barbarians, who
lived for the pleasures of sacking a defeated city. The Eagles
were like surgeons. They did the job they were paid to do, and
nothing more. Cain's men would not run wild in an orgy of
rapine and looting. They would simply destroy the enemy's will
to resist and turn control of the planet over to their employer's
forces. How much destruction that required largely depended
on how long the enemy resisted before surrendering.

If the residents of Petersburg had anyone to blame for
their misfortune, it was themselves—and the inferior men
and women they had chosen to lead them. Cain's soldiers had
attacked this dying city, not out of enmity for the terrified and
suffering civilians, but because the actions of their leaders had
provoked an enemy. Not just any adversary, but one wealthy
enough to hire Darius Cain and the Black Eagles.

Petersburg's citizens were now paying the price for

electing corrupt and irresponsible leaders to rule over them. They had listened to empty promises, rallied behind elitist politicians who viewed them as little more than voting blocks, to be lied to and manipulated at will. And so it had gone on Karelia just as it had so many other places in Occupied Space, where a 30-year experiment in republican government had produced an elite class little better than that which had ruled the Earthly Superpowers.

Democracy, Cain thought, was something that worked in theory—but not so well in reality. The people tended to greedily claim the perquisites of their society while abandoning any responsibility to educate themselves or watch over and control those they put in power. They complained about the men and women in charge while repeatedly re-electing them. They sold their votes to any politician who offered to pay for it, usually with the wealth of those who voted for the opposition. They empowered a class to rule, formed from the most manipulative and rapacious among them. Now, on Karelia at least, they were paying the price for their foolishness.

This particular group of leaders, trying to create a crisis to further consolidate and increase their power, had picked a fight with the far wealthier Raschidans. They challenged their rivals for control of the Allagaran Asteroids and their vast mineral resources, and they captured and imprisoned Raschidan miners in a misguided show of strength. They whipped the population into a patriotic fervor and imposed a whole series of new laws and taxes, all in the name of planetary security. They branded those who resisted as traitors, as dangers to society and security, and they began to imprison them. The power of the ruling class increased sharply. Sitting minsters used the crisis to unilaterally extend their terms of office, cancelling elections and ramping up arrests of political opponents.

But the politicians, drunk on power and greed, had overplayed their hand, taken their brinksmanship too close to the edge—and the Raschidan Emir lost both his patience and

his temper. He hired Cain and his people to teach his enemies
a lesson. The citizens of Petersburg were now getting just
that—a hard tutorial in civic responsibility.

The rank and file, the line troops of the Black Eagles who
had won this fight, largely shared their commander's attitude
and demeanor. They did their duty with ruthless efficiency—
and little consideration to the politics and arguments of the
respective sides. They were cold-blooded and didn't allow
pity or sentiment to interfere with what had to be done. But
they committed no atrocities either, killed no more than the
completion of the operation required.

The Black Eagles were the most professional of the
mercenary companies, indeed, the most effective combat
force of any kind in human space. They fought for gain, for
wealth—and once they took a contract, they completed it, no
matter what it took. Most of them had come from the worst
hellholes in human space, and they had spent their entire lives
fighting one kind of struggle or another. For soldiers who had
come from slums where men killed for a crust of bread, war
held no shocking revelations. Death and danger had become
routine for them, horrors they had faced since childhood. It
was part of the job, nothing more.

Cain's eyes moved to the north of the city. A large
and unruly group of soldiers had caught his eye. They were
moving forward, looking more like a mob than a military
formation. He frowned. The Raschidans had sent a force to
take possession of the conquered world from Cain's people.
They were supposed to remain in orbit until he had declared
the planet secure, but their commander, jealous to lay claim to
some credit for the victory, had jumped the gun.

The Raschidans had just deployed, and already they had
made a mess of Cain's meticulous operation. The Emir's
warriors lacked the standards and code of the Eagles, and it
showed in their conduct. They ran wildly through the ravaged
city and the half-wrecked suburbs surrounding it, worked into
a lusty, uncontrolled fit of rape and pillage. They were already

drunk, most of them, and Cain wore a scowl of disgust when he considered their shoddy performance.

He didn't approve of the brutal sack of the city they initiated, nor of the unnecessary brutality, but what most offended him was these so-called soldiers allowing themselves to become so undisciplined and disorganized. War to him was a profession like any other, and as such, he expected it to be practiced with excellence and efficiency.

"It's a good thing we're here to destroy the rest of the Karelian forces for them." He spoke softly into the command comlink. "One decent counter-attack could bag their whole useless army." His voice was thick with disgust. *A few dozen of them will die even without an enemy attack—in the fires, too drunk to find their way out...*

Any soldier of his who behaved that way would do well to be lost in the conflagration. It would be a better fate than that which awaited him at Cain's hands. Darius Cain was idolized by his men, but not because he was easy on them. He disciplined them mercilessly, not hesitating to execute any who broke the code of conduct he had established. They loved him because he had taken them in as scum, the detritus of a hundred worlds, and he'd made them into the best, a legion of brothers and sisters feared everywhere men dwelt among the stars. It was his iron hand that had turned this group of refugees and misfits into the most respected warriors in human-occupied space.

Erik Teller stood next to Cain, looking out over the dying city. He sighed, the sound of his breath coming through the com slightly amplified. "You sound tempted." He snorted with an abortive laugh. "I don't imagine it would take us more than an hour." His voice was dripping with contempt for their allies and employers, just as Cain's had been. "Still, I suppose that would be a breach of contract, don't you think? The spirit of the agreement, at least. I'm not sure the document itself expressly forbids firing on the Raschidans."

Cain didn't respond right away; he just stared out over

the city and its environs. Finally, he turned toward his second-in-command—and only real friend. "I guess we need fools like this. If they had any idea how to fight a war, the Emir wouldn't be paying us 60% of his GDP to do it for him now, would he?"

"No," Teller replied. "I don't imagine he would." He paused, taking a quick look out over the field. "Speaking of which, the contract calls for us to capture Petersburg and reduce the enemy armed forces below 10% effectiveness." He turned and looked toward his friend and commander, though the gesture was a relatively pointless one in armor. "I think we're already there, but we will certainly be by dawn. That makes the final payment due."

"The Emir will pay." Cain sometimes wondered which of the two had affected the other more. They'd been friends for as long as either could remember, inseparable almost from birth. Cain was the colder of the two, at least in most circumstances. But Teller always knew to the milli-credit what they were owed and when it was due—and he had no patience for deadbeats or excuses. He'd made some truly horrifying threats against employers who'd tried to get out of making payments and, to date, no one had dared to call his bluff. Stiffing the Black Eagles took more courage than most politicians or petty dictators possessed.

"Send a message to Commodore Allegre. He is to send down the first retrieval wave at 0700 planetary time tomorrow." Cain had considered ordering his forces to break off immediately, but he was meticulous about meeting the terms of a contract. If the Eagles had agreed to a 90% degradation of Karelian combat capabilities, that is what they would deliver. "And order Vandeveer and Cornin to pursue any enemy military units that attempt to flee from the city. Two regiments should be enough to round up any holdouts by morning. I want the rest of the troops out of the city tonight. Raschid's toy soldiers will be running wild, and I don't want our people anywhere nearby when it happens."

"I'm on it, Darius." Teller's voice went silent. Cain knew his friend was switching channels on his com, sending out the orders.

He saw sudden movement off to the right, and his head snapped around instinctively. Half a dozen Raschidan soldiers were chasing someone. He'd seen a thousand incarnations of something similar and, while he didn't approve of such conduct, he knew it was part of war. But something caught his attention this time, and he cranked up his visor magnification to get a better look. It was a young woman running from the soldiers, and his eyes fixed on her the second she came into his view.

She looked to be in her early twenties. She was caked in mud and bleeding from a wound on her arm, but even so, Cain could see she was beautiful. Still, he wasn't one to be distracted from his work by a pretty face—or anything else she might have to offer. He had half a dozen mistresses back at base, and no taste for anything more binding than a night's passion. Indeed, he had multiple partners for just that reason, to prevent any problematic attachments or emotional baggage from developing.

Nevertheless, he found himself walking slowly down the hill, directly toward the approaching party. His eyes moved from the girl to her pursuers, and he quickened his pace. He knew what would happen when they caught her. The Raschidan animals would do it right on the ground, wherever they managed to take her down. And for some reason, Darius Cain decided to stop it.

"Darius, where are you going?" There was concern in Teller's voice. The Karelians hadn't put up much of a fight, but it was *still* a warzone.

"Just walking down here a bit," Cain replied, clearly distracted. "I'll be back."

Teller turned and gestured for Cain's guard to follow him. There were half a dozen on duty at any time, the pick of the Black Eagles. It was the one item on the organizational chart that Cain himself hadn't specified. The bodyguard had been Teller's idea, and he'd argued for it until Cain had gotten so sick of hearing about it, he'd agreed.

The heavily-armored soldiers trotted off down the hill after their commander. Two pushed forward, running ahead of Cain, while the others fell in around him. They carried their assault rifles at the ready, prepared to blast anything or anyone that threatened their commander.

Cain moved swiftly down the hillside. "Hold, you men," he yelled to the approaching Raschidans. The AI in his suit translated the command into the soldiers' native Arabic. They ignored him, and a few seconds later, he repeated the order. The AI translated again, but it failed to replicate the frigid threat embedded in Cain's tone.

"Who the hell are you?" one of them shouted back, still chasing the girl. "Go fuck your brother, mercenary. We are the Emir's men. This planet is ours now. And this woman is for us." The AI was translating for Cain as well, though multiple jobs done for former Caliphate colonies had given him a working knowledge of the language. His accent was terrible, so he rarely tried to speak it, but he was fairly adept at understanding what he heard.

Cain ran up the rest of the way, reaching the girl just as one of her pursuers managed to grab her and knock her to the ground. The Raschidan was worked up into a frenzy of rage and lust, and he barely paid attention to Cain, reaching down toward his victim and tearing at the simple dress she wore. He had it halfway down when Cain's armored hand grabbed him like a vice and tossed him three meters across the ground.

The others reacted, reaching for their guns. Cain's guards were faster, and two of the Rashidans burst into clouds of red mist, their bodies almost disintegrated by the hyper-velocity rounds of the Eagles' assault rifles. The others dropped their weapons and raised their hands, staring at the armored soldiers in abject terror.

Cain looked at the motionless soldiers, his eyes quickly

picking out the commander. "Now, who was that you wanted me to fuck?" His voice was like the cold of space itself, but the AI's translation spared the Raschidans the worst of it.

"I...we...are sorry. Sir?" The hapless soldier was guessing. The Eagles' suits were identical, from the lowliest rookie private to their general and commander-in-chief. Cain had never had the ego-driven need for fancy uniforms, and he saw no reason to give gifts to enemy snipers. He knew what his people did to enemy officers kind enough to advertise their presence on the field, and he had no desire to see that done to him—or any of his people.

Cain ignored the petrified soldier, and he knelt down next to the woman. She'd fallen hard, and it looked like her arm was broken. She'd been shot too, and while it didn't look life threatening, he was willing to bet it hurt like hell. He flipped the com to his guards' channel. "Get a med unit over here immediately. He toggled the com back to the external speaker. "Are you OK?" He could see she was in pain—and terrified as well. "Stay calm. No one is going to hurt you."

She turned and looked back up at him with hatred in her eyes. "Do you think I'm scared of you?" She spat at him. "You are murderers, barbarians. You only know death."

Cain let her continue her tirade. She was even more beautiful than she'd looked from a distance. "Yes, I am all those things, I suppose, but for right now I intend to help you." There was something about her that piqued his interest. He had just saved her from being gangraped and probably murdered, but she'd launched right at him with all the piss and vinegar she could muster. There was little Cain respected more than courage, and this young woman seemed to have more than her share.

"Is that why you came here? To help?" She leapt toward him and slammed her fist into his armor, recoiling in pain as she did.

He waved off his guards, who he thought just might shoot her when she moved toward him. "My armor is extremely tough. I wouldn't do that again." He glanced up at his tactical display, watching the med team approaching. "I'll make a deal with you, though. My medics are going to take you back to one of our field hospitals so we can do something about that gunshot wound and that broken arm." He smiled, though his armor hid it. "Go along with them quietly and, later, I'll give you another shot once I'm out of my armor."

"No," she yelled. "I can't go. I have to find my sister. She's alone in the city."

Cain imagined her staggering through burning ruins, wounded and in pain, but refusing to give up the search. His admiration grew. This woman was no pathetic sheep, like most of her fellow Karelians. "You're never going to find her. You'll just end up dead somewhere in the middle of the chaos." He gestured toward one of his guards. "But I will send this man with you to the hospital. Tell him about your sister—her description, where you last saw her…everything. And I will send a company of soldiers to find her and get her out."

She stared at him, her expression a mixture of contempt and confusion. "Why would I trust you?"

He stared down at her, though he knew all she could see was the bright reflective plate of his visor. "Because you seem like a realistic woman…and I'm the only thing you've got right now. And I have no reason to lie to you. There is nothing you have that I couldn't take right now. Nothing I couldn't make you do. But I am just going to see that your wounds are treated…and send a party out to find your sister." He waved toward his guard, flipping his com unit as he did. "Sergeant, accompany this woman to the aid station. Get as much information about her sister as you can, and dispatch a special ops team into the city to find her."

"Sir!" The guard spun around and gestured to the med team, pointing toward the woman.

Cain watched as the medics moved to pick her up and lay her on the stretcher. She stared at them suspiciously, but she didn't resist. The gurney had been designed to carry a fully-armored soldier, and she looked tiny laying in the middle.

"They won't hurt you," he called to her. "And tell the sergeant everything you can about your sister. My people will find her for you." He paused then added, "What is your name?"

"Ana," she replied, her tone still bitter, but now also confused. "Ana Bazarov."

He watched as the medical team carried her away then he turned back toward the Raschidan soldiers. His normally clear mind was clouded with anger. *Ana Bazarov*, he thought, the image of her face lingering in his mind.

"What shall we do with them, sir?" The commander of his guard stood at attention. The Raschidans hadn't moved. They cowered under the guns of his troopers.

Cain stared at the pathetic creatures. They had dropped their weapons and given themselves up. But the image of them pursuing Ana was still in his mind. They were creatures, and if he let them go they would just torment and kill more civilians. He imagined what they had been about to do to Ana, and anger coursed through his body.

Ana Bazarov.

"Kill them," he said coldly. Then he turned and walked away.

*   *   *   *   *

"Let's move. If we catch them at the river, we'll bag the entire force. And then we can all take a nice leisurely ride back to the ship." Sergeant Reaves was jogging along, shifting from side to side to keep from launching himself into the air. His armor magnified his own strength exponentially, and a slow jog would bounce him 5 or 10 meters up if he wasn't careful. That was bad news on a battlefield, where it tended to make you a target for every bogie within half a klick. *Not that any of this bunch is likely to shoot straight enough to pick me off.* It was the general opinion of the regiment—and the rest of the Eagles, he'd bet—that these Karelians were just about the worst fucking soldiers they'd ever seen.

Still, if General Cain had drilled one thing into their heads, it was *always be careful!* The worst half-assed toy soldier in Occupied Space could scrag your ass if you let your guard down, and none of the Eagles wanted to be some other fool's lucky shot.

The whole section was moving quickly. The Karelians were unarmored, and there was no way they could outrun the Eagles. With Reaves' section on the left, and Dolan's on the right, there was nowhere for the refugees to run but straight for the river. And they'd never get across before they were captured. Or wiped out—that would be their choice.

The ground beyond Petersburg was mostly lowland plains, boggy in a few places, and wide-open everywhere. There was no place to hide, no way to even try to evade pursuit. The whole thing was a waste of time. If the damned Karelians would just surrender instead of trying to run, they might make it back to their families. If they insisted on putting up a fight, Reaves knew his troops would wipe them out in a heartbeat. His people just wanted to wrap up the operation; they weren't out for blood. This was a job to them, nothing more. But the Karelians were so scared shitless, they probably expected the Eagles to massacre them.

Reaves' best guess was they were chasing eighty enemy troops, maybe a hundred tops, one of three or four forces that size the enemy still had in the field, all that was left from maybe 5,000 half a day earlier.

"We're half a klick from the river," he snapped into his com. "Squad B, push forward and make contact with the water. When you get there, turn and start moving in. I want one team on point, the other in support 500 meters back." He looked out in the direction of the enemy. "Squad A, with me.

We're going to move in slowly at an angle and link up with B Squad's forward team."

It was dark now, and visibility was for shit. Karelia didn't even have a moon, and the starlight was next to useless. It was only a minute or two before Squad B disappeared into the darkness.

"Corporal Weed, pop a recon drone. I want to know where these fuckers are. Exactly."

"Yes, sir."

Reaves knew Corporal Weed thought it was a waste of an expensive piece of hardware—and their cuts would be calculated after the costs of the expedition were deducted—but he didn't care. Better safe than sorry, and if it saved one of his troopers it was worth ten times the cost. Besides, General Cain had charged a king's ransom for this job, and they all stood to make a pretty pile for a battle that looked like it wouldn't last longer than a day.

A few seconds later, Reaves heard the popping sound of the drone's engine igniting, and the watermelon-sized device shot off into the night sky, leaving a trail of fire and smoke in its wake.

"Alright, let's move." He pushed forward, his pace slow and cautious now. "Drone input to my display," he snapped to his AI. An instant later, a handful of small gray ovals appeared on the inside of his visor—the Karelian troops, exactly where they were supposed to be. And something else too. "Sergeant Ving, what do you make of…"

His com unit crackled with feedback. "Outside jamming has interdicted all communications, Sergeant." The cool, even voice of his AI reported before he could even ask.

"Increase power to the com." Reaves had his assault rifle in hand, and a quick glance around confirmed his troopers were on alert as well.

"Negative, Sergeant," the AI responded. "Your power plant in incapable of producing sufficient power to override the jamming."

"But that's impossible…" Reaves' voice trailed off. *What the hell is going on?*

"It is unlikely, certainly, given all intelligence regarding Karelian military capabilities, however the fact that we are indeed being jammed proves it is possible."

Reaves opened his mouth, but he closed it again without saying anything. He'd argued with his overly literal AI more than once, and he knew it was the very definition of futility. He had more important things to worry about now. Like who the hell was jamming his com.

"Open visor," he snapped to the AI. An instant later there was a loud popping sound, and the front of his helmet retracted. Mission parameters called for closed suits even with breathable atmospheres. The protocol protected against radiation and undetected chemical and biological weapons, but right now Reaves had to communicate with his people.

He gestured, moving around to show them all his open helm. One by one they popped their visors and moved in closer.

"What is happening, sir? Can this be the Karelians?" Ving was the first to ask what they were all thinking, and the rest stayed quiet and listened. The Eagles were too disciplined to start talking over each other.

"I don't know, but I don't like it." He turned toward the section's scout. "Corporal Kyle, go after B Squad. I want them back here ASAP." Reaves didn't know what was going on, but he didn't like it. Not one bit. And he wanted his people all together.

"Sir!" the scout replied, and he turned and disappeared into the inky blackness.

"I want everybody on alert." He moved his head, looking at each of his soldiers in turn. "We don't know what's going on, but I'm betting it's not good…so nobody gets surprised, you got me?"

There was a chorus of yessirs, and the troopers turned outward, staring off into the darkness, rifles in hand.

Reaves squinted, trying to see anything at all in the direction of the enemy. His eyes darted up to his display, but the jamming had knocked out scanning too. He felt a chill, a cold sweat dripping down the back of his neck. It was quiet, almost eerily so, and he couldn't see anything. *Something's out there*, he thought, straining to listen for anything at all. *They're not jamming us for nothing.*

He heard a shot, and an instant later he spun around to see Ving down, a hole the size of a grapefruit in his chest. "We're under attack," he shouted, almost instinctively. Then all hell broke loose.

Chapter 2

"The Cape"
Planet Atlantia, Epsilon Indi II
Earthdate: 2288 AD (3 Years After the Fall)

Erik Cain walked silently up the stone steps from the beach. It was deep into the long Atlantian night, and he hadn't slept at all. Not for the first time, he wondered about the wisdom of an insomniac settling on a world where night was a good hour and a quarter longer than on Earth. Cain's sleeping problem was nothing new, though it had gotten worse over the years. It was just one of the wounds from a lifetime spent at war, one he suspected he would carry to his grave.

He'd taken to going on long walks at night. Atlantia's Cape District was one of the most beautiful areas he'd ever seen on any of the planets he'd visited. The coast was long and rocky, with small outcroppings perched between white, sandy beaches. Atlantia's single continent was shaped like a multi-pronged star, with a series of long, winding archipelagoes extending hundreds of kilometers into the planet's great ocean. It was the closest thing to a perfect place Cain could imagine, and when he'd chosen Atlantia as his new home, he'd hoped he would find the calm and peace he craved. But his demons had followed him, even into paradise.

Cain wondered if there came a time when a man had

simply seen too much evil, too much death. When he'd looked into the eyes of too many friends and watched them slip away, pouring their lifeblood into the sands of an alien world. When he'd held the hands of grizzled veterans as they breathed their last, and pimply-faced kids trying to hold their guts in with bloodsoaked fingers. Cain had enough material for a lifetime of nightmares.

He looked up at the moonless vista above, hypnotized as he often was by the sheer beauty of the night sky. He'd made a hobby of identifying the stars visible from Atlantia's northern hemisphere, but even that small joy had been marred when he realized half a dozen of them had planets on which he'd fought. He'd been surprised how many of his battlefields were visible with the naked eye.

His lost comrades sometimes visited him on his walks, though tonight they had been silent. Cain had a few surviving brothers in arms too, James Teller and Augustus Garret among them, but he had buried most of his friends. Darius Jax, Elias Holm, Terrance Compton, William Thompson—the list was long. And he felt guilt about surviving too, always asking himself the question, "Why am I alive, when they all died?" Cain didn't wish that a bullet had found him on one of his battlefields—it was a far more complex feeling than that. He was grateful he had survived, but there was a loneliness to it he sometimes found almost unbearable.

He took a deep breath and listened to the sound of the waves crashing against the shore. It was one of the few things he found truly relaxing, and he often sat out on the rocky point and listened for hours. It didn't put him to sleep, but it did quiet the inner turmoil, at least a bit. He sat for a few minutes, breathing deeply, savoring the cool ocean air. It was a couple hours before dawn, and generally, if he was going to get any sleep at all, that was when it came. Especially after a bracing walk in the cool night air. He was just about to head back when he heard soft footsteps on the gravel pathway.

"Out here again?" Sarah walked up behind him, putting

her hand gently on the back of his neck as she so often did. "I'm starting to think I've lost my appeal. It's getting harder and harder to keep you in bed." She smiled and sat down next to him on the low stone wall. "I understand," she said teasingly. "I'm as big as a house."

He returned her smile. After all the years they'd been separated, thrust in different directions through decades of brutal warfare, she was the one thing in his life that had never changed. Both Marines, they had been compelled by duty to answer the bugle first and foremost. But even when they'd been apart for years, the instant they were reunited, it was as if no time at all had passed. She was the one good thing that had come from his life at war. She'd been his doctor, and she had somehow managed to put him back together after he'd strayed recklessly close to a nuclear explosion. He often wondered what his life would be like without her, how lost and alone he would feel.

"I'm sorry if I woke you. You should be asleep." He looked at her and smiled again. "Especially now."

Sarah leaned back, stretching uncomfortably. She was pregnant—very, very pregnant. Indeed, she was due any day. Erik had tried to take her to the hospital in Eastport for a scheduled delivery a few days before, but she'd nixed that idea and declared that she would have the babies—she was carrying twins—when they came naturally. It was hard to argue a medical matter with the best trauma surgeon in the history of the Corps, but that didn't mean he didn't try. But Sarah was one of the few people who had ever been able to get her way in a debate with Erik Cain. Over twenty-five years together, she hadn't prevailed in every struggle, certainly—nothing close. But she'd won her share, including this one.

Indeed, when they'd decided to have children, her medical colleagues had expected her to artificially inseminate and use an AI-controlled crèche to carry the child to term. As a Marine on reserve status, she had access to state of the art healthcare. But she'd shot that idea down immediately, declaring she was going to do this old style—every step of the way. She was fifty-eight years old, but the Corps' program of rejuv treatments had slowed the aging process throughout her adult life, and she was the physical equivalent of a healthy, fit woman in her mid-thirties.

After a quarter century of almost non-stop war, Sarah had declared her intent to slow down and experience a life that didn't involve constant stress and bload-soaked rituals under the harsh lights of the operating room. She'd seen enough shattered men and women to last a lifetime, and then some. All she wanted now was to live like a normal Atlantian, a peaceful life by the sea, with a family she could hold onto. Erik knew her memories of childhood were as nightmarish as his own, and he was determined that she would finally have the peace she craved.

"I'd never have married you if sleeping through the night was that important to me." She laughed softly.

Cain looked at her and smiled. They'd been together twenty-five years when they'd finally gotten married. Erik hadn't cared one way or another. He intended to spend the rest of his life with her, and that was all that mattered. Most rituals and social customs meant very little to him. Cain judged people on their actions and behaviors, and he placed almost no value in society's artificial constructs. But many of the colony worlds, newly freed from the yoke of their parent Superpowers, had begun to revive old social customs, and Sarah was determined to become a normal Atlantian any way she could.

Their wedding had been a simple affair, with only a few friends. General Gilson had wanted to bring them to Armstrong so the Corps could host a massive celebration, but they had politely refused. Cain's thoughts were already on empty chairs, places where old friends should have been, but weren't. He had a way of seeking out the dark side of even the happiest occasions, and he didn't want to feed that tendency. In the end, it had been a good day, and virtually everyone Erik and Sarah cared about had come.

"Well, you certainly knew what you were getting by then."
He leaned back and closed his eyes. She had her hand on the
side of his neck. Her touch still had the same effect on him,
even after thirty years, driving away the demons, at least for a
little while.

"I certainly did." She smiled for an instant, and then her
eyes widened and she moaned softly. She put her hands on her
belly and turned and looked over at Erik. "Ah, not to interrupt
the conversation…but, in my expert medical opinion…it is
time…"

Cain leapt to his feet. "I knew we should have had you in
the hospital," he stammered, putting his hand on her arm and
leading her up the path. He was nervous, tense. His combat
reflexes were responding, and he could feel the adrenalin
pumping through his blood. "Let's go."

She laughed softy. "Relax, General Cain. This isn't a
Marine operation. People have been managing this for a long
time." She turned and walked slowly back toward the house.

Erik followed closely behind. Through all the years at
war, he had never imagined this day would come. In a few
hours he would be the father of twin boys. He thought
about what they would be like, who they would become. He
imagined many men dreamed of their sons following in their
footsteps, but that was Cain's worst nightmare.

Please, he thought. *Let them be doctors or scientists or
engineers…or let them drive a truck. But not a life of war, a life like
mine. Anything else.*

*   *   *   *   *

Augustus Garret stared out the viewscreen. *Pershing* was a
mighty vessel, a testament to the herculean efforts men could
put into war. And she had served well, in the struggle against

the First Imperium, and later against Gavin Stark's Shadow
Legions. His eyes were fixed, his mind lost in old memories,
as he bid a final farewell to the vessel that had been his last
flagship.

He knew three of her sister ships were out there too,
but they were too far away for him to see with the naked eye.
It was a fluke that *Pershing* was the closest to the station, but
Garret was grateful for a last look at her.

"Saying goodbye, Augustus?" The voice was familiar, and
Garret turned abruptly.

"Yes, I suppose. In my own way." Garret nodded to
Roderick Vance. "I want to thank you for your help with this,
Roderick. "There's nowhere else we could do this, at least no
place secure enough."

Vance looked out the viewscreen toward the hulking
battleship. "They were a great design. Even after we built
Sword of Mars and John Carter, I always thought ton for ton
the Yorktowns were the toughest warships ever built."

Roderick Vance was the head of the Martian
Confederation's spy services, and a member of its ruling
council. He'd been an ally to Garret and the rest of the
Alliance military for some time, though less so with the Earth-
based Superpower itself. In the years of warfare leading up
to the final battle, the Alliance's navy and Marine Corps had
grown into quasi-independent organizations, as answerable to
the colonies as to the Earth government.

None of that mattered now. The Alliance was gone,
along with all the other Earth-based Superpowers, consumed
in the disastrous nuclear finale of their last war. Earth
was a ruined planet, poisoned, radioactive, its cities utterly
obliterated. Vance's people had estimated that 90% of the
population had died over a 36 hour period of intense atomic
warfare, a figure that had left Garret speechless the first time
he'd heard it.

It was almost impossible to account for the further losses
from sickness, starvation, and fighting that had occurred in the

three years since, but the best estimate was one to two percent of the pre-war population was still alive—fifty to one hundred million people scattered around the globe, eeking out some type of marginal existence. But no one thought that would be the final figure. The population was almost certainly still declining, and only the wildest guesses could be made about the long term effects of radiation exposure on longevity and fertility. An entire population was difficult to eradicate, but Earth was still teetering on the edge.

"I just wish we could keep more of your fleet in space. Everybody is fought out right now, but we both know there will be new disputes." Vance's voice was sincere. He'd been an unemotional man when Garret had first met him, almost robotic in his demeanor, but the sacrifices of the last few years had changed him, and the former Alliance admiral could feel the empathy—and the pain—in his friend.

"Well, you can't afford that now, any more than we can. Mankind took it to the edge, and now we need to scale back. I don't think two-kilometer long battleships are necessary for prosperity and economic growth, and without any Superpowers to fight, they are an extravagance we simply can't afford." Garret felt torn. He was disgusted that humanity had fought one war after another, building ever greater engines of destruction to hurl at each other. That side of him welcomed the drastic reductions in armaments compelled by the destruction of Earth's industry. The colonies couldn't come close to supporting on their own the vast military organizations the terrestrial powers had built.

But he himself was a creature of those wars. His career, his fame, even his own image of self-worth was tied up in the persona of the great Admiral Augustus Garret. He had sacrificed everything to his duty, and now he had nothing else. War had been his life. That didn't make him proud, but he couldn't deny it. He'd been busy seeing to the downsizing of the massive war machine he had led, but he wondered what would happen when he was done. Would there would be a place for him with no war to fight?

Vance sighed. "That may be true, but we certainly can't build anything like this anymore...and I suspect it will be a long time before we have that kind of capacity again." His eyes narrowed, and his voice deepened, became more serious. "And we both know there are greater dangers out there than colonial disputes."

Garret nodded. He knew, perhaps better than any living being. Man's first contact with another species had been disastrous. The war against the First Imperium had been a holocaust, and humanity had only escaped destruction by the barest margin. But the enemy was still out there, somewhere, and it was only a matter of time before they returned. And no one knew what other horrors existed in the depths of unexplored space. But, whatever was out there, men like Garret and Vance were determined to be ready.

"It was hard to convince some of the other officers, but I finally managed it. The First Imperium put a hell of a scare into them, and it hasn't worn off yet." *No surprise there...those robot legions were the closest thing I've ever seen to a nightmare from hell.* "None of them could argue we didn't need to be ready. Besides, they were all facing the same option—scrapping the ships instead of entrusting them to your care. Still, there is much suspicion, even between allies. Most former Alliance officers don't like the idea of 'giving away' our most powerful ships."

Garret had led humanity's united forces against the First Imperium, and in the aftermath of the final battle on Earth, he'd gathered the naval commanders of the former Superpowers to a summit meeting. Even after the horrendous losses of the final war, they had far more vessels than the economic output of the colonies could support. And the political bonds between those worlds were rapidly dissolving. Without the oppressive Earth governments, planets were declaring independence everywhere. The surviving military forces were quickly finding themselves without nations to serve.

It had taken weeks of debate and negotiation, but Garret was still a larger than life figure, renowned by all as the man who had saved humanity from the First Imperium. He had always been uncomfortable with the share of credit he'd been given for a victory won by the sacrifice of thousands of men and women, but he was a master tactician, and he didn't hesitate to use the adoration to gain acceptance for his plan. In the end, he'd won widespread approval, and it was agreed that hundreds of mothballed vessels—battleships, cruisers, destroyers—would be stored on the Martian moon of Phobos, a reserve against the day when all mankind would again face the prospect of doom at the hands of an alien enemy.

It was an ideal location. The Sol system was deep in human-controlled space, insulated from any hostile future contact. Mars was the last Superpower, and though the destruction of her four largest cities late in the war made her power a shadow of what it once had been, she still wielded far greater strength than any of the colony worlds. The Martians could defend the stored vessels, ensure that no rogue parties took control of them. Though the Confederation had sided openly with Garret and the Alliance Marines in the last war, her history had been one of cautious neutrality. The Confederation was the natural choice to be custodian of mankind's surplus weaponry.

"I will do everything in my power to keep all of this safe, Augustus. And ready." Vance sighed softly. "For the day we need it again." There was sadness in his voice, but not a shred of doubt that day would come.

*   *   *   *   *

"Three days isn't much of a honeymoon, is it?" Jarrod Tyler was sliding his neatly folded clothes into a small duffle bag. The room was pleasant, a small bungalow on one of the tropical islets that dotted Columbia's equatorial zone. Tyler had known Lucia his entire life, but it had been much more recently he'd realized he loved her—and even less time since he'd discovered she reciprocated his feelings.

"Indeed it is, my love, but duty calls. A soldier like you should know that. The election is less than three months from now, and I can't spend my days basking in the sun while Walker and his people slander me mercilessly, now can I?" She lifted her head and gave him a warm smile. The sun had lightened her normally dark brown hair, and her nose and forehead were dotted with pink, peeling skin. Three days in Columbia's searing equatorial sun had certainly been enough to give her a sunburn.

"Like you can lose. I'm not even sure why that fool is running against you." Lucia had been the president of Columbia before the final war against the Shadow Legions. She'd yielded her powers to Tyler, in accordance with the crisis provisions in the planetary constitution, and the erstwhile general—now her husband—in turn yielded his dictatorial mantle as soon as the enemy was defeated. Lucia had spent most of the past two years struggling to hasten the recovery of her battered world. Indeed, even her wedding had been delayed, continually postponed to make way for her herculean workload.

"You can always lose, my love. Neither one of us should ever forget that." Her voice was pleasant, teasing, but there was a nugget of seriousness there too.

"What were you up in the last poll? Forty points?"

"Forty-one," she replied. "But people are fickle, Jarrod. A smart politician takes nothing for granted."

Tyler made a face. He detested politicians with a roiling passion. He'd never thought of Lucia as one, but of course that was foolish. She'd been a politician for years, and an enormously successful one at that. And one of the very few he'd ever seen who always seemed to stay focused on the good of the people and not the accumulation of personal power. He couldn't imagine the population turning on a leader like that, not when most of the others were corrupt and focused on their own political gain above all things.

He glanced down at the chronometer on his wrist. "You don't have anything scheduled until tomorrow, right?"

"No," she said, some confusion in her tone. "Why?"

"Well…" He moved quickly across the room. "I thought maybe you could squeeze in a small—very small—political rally down here…"

"On this island?" She stared at him questioningly.

"In this room." He slid up behind her and slipped his arms around waist. "After all, you will be wanting my vote, won't you? How do you plan to earn it?"

She turned her head and leaned back. "Oh, so is that how it is?" She leaned back into him, a wry smile on her face. "Well, I suppose I can spare twenty minutes for a loyal voter."

He pulled her closer and kissed the back of her neck softly.

"Ok, ok," she said softly. "An hour."

Chapter 3

Outskirts of Petersburg
Planet Karelia, Gamma Hyrdus II
Earthdate: 2317 AD (32 Years After the Fall)

"With all due respect, General Akeem, over fifty of my Eagles are missing, and contract or no contract, we are not leaving until I know what happened to them." Cain stared at the Raschidan officer, not even trying to mask his contempt.

"General Cain, while I understand your forces suffered some unanticipated casualties, may I point out that your losses for the entire campaign were still extremely light. Perhaps this platoon was careless in rounding up the Karelian stragglers and was taken by surprise and wiped out." Akeem had an irritating voice, and it wasn't doing anything to improve Cain's mood.

Cain stared back at the Raschidan commander with molten eyes. *Careful, you inbred piece of rat shit.* "My soldiers are not careless, General." Cain saw Akeem twitch uncomfortably, an irritated look crossing his face. *You want me to call you Lord Akeem, but that is never going to happen, asshole.* "There is something unexplained here, and I have no intention of going anywhere, not while there is the slightest chance my troopers are alive." He paused. "That is to your benefit, as well, since you will have to administer Karelia when we do leave." *And anything that can wipe out fifty of my people can obliterate half of your pathetic little army.*

Cain could see Akeem was fighting to control his anger. He'd have found the whole thing laughable if he hadn't been so focused on his lost platoon. If Akeem decided to bet that he was untouchable, the pompous ass was in for a rude awakening. Cain would drop the Raschidan general in a heartbeat, and the Emir would accept his utterly insincere regrets before he'd make an enemy out of the Black Eagles. *Skulk back to your headquarters, Akeem…stay alive.*

"But fifty soldiers?" Akeem sounded genuinely confused as well as annoyed. "I cannot imagine what your continued operation is costing." He paused. "The planet is pacified. Per the contract, we are no longer responsible for your expenses. Why would you remain here at such cost over fifty soldiers?"

Cain felt a rush of anger, but it was quickly overwhelmed by disgust. Akeem wasn't worth his rage. "I do not expect you to understand this, Akeem, but I do not place a monetary value on my soldiers' lives. Death in battle is a hazard of our trade, but when I lose Eagles, I know why. Always. And there is something going on here that I do not understand. Yet." There was a cold edge to his voice, a non-verbal message. *Get the hell out of my headquarters. Now.*

Akeem didn't look satisfied, but he took the hint. "I will be in my command post," he grunted, and he turned and walked away.

Cain was already ignoring the Raschidan commander. He was deep in thought, going over everything he knew about the missing platoon. They'd been approaching the river when they had last reported in. A few minutes later, the command post lost their signals. Something must have jammed their com, because there had been no warning, nothing. One instant their transponders were relaying their locations per normal procedure, and the next they were gone. And by the time the scouting party arrived to investigate, there was nothing left but a few scattered signs of fighting.

The Karelians didn't have anything like jammers that

powerful. If they had, they'd have used them in Petersburg where they could have seriously messed with his forces. Even if he considered the possibility that it was a Karelian force that had attacked his Eagles—something that still didn't pass the smell test—they had used weapons and equipment he knew damned well the locals didn't possess. No matter how he looked at it, there was tech at play that had come from someplace else, even if Karelian soldiers had pulled the triggers.

"Erik!" he called out to the anteroom. "You out there?"

"Here, General." Teller came rushing through the door. He rarely used rank when addressing Cain, usually calling his childhood friend by his first name. But the Raschidan commander had just left, and Teller was always crisp and proper around Cain in front of outsiders. The less trusted the visitor, the more formal he was. And Erik Teller trusted Abdullah Akeem as much he did an Arcadian hill viper.

"Erik, I want more search parties out there. I want every square meter from Petersburg to the river scoured. There is something strange going on."

"I'll give the orders, Darius." Teller turned to walk back out.

"And Erik?"

Teller spun around again. "Darius?"

"I want patrol sizes tripled. Whatever is out there, I don't want any more of our people getting picked off."

Teller nodded and trotted out the door.

Cain stood for a few minutes, staring at the spot his friend had occupied. He had a bad feeling. Something was going on. He had no idea what it was, not even a clue. But something in his gut told him it was bad. And that it was just beginning.

*   *   *   *   *

"How are you feeling?" Cain knelt down next to the cot. The field hospital was quiet. There were perhaps half a dozen beds occupied, but the Eagles' losses had been mercifully light, and most of the med staff were wandering around without much to do. The Karelians were amateur soldiers, outmatched and outgunned, and few of their weapons could even hurt the heavily-armored Eagles.

He was still clad in his fighting suit, but the helmet was fully retracted. He suspected he was a mess. A few days in battle armor tended to make one less than presentable. It was a common joke that a powered infantry soldier would trade a campaign's worth of plunder for a hot shower. It was an exaggeration, of course, but there was a kernel of truth to it—as anyone who had ever smelled a landing bay after a long battle could attest.

Cain spent a considerable amount of time in his hospitals. He had a habit of moving too far forward, at least in the opinion of Erik Teller, and he'd been wounded himself five times in the nine years since he'd fielded his first force of Eagles. But mostly he came to visit his soldiers. The men and women who served under his banner knew he enforced iron discipline, that he expected them to follow his orders with the last bits of strength they possessed. They understood that his justice was harsh and often brutal, but they knew one other thing too. That he watched over them like a father. The Eagles didn't leave their own behind, and wounded troopers could expect the best possible medical care. And they also knew they would see their leader walking the aisles of their hospitals, checking on them, making sure they had all they needed.

But this time he was there to see someone else, an outsider. Someone who had affected him oddly, who had been on his mind since he'd first set eyes on her. Outside of his Eagles—and his enemies—Darius Cain tended to ignore and forget those he met, but not this time. He stopped at one of the hospital's cots and looked down at the occupant.

Ana Bazarov glared back at him, her blue eyes glittering with rage. "Is this a sick game of some kind? You bring your butchers here to kill my people then you take me to your hospital and heal me?" She was lying back, propped up on a pair of pillows, a light sheet stretched over her.

She spoke English, which was a surprise. Karelia's original settlers had been ethnic Russians, and few spoke anything but their native tongue. Cain's interest grew. She had a heavy accent, one he found oddly appealing. He felt a smile trying to force its way onto his face, but he held it back. He didn't think it would be well received.

He'd been strangely distracted when he'd first seen her, but now he realized she'd been injured more severely than he had thought. It looked like she had broken bones in both her arm and leg, as well as half a dozen lacerations. Her breaks and cuts had been fused, and wrapped in sterile dressings. He suspected she was sore as hell, but she'd be up and around in a couple days, and back to normal in a week.

He paused for a few seconds, his eyes moving from bandage to bandage. Cain was normally indifferent to collateral damage in war, but he found himself feeling regret for her suffering. He wondered if the Eagles had caused any of her wounds. Certainly none of his people had assaulted her directly, but bombardments were indiscriminate things, and bystanders were killed and injured all the time. He'd never tried to calculate how many civilians his people had killed in their operations. He'd never cared. But now he realized it must have been thousands. Tens of thousands.

"No, it is most certainly not a game," he said softly. "But it was your government's actions that brought this down on your world. At least they shared in the responsibility. My Eagles were merely the instrument used. I can assure you, this would have been much worse for your people had it been any other force sent here. Indeed, it was a group of Raschidan soldiers who were pursuing you, and mine who rescued you. Perhaps you see some meaning in that fact?"

He was hoping to reach her, but she just scowled at him. "Rescued me for what? To be your slave, your spoil of war instead of theirs? Her voice was heavy with disgust—and fear she was clearly trying to hide—but her eyes remained fixed. She was scared and angry, but she wouldn't look away.

"Well, you are technically my captive, I guess, but I can assure you that no harm will come to you under my stewardship. Indeed, you are safer in my custody than you would be anywhere else on Karelia right now." He paused then added, "Nothing approaching slavery, and certainly not a… how did you put it? Spoil of war?"

"Why would I believe anything you say? If I am not your slave then let me go."

Cain admired her spirit, even if it was mostly directed toward hating him at the moment. "I am not even sure you can stand right now, but I am positive that you wouldn't get a hundred meters before you collapsed. The Raschidans have taken over the city, and I am afraid their conduct is less than admirable. I would hate to see you end up victimized by another group of drunken looters." He allowed a fleeting smile. "So, let's say that you will accept my hospitality for now, at least until you are healed. Then we will discuss your status."

She nodded but didn't respond right away. The hatred in her gaze had faded for an instant, but then it flared back with renewed intensity. "So, I am safe here with you…while people all over the city are raped and robbed and murdered—by the animals you placed in power."

"I'm afraid the Raschidans are not my concern. My people have completed their part of the operation. We have some…ah…unexpected business to attend to, or we would have departed already." He saw the anger in her eyes, and he knew what she was thinking. *My soldiers could stop the sack of the city, restore order. Perhaps, but we cannot change the ways of the universe. In the end, these people had made an enemy and allowed themselves to be conquered. Vae Victus. Woe to the defeated. It is how things have always been, and protestations to the contrary are nothing but lies. Perhaps she thinks I like it, the suffering, the destruction—that I want things to be as they are. But it is not my choice, Ana Bazarov. It is inevitable, like storms and earthquakes. Mankind's eternal curse.*

He kept his thoughts to himself. He'd found people were rarely prepared to accept the universe as it truly was, preferring to exist under varying levels of self-delusion. Cain had never seen a use for anything but cold realism, but now he found himself hesitating. He normally didn't care what people thought, but he found that he didn't want Ana to view him as a cold-blooded monster.

"But I can promise that you will remain safe." He turned back toward the entrance. "Sergeant," he yelled. "And I have something else for you as well," he said, looking back at her. He watched her reaction, confusion at first then shock.

"Tatyana," she squealed. She threw her arms out, wincing at the pain as she did.

"Ana!" A young girl ran toward her. She had the same flaming red hair, but she was no older than 13 or 14. She ran to the bed and wrapped her arms around her sister.

Cain turned and walked away, allowing himself another uncharacteristic smile as he listened to the joyful reunion behind him.

*   *   *   *   *

"Black Eagles don't just disappear," Cain roared. "They don't run, they don't desert, they don't hide." He stood at the head of the folding table, staring out at the assembled officers. "I want to know what happened to those men, and I don't care if you have to take Karelia apart down to the mantle to find out."

Teller sat to Cain's right, silently listening to his friend's tirade. Most people in Occupied Space had heard of Darius Cain and the Black Eagles. The vast majority of them knew

him as a dark figure, a butcher—a conqueror whose trade was
human suffering. But Teller knew this was the real Darius,
his concern first and foremost for his soldiers. He knew Cain
didn't care what people thought of him, but it upset him to
see his oldest friend so mischaracterized. Cain had spent years
training his troops, honing them into a scalpel rather than a
sledgehammer. The Eagles ended confrontations quickly, with
far less death and destruction that the other companies, or
worse, the amateur armies of the colony worlds.

"General, we have searched the area twice. We found
traces—a few fired rounds, some scorched areas on the
ground, but someone did a pretty fair job of cleaning up after
whatever happened there." Colonel Evander Falstaff was the
senior regimental commander, and he'd personally directed his
people in scouring the apparent battle area. "We also found
some scraps of armor, mostly bits and pieces. Some of it
ours…" He stared right at Cain. "…and some of a different
design." He paused. "I'd bet the pay from our last ten jobs
there was a nasty fight there, and whoever hit our troops…they
were also powered infantry."

The room was silent. The implications were sobering.
Powered armor had become rare in Occupied Space since
the Fall. Few planets had the economic might to fund such
expensive military units. It was a major cause behind the
growth of the mercenary companies, but even among those
professional forces, only a few, the Great Companies, could
field more than a handful of powered troops.

Teller looked up at Cain. The commander of the Black
Eagles was deep in thought, no doubt reaching the same
conclusion as his second-in-command. This was no rogue
group of Karelians surprising one of their platoons. Someone
was fucking with the Black Eagles. One of the other big
companies—or another power, one that possessed secret
military tech. Either way it was trouble.

"I want to know who was behind this. I want every scrap
of that armor inspected. I want every scorched patch of grass

analyzed. I want to know what kind of explosives these people use, the alloys in their armor, the types of guns that fire their ammunition. And I want it now!"

"Yes, General." Falstaff's voice was hesitant, and he looked at Cain nervously.

"What is it, Colonel?" Cain's eyes drilled into the regimental commander's. "Speak!"

"Sir, we are not properly equipped to analyze these materials here. We did not come prepared for scientific study." He paused. "I know you don't want to give up on those Eagles, sir, but I don't see how they could still be alive. We've searched everywhere. Whatever was out there is gone." He hesitated again. "But if we get everything back to the Nest, Dr. Sparks can get a lot further than we can out here."

Cain stared silently across the table. He could see his officers all agreed with Falstaff. Cain had always found it difficult to give up on anything. He'd inherited his immense stubbornness from his father, who had long been the most pigheaded Marine in the Corps. But Darius knew when to rely on the few people he trusted for perspective. And if someone was beginning to fuck with the Eagles, the sooner he could identify them the sooner he could blast them to atoms.

"Do you all agree?" There was a half-hearted chorus of yeses around the table. Cain's people didn't like disagreeing with the commander they all idolized. But Darius hadn't assembled a weak-willed corps of yes men to lead his beloved Black Eagles.

"Very well. We will leave in 48 hours." He panned his eyes down the table. "But I want one last intensive search. If there's any debris out there bigger than a molecule, I want it collected. And I want every potential refuge within fifty klicks checked out." He paused. "Understood?"

"Yes, sir," they replied, almost as one.

"Then get to it. All of you."

Everyone in the room jumped up and snapped off a salute before racing to the door.

"Not you, Erik."

Teller stopped and turned toward his friend. "Darius?"

"We need to be considering the possibilities if someone is targeting the Eagles."

"Who would dare to come after us?"

Cain looked up, his eyes finding Teller's. "I don't know, but that platoon didn't just vanish. Maybe it's some freak thing we'll never be able to answer…" His voice trailed off. It was obvious he didn't believe that. "But a powered armor equipped foe? Could one of the other companies be coming after us?"

"What company could take us? Or convince themselves they had a chance?" Teller was shaking his head, but he stopped abruptly. "But what about an alliance of companies? With the Eagles gone, the way would be open for them to scoop up the best contracts—jobs that go to us now."

Cain nodded, his face twisting into an angry grimace. "Maybe…" His voice was deepening. "But why just a company? Why hit us in such a small way?"

"Testing us? Or trying out their tactics?" Anger was creeping into Teller's voice too. "We'd better be on our guard, Darius. If somebody is coming after us, the next time they will hit us a lot harder."

Cain glared into his friend's eyes. "Oh, we will be ready. If someone comes at us again, they will regret it…I don't care if it's every mercenary company in Occupied Space all together." His hands were clenched into armored fists. "By God, they will regret it."

Chapter 4

Inner Sanctum of the Triumvirate
Planet Vali, Draconia Terminii IV
Earthdate: 2317 AD (32 Years After the Fall)

"We must accelerate our plans. The Triumvirate
must complete preparations for the New Era as quickly as
possible. I fear we have little time left. We must accelerate
our harvesting operations on Earth. I propose we double
all bounties." One stood hunched over the end of the
table, holding himself up with frail arms. His face was pale
and spotted, his skin hung loose and sallow. He was thin,
wretchedly so, and his eyes were clouded and old. To any
observer, he appeared to be well past his hundredth birthday,
though in fact, he was only 36.

The Inner Sanctum was a large triangular room, ten
kilometers underground, cut from the solid stone of Vali's
deep crust. The ceiling soared thirty meters above gleaming
granite floors, and the center of the room was dominated by
a massive table, also a triangle, carved from a single block of
polished green stone and bearing the three interlocking rings
that symbolized the Triumvirate. There was a large door
on each of the chamber's three sides, the passages to the
Triumvirs' own private domains. Each of the three men who
ruled the massive, but utterly secret, Triumvirate had their

own offices and private chambers which, by three-decade old agreements between them, were off-limits to the others.

One of the other men nodded. He was called Two, and though, as with One, that was more of a title than a name, he had no other designation. "I concur, One, yet I still feel compelled to advise caution. We have been working many years on the Plan. Indeed, for much of this time, we hoped this Triumvirate would be able to continue to rule and see the Plan to its ultimate fruition." He looked across the table at One before turning his aged head slowly to face his other companion. "Alas, our greatest efforts have been in vain. The science we need to sustain life has eluded us, and despite my earlier concerns about moving too quickly, I must now agree with One. Time is not our ally. Let us double the bounties."

The third man took a breath as his colleague finished. "I also agree. While I still encourage that we move surely and without recklessness, I can feel the time running short as both of you do. I fear we must finalize the Plan by the end of the next two Earth years or see all of our efforts fall to nothing. Certainly we must, at the least, increase the productivity of our terrestrial operations."

"Then we are all agreed," One said. "The Earth bounties will be doubled." He nodded his head for emphasis. "Additionally," he went on, "we must continue to create incidents between the major colony worlds and the Great Companies until there is war throughout Occupied Space." He paused and drew in a deep, ragged breath. "Let us sow seeds of suspicion and distrust among the colonies, while continuing our campaigns to seize control of the targeted worlds. We have two years, my colleagues. Two Earth years to spread destruction and chaos, but after that, we can delay no longer." He coughed and took a few seconds to clear his throat."

"Agreed," said Three. "It is a short time to prepare for the final phase, but whatever has been accomplished—and whatever remains undone—before two years have passed, we must activate Black Fist." He paused for a few seconds then continued, "Then we will release Force Omega to sweep away the remnants of the mercenary companies and the planetary militaries. At last, we will achieve the final domination we have worked so long to bring about. All mankind will be ruled by a single force, one that will direct and guide his future."

One and Two both nodded. "We are all agreed," Two said grimly. "I suggest that we begin by reviewing our operations to date." He glanced around the table, acknowledging the nods of his colleagues. "Let us consider our most effective operation. As you are all aware, fifteen years ago, we discovered a dormant base of the First Imperium. That was a stroke of good fortune, facilitated by our decision to continue devoting moderate resources to exploration activities beyond the fringes of human habitation. Our subsequent success in activating its AI yielded considerable results when it immediately executed the twenty year-old directive from the distant Regent—destroy the humans."

Two cleared his throat, fighting back a coughing spasm as he did. "The war now called the Second Incursion devastated a considerable swath of human-occupied space. The casualties and physical damage inflicted set back the general development level of dozens of worlds, serving our purposes admirably. As a bonus, the remnants of the old Marine Corps, Janissaries, and other veteran formations suffered very heavy losses, further diminishing the pool of retired veterans available to be recalled to service—a process that the passage of time has also aided. The former colonies are incalculably weaker than they would have been had they been allowed three decades of unfettered growth."

"Indeed, Two, the discovery of Zeta Omicron was a stroke of fortune, though it was not without cost. The war pushed the colonies together again to face the alien menace, interrupting the natural progression toward rivalry and warfare among themselves. Considerable efforts have been required to accelerate that trajectory and create and encourage conflict." Three leaned back in his chair, shifting his gaze between his two companions as he spoke.

"Indeed," he continued, "our efforts helped to bring on the development of the mercenary companies, assisting in their founding and growth, if in clandestine ways. The companies, while they also represent a potential military threat to the Plan, were an essential component to bring us to this point. The colonies were too weak, especially after the battles of the Second Incursion, to project strength against rival worlds. But the development of the Companies provided a way for them to strike at enemies, even to subjugate them. And the costs they were compelled to pay bankrupted their treasuries and exceeded the economic value of the beaten and devastated worlds they conquered."

One nodded. "Your analysis is correct. While the companies do represent a potential threat to the Plan, they have also contributed enormously to weakening the colonies. Indeed, if you will review the most recent analysis of the development of Occupied Space, you will see that both total economic output and aggregate technology level have been declining at an accelerating pace for the last ten years. The Second Incursion, and our subsequent encouragement of internecine conflict has created a tipping point, a reversal from advancement to decline. Mankind is slowly sliding toward a dark age, though it is unlikely anyone outside of this room fully understands this."

There was a brief silence before One continued. "Moving onto other matters, Three, perhaps you can update us on the status of our operations regarding the Black Eagles?"

Three bowed his head slowly. "Certainly, One. As you are both aware, we unanimously agreed that the Black Eagles mercenary company has become dangerously proficient, representing an intolerable risk to the Plan. Darius Cain has proven to be an extraordinary military leader, more proficient perhaps, than even his father. This has been an unforeseen development, one we decided required immediate intervention."

He paused for a few seconds, clearing his throat and taking a deep breath. "Our subsequent operation to collect prisoners from the Black Eagles during their invasion of the planet Karelia was less successful than we had hoped. We deployed two stealth vessels, each with a full Omega company aboard to ambush and capture a Black Eagles patrol. Despite the fact that our forces were engaged with only a platoon-sized unit, they were fought nearly to a standstill. In the end, they were barely able to withdraw undetected. They were unable to compel any of the Black Eagles to surrender, and they only took three prisoners, all enemy soldiers who had been wounded and rendered unconscious in the battle. Our casualties were extremely heavy, well over 50% of engaged strength, a loss ratio of five to one despite our numerical superiority."

Two sighed. "This is disturbing news on multiple levels." He flashed his eyes toward One then back again to Three. "It appears we have underestimated Darius Cain, an error I fear is unforgivable in light of our knowledge of his father. The younger Cain has succeeded in creating a fighting force vastly superior to any in Occupied Space, apparently including our own Omega warriors." He paused, looking briefly again at each of his colleagues. "It is apparent we must escalate our efforts to destroy—or at least degrade—the Black Eagles."

"I concur," said One.

"And I," added Three.

"Very well." He glanced down at a small tablet on the table in front of him. "Our most recent intelligence reports suggest that war is brewing between Lysandria and Albemarle. What is not generally known is that the Albemarlian Senate has just ratified an agreement with the Black Eagles to invade Lysandria for them. One questions how they were able to afford it. They must have pledged everything of value on the planet to fund the contract." He paused. "Although the Lysandrians do not yet know of this development, it renders their position hopeless. As a largely agricultural world, they simply do not have the financial resources to mount a defense that has any hope of stopping the Black Eagles. They will be crushed, and Albermarle will be bankrupted...both desirable results for us."

His voice began to fade, and he paused to regain his breath. "However, I believe we can achieve an even greater benefit and thoroughly increase the effectiveness of this dispute. As you are aware, we control a number of clandestine enterprises on Lysandria, local operations of interplanetary underworld syndicates, mostly. I propose we arrange to provide financial support to the Lysandrian government, allowing them to hire one of the Great Companies to defend them. Indeed, I suggest the Gold Spears. They are among the strongest of the companies, one of the two or three that are even close to a match for the Eagles. And, I believe there is bad blood between the two forces, which may serve to increase the intensity of the fighting and ramp up losses on both sides."

"Brilliant," One said. "Though I suspect the Gold Spears are rather less a match for Cain's people than they style themselves, they will no doubt inflict considerable losses on the Black Eagles. We will not neutralize Darius Cain with a single operation, but your proposal is an excellent start." He turned his head. "Three?"

"I agree entirely. Let us commence the operation at once."

He paused, a troubled look on his face. "Before we proceed to reviewing the operations reports from the various planets, I suggest we discuss the other Cain son. Elias Holm, as you all know, is a senior officer in the Atlantian patrol. We have long considered him less of a threat than his brother since his efforts have been mostly in law enforcement and not military operations. However, his investigative abilities have proven to be extremely effective. He has penetrated several of our enterprises on Atlantia and, while they represent only a tiny portion of our revenue, I have become concerned he will discover the connections to our wider network. And that would be a *significant* problem."

"Indeed it would, Three." One looked troubled for a few seconds, but when he continued, his tone was more hopeful. "His follow up beyond Atlantia's system will be greatly hampered by jurisdictional issues. Perhaps we needn't be overly concerned. With increasing interplanetary tensions, he will likely find it difficult to obtain the cooperation he will require to truly penetrate our organization at anything above the lowest levels."

"I am inclined at first to agree," said Two, "but then I ask myself, do we truly wish to once again underestimate a Cain? We are in the unfortunate position of trying to put remedial action in place to address the power that Darius Cain has amassed under our noses. And let us not forget how Erik Cain was able to defeat our predecessor on the eve of his triumph." He swallowed hard, and continued in a raspy tone. "Perhaps it is wise to deal with Elias Cain now. Just to be safe."

"What do you propose?" asked One.

"I think the most direct option is probably the best. Darius Cain is virtually untouchable, surrounded at all times by his fanatically loyal army. This is not the case with Elias. For all his ability and the law enforcement resources at his command, he is far easier to reach."

"An assassination?" Three sounded intrigued. "Yes, that may be possible. Even more so if we create a diversion, a way to draw him into an exposed location." His face slowly contorted into a twisted smile. "And I have just the plan…"

Chapter 5

Starship Eagle One
In Orbit Around Lysandria, Delta Sigma III
Earthdate: 2318 AD (33 Years After the Fall)

"How did the Lysandrians manage to hire the Gold Spears?" Darius Cain sat at the small table, staring across at Erik Teller. "Tomlinson did a full financial analysis. There is no way Lysandria could have put together the Spears' price... even assuming the most extreme range of contingencies. We'd allowed a 10% probability they would be able to retain one of the lesser companies, but none at all that they could afford another Great Company."

Teller was staring across the table at his friend. Darius was usually as cool as they came, but he could see the leader of the Eagles was agitated. Teller understood—he felt it too. The Eagles had faced the Spears before, three times, in fact. Each contest had been a victory for Cain's soldiers, as every battle the undefeated Eagles had fought had been. Most companies were quick to surrender to the Eagles. Battles to the bitter end were unprofitable, and a company that fought to utter destruction was out of business. But the Spears wanted the Eagles' perch; they wanted to stand atop the heap as the undisputed best of the Companies. And they knew that could never happen, not when their hated rivals were still in the way.

The rivalry had grown over time until it had become extremely bitter. When the two forces had last met, Cain warned the Spears—the next time they faced each other there would be no surrender, no quarter. The fight would be to the death. If the Black Eagles found the Gold Spears once again arrayed against them on the battlefield, Cain had sworn it would be the last time. Erik Teller knew his commander and oldest comrade never made a threat he wasn't willing to carry out. He wondered if the senior officers of the Spears understood that.

"I don't know, Darius. It doesn't make sense to me either. The Lysandrian government was almost bankrupt even without the prospect of war. I can't conceive of any way they could have raised such a sum. Unless they had help."

"Help?" Cain replied. "You mean another planet? Maybe someone with designs on the Albemarlians?" His face twisted into a frustrated grimace. "No, that doesn't make sense either. It really doesn't matter to the Albemarlians if we get banged up in the fight. They paid us to subjugate the defenders. The only way they come out behind is if we lose outright." Teller knew Cain tried to avoid arrogance at all costs, but he found it difficult to imagine the Eagles actually losing the upcoming fight, and he suspected Cain felt the same way.

"Could it be someone targeting us? Trying to interfere with our contracts? Or to wear us down?" Teller had just been thinking out loud, but now he paused and looked right at Cain. "That has to be it. Somebody *is* after us, Darius. They want to inflict heavy losses, wear us down. There's nothing else that makes sense."

"But who?" Cain was nodding. "I agree with your thinking, but I can't come up with a guess at who. I wouldn't put it past that piece of shit Ling to convince himself his Spears could take us, especially with someone encouraging him, but I don't see anybody else buying into that. We might get shot up pretty badly down there, but we will win…and by the time we leave, no one will even be sure the Gold Spears ever existed." There was venom in Cain's voice. Any doubts Teller might have had about Darius following through on his earlier threats evaporated instantly.

"I suggest we revisit the assault plan, at least. We're going to be facing a much stronger defense than we'd expected."

"Agreed. Let's move Cyn Kuragina's regiment into the vanguard." Kuragina was a refugee who'd fled from the colony world of Vostok, one step ahead of the law. Neither Cain nor Teller knew what she had done, and neither cared. Black Eagles were born again when they took the company's oath of service, their prior sins forgotten and forgiven. Such absolution came at a price, however, and Eagles were held to an onerous standard of conduct and duty. They were sworn to serve their brethren, and any who failed in that sacred trust could expect to deal with Darius Cain at his merciless worst. Every Eagle knew their commander would run into the middle of enemy fire to retrieve a wounded private, but they were just as certain he would repay treachery with a cold and merciless justice.

"White Regiment first. Got it." Teller agreed with the decision. Cyn Kuragina was an odd duck, a woman who looked and acted like she'd been raised as a diplomat's daughter but who took to soldiering with a gritty vengeance. She was tough as nails and as strong a tactician as the Eagles had, besides Cain and Teller.

"The Teams will go down with her people. I want the area scouted immediately, and I want snipers in place as soon as possible. The Spears' officers are all strutting peacocks just like Ling. We should be able to put half of them down in the first few hours." Like all serious military units, the Gold Spears issued the same armor to their officers and key personnel. But their commander, General Ling, was an arrogant man, and his leadership style permeated his unit. And Darius Cain had trained his Special Action Teams to search for any indication a target was an officer – posture, positioning, behavior. His elite snipers were utterly without peers in Occupied Space, and he was confident they would wreak havoc on the Spears' command structure.

"Falstaff next?" Teller asked. Evander Falstaff's commanded the Eagles' senior unit, the Black Regiment. After the Teams, Falstaff's people were the most experienced veterans, and they served almost as a guard unit.

"Yes, right behind Kuragina." Cain's voice was stern. "And I do mean *right* behind, Erik. If we mess around with the Spears, they can hurt us. And I don't want Kuragina's people down their alone a second longer than necessary."

"Understood. I'll run the launch sequences myself."

"Good." Cain paused for an instant. "Let's land Cornin's Red Regiment next and keep Vandeveer's Blues in orbital reserve. But I want them ready to land immediately if we need them."

"Got it, Erik. Still good for launch at 0800?" The Eagles ships ran on Earth time, just as the fleets of the Superpowers had. Earth was a radioactive wreck whose survivors clawed out a miserable existence in the shattered ruins, but she was still man's original home, and her clock and calendar were still in use across much of human space.

"Yes." He stood stone still as his executive officer nodded. "And I'm going in with Kuragina."

Teller's eyes snapped back to Cain's and his mouth opened to argue. But he got one good look at his commander's face, and he held his tongue. He'd known Darius Cain most of his life, and he knew that expression. He knew it far too well.

*   *   *   *   *

Cain walked down the corridor of his flagship toward his quarters. The landing was commencing in three hours, and if his Eagles were going to have their final showdown with the Gold Spears, he was damned sure going down with the first wave. He'd originally expected the campaign against Lysandria to be relatively quick and easy, but now he knew it was going to be a hard fight. He had most of his strength with him— about 6,000 ground troops in total—and preliminary scanning reports suggested the Spears had roughly the same. Of course, his people were invading, and their enemies were down there, dug in and waiting.

He was stressed, worried about the campaign, and his anger toward his rivals was gnawing at him. But there was something else too, something he couldn't put out of his mind. Tom Sparks had researched the debris he'd brought back from Karelia, and he'd confirmed the few bits and pieces came from state of the art fighting suits, as good or nearly so as the Mark VIII units his people wore. But there was no indication of who had fielded units so equipped or why they had ambushed a party of his troopers. He'd reluctantly accepted the likelihood that his missing people were dead, though it had still stabbed at him to leave Karelia without being sure. He'd hoped Sparks would be able to ID the source of the equipment, but the brilliant scientist had been stumped.

Now he was facing another anomaly, something else that didn't make sense, and on the very next campaign. Cain always researched his opponents thoroughly, and he didn't make mistakes. If it had been remotely feasible, possible even, for the Lysandrians to hire a company as costly as the Spears, he would have known it. Events were never entirely predictable, but this was the second consecutive campaign that had him analyzing bizarre occurrences. Darius Cain didn't believe in much, and certainly not coincidences. Something was going on. He had no idea what it was, not even a starting point. But he knew there was some kind of trouble coming.

"Erik told me you were going down with the first wave?" The familiar voice came from behind. He turned and saw Ana Bazarov walking up behind him. He usually had a smile for her, but he was too troubled this time, and he just nodded. "Yes," he replied simply. Cain had become quite fond of the refugee since he'd saved her from a brutal assault on Karelia. Even he didn't understand the effect she had on him, but the thought of seeing her hurt—or left behind on a planet destined for servitude and economic depression—was something he'd found upsetting, and he'd taken her with him when the Eagles departed.

She'd been hostile to him at first, feeling she'd merely traded one assailant for another. But when it became apparent he had no intention of harming her or her sister, she began to warm up to him, slowly at first. Now there was real warmth in her voice, and worry as she thought of him leading his vanguard into the teeth of heavy resistance. The news that the Gold Spears were waiting down on the surface had spread rapidly through the fleet.

"Why?" she asked softly, reaching out and putting her hand on his arm. "You don't usually land with the first wave, do you?"

He felt an urge to pull away from her, but it vanished quickly, replaced by the calm feeling she usually gave him. He resisted his initial impulse to snap back at her. He was tense, and his mind was deep in thought, trying to understand what was going on. Darius Cain had a paranoia as strong as his father's. He was sure the suspicion he felt was warranted, but his efforts to develop a hypothesis had so far produced only frustration. He was fond of Ana, perhaps even infatuated, but he didn't have time for her now.

"I land at whatever point I feel is best for the operation. When I drop later, it is because it is tactically advisable to direct early operations from the fleet. Physical safety is not a concern in the decision. I am prepared to go anywhere I send my soldiers."

"Shouldn't you make sure your soldiers have secured the area before you land? I'm not military expert, but…"

"No," he said, more harshly than he'd intended, "you are not a military expert." He paused, softening his tone before he continued. "Look, Ana…" He forced a smile. "…I appreciate your concern, but you have to trust me on this. War is my business. And I'm good at it. Very good."

She didn't look convinced, but she just nodded and looked up at him with watery eyes. "Be careful, Darius." Her voice was soft, affectionate. "Please."

"I am always careful, Ana." It was the first lie he'd ever told her.

*   *   *   *   *

"I want your people to form a large perimeter and dig in as soon as we land. I wouldn't put it past Ling to send his people in to try to pinch out our LZ as soon as we hit ground."

"Yes, sir." Cyn Kuragina stood next to Cain, fully armored except for her retracted helmet. She'd had long blonde hair when she'd first arrived to join the Eagles, but she'd been shaving her head for years now. She stared back at Cain with piercing ice blue eyes. Kuragina was a very attractive woman, but she'd given herself over completely to the martial life. Cain pitied the man who tried to pick her up when she was on leave. He'd be lucky to keep his teeth. Kuragina loved men, at least the ones who made up 80% of her regiment, but for most other purposes, she preferred women.

"The Teams are going in on the lead wave too, so make sure your people know they're there. I don't want them seeing bogies when it's just our scouts and snipers." Nothing made Cain as crazy as friendly fire incidents. He mourned every one of his soldiers lost, but the ones caught in the crossfire cut the deepest. The Eagles all had friend or foe transponders, but jamming and other battlefield confusion sometimes overrode precautions. No matter how good a unit was, no matter how well trained and equipped, when the shit got really nasty, troops got hit by their comrades.

"Understood, sir." She paused, staring at him with those

glacial eyes. "And prisoners, sir? Is it true we're not to accept any surrenders?"

Cain returned her stare, and his eyes were no less frozen than hers. "There is to be no quarter given to the Gold Spears, Colonel. They have had their warning, and they have chosen to disregard it." His voice was like ice. "You may accept the surrender of local forces, but only if you are confident you can do so without compromising the security of your command."

"Understood, sir." She snapped to rigid attention.

"Very well, Colonel Kuragina…you may see to your regiment's dispositions."

She saluted crisply and turned on her heel, a difficult maneuver in armor. Cain watched her walk briskly toward the launch bay. He'd always liked Kuragina. When he'd first seen her, straggling in with a shipload of new recruits, he'd bet himself she would wash out in less than a week. She was the shortest of her trainee class by a good quarter of a meter, and half the men outweighed her by 50 kilos. But she was the toughest of them all, and she finished at the top of the class. She'd risen through the ranks faster than anyone else in the history of the Eagles, and she was the only regimental commander who had started as a trainee instead of coming to the unit with previous combat experience. He still remembered watching her kick the living shit out of a male trainee almost twice her size. She'd walked away almost without a scratch, and her opponent ended up in the infirmary.

Cain walked toward a long wall at the end of the ready room. There were empty racks stretching for a hundred meters, with one suit remaining in place. He walked over toward the hulking black armor, sliding his shirt over his head as he did. "Open," he said, as he continued to undress.

"Open," the AI responded as the suit popped like a clamshell.

"Diagnostics?" Cain pulled the last of his clothes off, stowing them on the small shelf next to the suit.

"All systems confirmed 100% functional, General."

The AI's voice was calm, almost human-sounding, but not quite. He had a passing memory of Hector, his father's AI. Hector had accompanied the elder Cain during most of his career. Darius could remember his father's stories, liberally laced with complaints about the poor attitude the AI had developed. It had all been part of a program implemented by the Corps, an elaborate experiment with enhanced personality AIs designed to adapt to their individual officers to lower stress and improve interaction. Darius didn't know if it had been a success, but he suspected it had been, at least to a greater extent than his father had ever admitted. Erik complained about Hector, but he'd also brought the AI with him when he retired, and he spent the next fifteen years sparring with it about one thing or another, as the computer presence went about the mundane tasks of running the Cain household.

"Very well, begin power up sequence." Darius' AI had substantially less personality than Hector. When he'd had the Mark VIII units put into production, he hadn't worried about esoteric details like customized AIs. His suits' systems served their purposes and did their jobs, without excess banter with their wearers.

Cain backed into the suit, pushing himself upwards and into place. "Close," he said, and he prepared himself for the inevitable pain as the suit shut and a series of probes and intravenous connections jabbed into him. The Mark VIII suits were the ultimate union between man and machine, but the interface that made all that possible was not a gentle one.

"All systems activated. Neural interface established and functioning."

No shit, it's established. The neural connection was the worst part of suiting up—a thick probe that drove into the top of the spinal column. It was something new in the Mark VIII armor, an innovation that no one but the Eagles had, at least to the best of Cain's knowledge. It allowed direct communication between the wearer's thoughts and the artificial intelligence controlling the armor. It came close to allowing an

Eagle trooper to control the mechanicals of his suit the way he moved an arm or a leg—or took a deep breath. But it hurt like a motherfucker going in.

"Let's go," he snapped to the AI. An instant later he felt the suit moving down the track toward the launch tubes. Landing was one area where the Mark VIII suits were a step ahead of the Mark VII's his father and the Marines had worn. The "eights" as they were called, were capable of individual orbital insertion, while the Mark VII's had been designed for use with landing craft.

Darius could feel himself moving down the launch prep track. He knew the procedure so well, he could imagine every step of it as he stood silently inside his suit. First, the disposable thrust pack would be bolted to one of his armor's multi-use hardpoints. Then, the three braking parachute modules would be attached, after which he would be encased in a thin metal launch pod. The cocoon would then be force-filled with expanding, heat-resistant foam before he was placed in the electro-magnetic launch tube.

A Black Eagle ready for launch was almost like a bullet in a gun, ready to be blasted out of the ship into the upper atmosphere of the target world. It was a streamlined system, requiring far less tonnage of support materials than the old Gordon and Liggett landers the Marines had used. It allowed Cain to carry almost twice as many soldiers per ton on his transports, a huge advantage in the leaner times that had come upon mankind.

He felt the pod moving to a horizontal position as it fed into the catapult. He was not only in the first wave, he was in the initial group of that wave. He knew his people were going to have a tough fight on their hands on Lysandria. There was nothing he could do about that. But he could damned sure be on the front lines with them, and nobody was going to keep him from that.

"*Eagle One* command center, this is General Cain… commence landing operations."

Chapter 6

Settlement Jericho
Planet Earth, Sol III
Earthdate: September, 2318 AD (33 Years After the Fall)

"We just got word on the com unit. The Martians are making another series of aid drops. We should have ours sometime tomorrow." Ellie was walking up the path toward the small shelter she and Axe had shared for 25 years. She had a big smile on her face. "That's really going to help us with our winter stores."

Axe turned abruptly when he first heard her, and he slipped something behind his back, hiding it before she rounded the corner and looked up at him. He stifled a cough and gave her his own smile. "That's great news. We can really use it." Jericho's population had been growing steadily over the past few years, and now there were over a thousand men, women, and children crowded within its makeshift walls. Axe had been determined to turn away the last few bands of refugees, but Ellie had convinced him to take them in.

He understood her sympathy, but he also knew there was a limit to what they could do. Thirty years after the Final War, Earth was still a ravaged wasteland, its poisoned hills and fields traversed by wandering bands, survivors of the doom that had

claimed most of mankind. Axe knew how tenuous life was
for the scattered groups, but he felt his first responsibility was
to Jericho's existing residents, many of whom had been with
him for years and who had helped to build the settlement to its
current state of relative prosperity. It was a constant challenge
to feed the people they already had. If it hadn't been for the
Martian drops…

He remembered the early years, right after the war, the
nightmare just to survive from day to day. Axe had been
about 40 klicks from the city when the bombs hit. New York
had shrunken considerably since its peak centuries earlier
as a massive metropolis, but the Manhattan Protected Zone
had still occupied a prominent place on the target lists of
the enemy Superpowers. Half a dozen of the big city-killer
warheads had impacted by the time the attacks ceased, leaving
nothing whatsoever of the kilometer-tall towers that had
reached into the sky.

Axe and his small band of followers had taken refuge
deep in the cellar of a long-abandoned factory, hiding
from bombs, from radiation—from the nightmare that had
descended on the world. But eventually they ran out of food
and water, and they were forced to leave the relative safety of
their hiding place in search of sustenance.

They didn't dare get any closer to the radioactive hell
surrounding the city, so they went east, eventually reaching
the very end of what had been called Long Island. Once a
densely-populated part of the massive New York metropolis,
the island had long been mostly abandoned, a sea of crumbling
suburbs where millions had once lived, before the government
decided people were easier to control in densely populated
cities than they were dispersed over hundreds of small towns.
Now there was little but the remnants of 150 year-old houses
and stores, all that still stood to attest that so many had once
called the place home.

Axe had realized his small band needed to get off the
island to survive. They'd managed to scavenge what they had

needed to survive in the short term, but Axe knew they had
to find someplace they could hunt and grow food if they were
going to survive in the years to come. His limited knowledge
of geography told him the route back west was out of the
question. There was no way off the island in that direction
that didn't come within the lethal radiation zone around the
city. In the end, they left from the east, building crude rafts
and barges to cross the narrow sound to the coast of what
had once been Connecticut. They'd then marched north for
weeks, staying away from the deadzones and finally settling in a
wooded area right next to a river.

Axe didn't know what the place had been called, what
state or government administrative unit had ruled over it, but
none of that mattered anymore. It was far enough from the
devastated and polluted areas closer to the old urban centers,
as good a place as any to stop fleeing, and that is what they
did, struggling to build their growing community through one
challenge after another. They survived the Great Dark, the
two-year long partial nuclear winter that followed the war, and
a hundred other calamities after that, but thirty years later they
were still there.

Axe had been a gang leader in the Brooklyn sector of old
New York, every bit as ruthless as any of his brethren. He'd
learned to kill at a very young age, and he'd murdered more
people than he could remember. He was ashamed of his youth
now, though he realized his experience had helped him lead
his band of refugees to this place, and to provide a haven for
countless others over the years. Had he been a normal Cog, he
knew he'd have died in Brooklyn when the bombs came. How
many of his thousand would also be dead in that scenario?
There was no way to know, but he suspected the answer was
most of them. He'd often considered the strange way life
worked, that his earlier brutality had given him the ability to
save so many lives later.

He shook out of his thoughtfulness as he felt Ellie sit
down next to him. "What's wrong?" she said. "You look

like something's bothering you." She smiled and put her arm around his back.

Ellie was another odd addition to his little band. He'd found her when he was scavenging the Manhattan Protected Zone just before the final attacks, robbing whatever he could in the wake of the Cog revolts that had swept the city. She'd been a captive of a member of the elite of the Political Class, and he'd found her locked up, brutalized and left behind to die when the politicians had fled.

She had been skittish and terrified. For months, he'd worried she might take off and die on her own somewhere, alone. But she had stayed with him. It took a long time for her to get past what had happened to her, but she found the strength she needed, and they'd been together ever since.

"Nothing's wrong." He was lying, and he suspected she saw through it. But she was used to him being overly protective. He tried to change his tone to something more cheerful, with very limited success. "You mind tracking down Horace and letting him know about the drop? Tell him to put a group together to go collect it." The Martians had been making humanitarian deliveries for twenty years now, air drops that usually came pretty close to landing at the designated coordinates. A Martian drop was full of useful items—food, medicine, and tools—and he knew if he didn't have his people out there and ready to load it up and bring it all back to Jericho, someone else would find it.

"I'll take care of it." Ellie looked at him strangely. Axe knew she could tell something was wrong. He never had been able to lie to her. She leaned in and gave him a kiss on the cheek then she got up and walked down the path toward the center of the village, looking back a couple times as she did.

Axe struggled to hold back the spasm until she vanished from view. Then he pulled the rag he'd hidden behind his back and coughed hard half a dozen times. He pulled it from his mouth, looking down at the blood soaked cloth. He wasn't sure what it was, but had a pretty good idea. He'd seen the long term effects of radiation exposure far too many times. Jericho had buried its share of residents who had died far too young, victims of compromised immune systems and various cancers. The Final War had been thirty years before, but it was still killing people.

Axe knew he and Ellie hadn't escaped all of the effects of being too close to New York. He was fairly certain one of them, at least, was sterile. They'd tried for years to conceive a child, with no success. But after decades of constant worry, he'd begun to hope they had been spared anything worse. Until now.

He coughed again. More blood, and pain this time too. Whatever it was, the symptoms were getting worse. *Cancer, I guess. Probably in my lungs.* Before the Final War, cancer was an easily cured disease, usually requiring just a few injections. It was such a simple treatment, it was even available to the lower classes. But targeted immunotherapy was part of the knowledge that was lost along with so much else, on Earth, at least, when man had finally tried to destroy himself.

Something else worried him too. The larger Jericho's population grew, the harder the settlement was to control. Axe had come up in the old gangs of New York, and he'd seen firsthand the brutality people could perpetrate on each other. The pathetic refugees he'd taken in had been enormously grateful, but Axe knew that kind of thing only lasted so long. Now he heard grumbling, complaints about allowing new people in, anger at his strict rules and heavy security. The newer arrivals clashed with the old residents, and there was a growing feeling of unrest.

He had maintained control for a long time, doing whatever was necessary, including executing several dozen of his own citizens over the years. He'd found those instances to be particularly difficult. After all the destruction, he knew the last thing the survivors needed to do was keep killing each other. But there was no room in his community for those who preyed on the others, as he had once done, and no resources to waste on keeping prisoners perpetually jailed. When the necessity arose, Axe himself had performed the executions. It wasn't something he felt he could order someone else to do.

Jericho wasn't a democracy, and he made that completely clear to every refugee he allowed to become part of the community. He'd seen the world people had created for themselves before, the poor judgment they'd shown, and he didn't intend to allow that to happen to his small settlement. But he also knew the dynamics of force and brutality. If he let his guard down, one day someone would unseat him and take control. He'd been confident that he could counter any threats, at least while he'd been strong and healthy, but what about when he was gone? What would happen to his people then? What would happen to Ellie?

*   *   *   *   *

"Boss, we found a settlement of some kind. It's about ten klicks to the east." Peter Barkley scrambled down the steep hillside, pushing his way through the heavy brush. He was clad in dark green fatigues, with heavy combat boots reaching almost to his knees. He had a martial look of a sort, but it was less like a soldier and more like a…hunter.

Rufus Grax turned and watched his lieutenant barreling down the slope, plunging through the heavy scrub. He winced as he saw Barkley plow through a particularly dense section of brush. "Careful, Pete, these bushes are a motherfucker."

Barkley stumbled to a halt right in front of Grax. "No shit," he said, pulling a large branch full of thorns from the side of his neck. He shook himself and yanked another handful of prickly leaves from his fatigues.

"Like I said, Boss, a settlement. A damned big one, built right alongside the river. The place has walls and everything." Barkley was obviously excited. "There must be close to a thousand people living there. And they got their shit together, Boss, so they're probably healthy, well fed. Good stock, not like that last bunch, half rotten inside. They'll fetch a good price."

Grax stood still, listening to his second-in-command. He glanced absent-mindedly in the direction Barkley had come from. He nodded, but his expression was full of doubt. "Sounds like a good haul, Pete, but I wonder if we can handle that ourselves. A village that size probably has at least some weapons. And that's a lot of people, even if they've just got clubs. It's gonna be a lot harder to take them than grabbing a dozen scavengers in the woods."

"There are a lot of them, Boss, that's true. But they're still Earthers...refugees. They may manage to feed themselves, but any fighting experience they have is just against wanderers. I doubt they've ever faced an organized attack. We'll blow a section of the wall out and be in there before they know what hit them." Barkley's voice was arrogant, dismissive. "They'll probably give up without a fight. If not, we'll take 'em out with the gas, and by the time they wake up, they'll be all chained up and halfway to the clearinghouse."

Grax stared at his second-in-command. "I just don't know. After thirty years, they must have had their share of scrapes." He paused. "I can call it in and get some help. Central Command can divert a couple more teams here, give us some backup." He hesitated, taking another look in the direction of the village. "Better to be careful than to get in too deep." His voice was far from certain.

Barkley frowned. "Yeah, but then we're splitting the pot more ways. And *we* found the place, Boss." Barkley glanced back over his shoulder in the general direction of the settlement. Then he swung back to face Grax. "They looked like prime candidates. If we take this down ourselves, we're looking at one hell of a payday."

Grax sighed and stood silently for half a minute. Then he smiled and said, "Ok, Pete. We could use a good payday like that. And they're just Earthers, after all." He sighed, a nervous expression on his face. "But I want this executed perfectly. No mistakes."

"No mistakes, Boss. We can hit them at dawn."

*   *   *   *   *

Axe sprang out of bed at the sound of the first shot. Ellie hadn't heard it, but he woke her up scrambling noisily across the small room, throwing on his clothes.

"What is it, Axe?" She stared at him with bleary eyes.

"Gunfire. Sounded like outside the south wa…"

The clanging of the alarm bell silenced him. Jericho had sentries in its guard towers 24/7. It was one rule Axe had always insisted upon, even though it drained manpower from the fields and the hunt. He'd been resolute over the years, though recently there had been more grumbling that the settlement's sheer size deterred raiders, and the labor wasted on the watch could be used to increase the village's small but growing food surplus. For years, the settlement had teetered on the edge of sustenance, and the promise of increased prosperity was appealing to most. But Axe ignored it all. Keeping his people alive was what mattered to him.

Jericho had seen its share of fighting in its earlier days, when roving bands of refugees frequently attacked, but it had been years since the last serious encounter. Jericho was large and surrounded by its wall, and the flow of wanderers had trickled to a crawl. Thirty years after the Fall, there weren't too many purely nomadic groups anymore, at least not large ones. They had either settled somewhere, built something permanent like Jericho, or they had died. But Axe had always feared the day would come when Jericho faced a serious threat again, and he'd never let his guard drop.

"Stay here, Ellie. There's a pistol in the small trunk, underneath the winter gear. A couple spare clips too."

He bolted out before she had a chance to say anything. There were a dozen of his people running around, and more coming out of their small huts every second. "To the arsenal," he yelled, waving his arms wildly. His eyes darted to the south tower. The mysterious shooting seemed directed mostly at the ten meter tall fortification. He couldn't hear any return fire, which probably meant his sentries were dead. He still had no idea who was attacking, but he had a bad feeling this was no normal raid.

"To the arsenal," he repeated. "Arm yourselves." He ran down the narrow path to the heavy log building and threw open the door. He slipped inside, feeling around in the dark for the battery-powered light. A few seconds later, the dim lamp cast a shadowy glow across the armory of the Jericho settlement.

There were a dozen rifles of various sorts stacked up along a makeshift rack. Other than the weapons issued to the tower sentries, they were all that remained functional after thirty years. Each gun had a varying supply of matching ammunition, ranging from a dozen rounds for the single military grade assault rifle to about three hundred each for the four police shotguns. Axe knew all of it together wouldn't get them through one decent fight, but it was all they had.

Twenty pistols, a hundred-odd knives large enough to be accounted weapons, a few boxes of explosives, and eleven stun grenades—that rounded out the armed power of Jericho. Axe knew a well-equipped section of trained soldiers could wipe his people out in twenty minutes. *It's a good thing there are no trained soldiers left on Earth. At least we hope there are none.* Something was still nagging at him. A raid was dangerous enough, but in his gut he was sure this was more. Jericho hadn't been raided for years. It was too big for any rival settlements to target. The cost of an attack would vastly exceed any supplies the attackers could steal. *So who is hitting us now?*

"Tommie, Randy…you guys each take one of the rifles." The two were both founding settlers, and good shots as well. He turned and caught a glimpse of long, blonde hair. "Jack, take this. It's the best weapon we've got, but you've only got a dozen rounds, so make them count." He grabbed the heavy assault rifle and handed it to the tall, grim man standing next to him. He was pretty sure Jack Lompoc had been a cop or a government enforcer of some kind before the Fall, and his suspicions had fueled a strong mistrust at first. But Lompoc had arrived at Jericho's gate starving and sick like so many had before him. He'd been in Jericho for fifteen years now, and Axe had long ago accepted him. There was no room in the new world for nurturing old hatreds. Not if mankind was going to survive on Earth. Axe himself had more than one thing in his past he wished he could erase, and he didn't assume he was the only one who felt that way. And Lompoc was the best shot in Jericho, by a considerable margin.

Lompoc reached out and grabbed the gun. "Thanks, Axe." He moved his hand across his face, pushing a long hank of greasy blonde hair out of his eyes. "I'll try to pick out their leaders." He nodded quickly and slipped through the door and into the darkness.

Axe finished handing out the firearms, trying to pick and choose those to whom he gave the precious weapons. "The rest of you, grab a blade or a club, and try to stay close to the guys armed with guns." He was about to rush back outside when he saw a familiar mass of brown hair come through the door. It was Ellie, and she had the pistol in her hand.

"What are you doing here?" he snapped, with more edge in his voice than he'd intended.

"I'm not going to cower in our shelter and wait to see if my home survives or not." Her voice was firm, defiant.

Axe stared back at her, ready to argue, but he held his words. He tended to try to protect her as much as he could, probably because of the way he'd found her all those years ago, so helpless and abused. But Ellie was 45 years old now, and a survivor of three decades of post-Fall life. He knew he didn't have the right to treat her like that tortured and terrified young girl he'd found so long ago. *Don't coddle her, Axe. She's going to have to be strong when you're gone. And that's not going to be long, even if you survive tonight.*

"OK, stay here then, and give out the rest of these weapons."

She nodded. "I will." She stared around the room, taking a quick mental stock of what was left. "You be careful."

He paused for a few seconds, just looking at her and nodding. There was so much he wanted to say, but so little time, so he just smiled at her and slipped out through the door.

*   *   *   *   *

"Grenade teams, open fire!" Barkley stood to Grax's side, staring toward the breached wall of Jericho. There had been a brief firefight with the guards in the tower just behind the settlement's ramparts, but he was pretty sure they had taken out the sentries. Grax would rather have spared them. Almost certainly, those tasked with defense were among the strongest and healthiest in the village—and thus the most valuable. The Traders paid ten times as much for captives that met their Prime parameters, and the men they'd just shot off that tower were probably all within that 3% portion of the population.

But the tower was well-positioned to cover the approach to the walls, and two of his men had already been hit trying to get close. In the end, he'd had no choice but to order his people to take out the sentries. There just wasn't time. The heavy fire had instantly roused the village, almost certainly, but that had been inevitable once the guards had spotted his scouts approaching.

Still, he wasn't here to kill any more than he had to. These villagers were his inventory, and every one his people killed was one he couldn't sell. And that cost them all. No, his men weren't here to get into a pitched battle. This was business, nothing more. It was hunting, not war.

Whoomp. He watched as the first grenade sailed over the walls. The tranq canisters made his job a lot easier. The modified nerve gas had a mortality rate of about 10%, which was somewhat wasteful, but that was well worthwhile considering it turned most raids into simple exercises in loading unconscious captives into the transports. Normally, his grenadiers could take all the targets down before the rest of his people closed in, but this settlement was much larger than anyplace he had raided before. There was a good chance the gas attack wouldn't take all the defenders down, which meant there might be some actual fighting to do. Grax normally preferred to avoid unnecessary risks, but greed had overruled his caution, and he'd allowed Barkley to talk him into the raid.

Whoomp. The second round of grenades flew over the walls. The gas was odorless, but it was visible as wispy white clouds where concentrations were heavy.

Whoomp. The third round was directed deeper into the village. Two volleys was all he'd ever used before, but he wasn't taking any chances here, and he'd ordered four. Plus his people were armed with smaller, handheld grenades. His teams were all equipped with gas masks, and every villager they could capture instead of kill increased the expedition's profit.

"Masks on," he barked, looking quickly to the left and right at his people. They were ready.

Whoomp. As soon as he heard the last round leave the launchers, he leapt to his feet. "Forward...through the breach. Take down anybody who is still standing in there."

He watched Barkley leap forward, leading his twenty men toward the breach. There was no fire, but that didn't mean there wouldn't be any once they got inside. He turned back toward the grenade teams. "Stow those and bring the transports through that breach. We should have a ton of prisoners to load."

Then he checked his rifle, and he moved forward,

following his raiders through the collapsed section of wall.

*   *   *   *   *

Axe slipped around the edge of the building. He'd
been up near the gate when the gas attack began. He'd been
surprised at first, but then he realized what was happening. He
didn't know why the raiders were there, but he knew they were
using gas. He'd seen the police in New York use gas on rioting
Cogs more than once.

"Get away from the gate," he screamed. "Gas!" He
stood in place and waved for any who could see him to follow.
Dozens of people were dropping to the ground, and he could
see the gauzy white clouds drifting his way. "Let's go," he said
again, and he rounded the corner of the building and headed
deeper into the settlement, about a dozen residents following.

He slipped down the narrow alley toward a row of large
structures, turning out into the dusty track that served as
Jericho's main thoroughfare. He ran past a series of long, low
shelters, mostly storehouses, stopping in front of the infirmary.
He pushed open the door, waving his arms as he did. "In here.
Now." It looked like about fifteen people had managed to
follow him.

He ducked inside, feeling around on the wall for the
battery-powered lantern he knew was there. It took him a few
seconds to find it and flip it on. "We need to make some gas
masks. Now." He ran to the crude racks along the wall, pulling
open the doors and ransacking them for what he needed. He
angled his head back toward the cluster of people behind him.
"Close that door, and jam some cloth underneath."

He grabbed some surgical masks and a bundle of gauze
from one cabinet and dropped them on the table. Then he
knelt down and pulled an armful of old plastic bottles that
had been cut up into makeshift flasks. He pulled out the knife

he wore at his side and started cutting them roughly in the shape of masks. He soaked a handful of cloth in water and put it inside the first bottle. He turned and handed it to the person closest to him. "Put it against your face. There are some elastics in one of those drawers over there. Go grab a handful."

"OK, Axe." Sid Wentz was one of the settlement's oldest residents. He'd been part of Jericho since the start. Axe knew Sid had been over 35 then, but he remained fit and strong, almost immune to the effects of radiation and hardships.

Axe knew Wentz had gotten a serious dose of radiation; he'd been a lot closer to ground zero than most survivors. But year after year, he'd failed to show symptoms. It was a game, a race between genetics and random factors. Axe himself had been relatively immune to side effects from the blasts, even as he'd watched hundreds die over the years. Now, he knew his luck—or his genes—had finally failed him, but Wentz was almost fifteen years older and still going strong.

He was making more masks as quickly as he could, handing them off one at a time as he finished. He knew he only had a few minutes, but he was determined to get one to everybody before they left the infirmary. He knew the attackers would wait until the gas attack had taken out as many of Jericho's people as possible before they moved in. That gave them a short while at least.

He could hear the sounds of more gas grenades impacting, closer now, right outside the door. The infirmary was a half-assed structure, thrown together like everything else in Jericho from whatever could be scavenged. He had no idea if it would keep the gas outside long enough—or if his primitive gas masks would even be effective at all. But he couldn't think of anything else to do, so he didn't waste time worrying about it.

Ellie kept passing through his mind, but he knew he couldn't get to her now. Hopefully, she had gotten away. If not, he knew his best chance to save her was to stay on his feet.

And one breath of that gas would take him out of the fight.

"Alright, let's go," he said as he pulled an elastic around his head, fixing his own mask in place. "Grab anything that looks like it can be a weapon, and let's move. We need to get an idea how many attackers we're dealing with."

He moved toward the door. "Make sure your masks are on. And try not to breathe near any of the white clouds… even though your masks." He put his hand to the door, but he paused and turned his head back around. "But that doesn't mean you're safe if there are no clouds near you. That gas is probably effective even when it is dissipated and invisible. Breathe slowly, carefully." He looked at the small group stacked up behind him. They looked terrified, almost panicked into shock, but they were still there. They weren't warriors. There were a few people in Jericho who knew how to fight— Jack Lompoc was one of them for sure—but none of them were with him now. For all he knew, the fighters were all captured already, or dead.

"He pushed open the door and slipped out into the street. The darkness was lit by a series of fires. Part of Jericho was burning, and there were clouds of dark smoke mixing with the wispy white plumes where the gas grenades had hit. Axe pushed his mask against his face, taking a tentative breath. He didn't know how effective it would be, but it was all he had.

"Let's go," he yelled, his voice muffled by the mask. He moved down the street, staying close to the wall. He stopped after about ten meters and looked around. He didn't see anyone, no invaders, none of his own people, but he could hear sounds in the distance, from around the corner.

He crept up to the edge of the building and peered around. There were more fires, and he could see people running in the flickering light. There were bodies covering the ground. He couldn't tell if they were dead or alive, but he saw half a dozen more drop as he watched. A few seconds later he saw a shadow fly through the air, and everyone still standing fell immediately. *Gas grenade.* A few seconds later he could see half a dozen armed men run into the scene.

"Let's go." He turned and gestured back the way they had come. "That's a dead end." He ran back, past the infirmary and the rows of grain storage buildings. His mind was racing, trying to figure a way to get to the armory. Ellie. She was there. Or at least she had been. Wherever she was, he had to find her. He could gather up whatever survivors he found and try to escape to the north. But not without Ellie.

He paused just before the main intersection, looking carefully around the corner. There were more armed men running through the streets. They were throwing gas grenades, targeting anyone still standing, but then a shot rang out, and one of them fell.

The others reacted immediately, opening fire on something off to the side. Axe couldn't see what they were shooting at, but he knew one of his people had taken down an attacker. He felt a surge of satisfaction, even as he realized that act of defiance was going to cost the shooter his life. There were half a dozen enemies firing, and it only lasted a few seconds. When they stopped, Axe knew another one of his citizens was dead.

He froze for an instant, as he watched the scene. Then he ducked back, but it was an instant too late. One of the attackers started yelling and pointing in his direction. Three men began moving toward the corner of the building, assault rifles at the ready.

Fuck. "They saw us. Everybody, run. Head for the north side of the village, and make for the woods beyond the wall. We'll meet up at the waterfall." He saw they were all hesitating, reluctant to leave him. "GO!" he roared. "Now!"

He peered around the corner and fired with his pistol. "Go," he repeated. "I'll hold them off." *My life's not worth shit now anyway. I'll be dead in a few months, even if I get out of here.* He ducked back as return fire slammed into the wall. He dropped lower, crouching, trying to stay as much in cover as he could. The shelter was flimsy, a combination of logs and thin sheet metal. He knew damned well those bullets could penetrate all of it with enough force left to blow his head off his shoulders.

He ejected the spent clip from his pistol, reaching around to the back of his belt for another. *Last one*, he thought as he slammed it in place. He leaned forward, hearing a volley of bullets blast through the building and whiz by just above his head. He had to move, make a dash for the other side of the street. It was dangerous, desperate, but he was in a death trap where he was.

He took a deep breath, and his lungs strained at the effort. He started coughing hard, but he took off anyway, running as fast as he could. He took his adversaries by surprise, but that only lasted an instant. If he'd been healthy, maybe he could have made it. But his tortured lungs strained for air, and he was too slow. He felt the round hit his leg like a sledgehammer. Then he was falling.

He spun around, trying to land on his back and bring the pistol to bear, but the impact of the fall was too much, and it knocked the weapon from his hand. He felt a wave of pain, first in his leg and then his back as he slammed into the hard ground. He was dizzy, half awake, but the adrenalin was still pumping, and he tried to reach to the side, to grab for his pistol.

His hand was almost there when a black boot came down hard on the pistol, kicking it out of his reach. "Got another one here," he heard a gruff voice yell.

He was lying on his back, trying to focus, his mind racing for a way to escape. "He should be out by now, but he's...oh, check this out." The heavy boot swept across his face, kicking the mask away. "Some kind of homemade gas mask. This one gets points for ingenuity, at least.

Axe heard coarse laughter, but it was soft, far off. He felt his consciousness slipping away. He started coughing hard, the gas triggering a bloody spasm. He could feel the warm blood in his mouth.

He was drifting away, floating slowly into the darkness.

The last thing he heard was, "Fuck it. This one's sick." Then he saw the shadowy image of the man extending his arm, pointing his gun. Pain. Then nothing.

Chapter 7

Dyracchium Plateau ("Dead Man's Ridge")
Planet Lysandria, Delta Sigma III
Earthdate: 2318 AD (33 Years After the Fall)

"Move it, Eagles! I want those things firing in one minute. You hear me? One fucking minute!" Lieutenant Dan Sullivan was crouched low along the top of the ridge. His people had paid for the miserable strip of high ground—they had paid dearly for it. And, by God, they were going to get everything they could out of it now that they had it, and their enemies were the ones out in the open.

He could hear the high-pitched sounds of his troopers' electro-magnetic projectiles, as more squads advanced to the ridgeline and began firing at the retreating Spears. The enemy had known as well as the Eagles how crucial the position was, and they'd fought like hell to hang on to it. Sullivan had begun the battle as a platoon commander, but Captain Hewitt had taken a bad hit early on, leaving him in charge of the 140 men and women of the 3rd Company.

"Get me battalion HQ," he snapped to his AI.

"Connected."

"HQ, this is 3rd Company. We are in possession of the ridgeline. Enemy is retiring in good order. Request immediate drone strike, coordinates 111.7 by 84.9 to 111.9 by 84.9."

"Request approved, Lieutenant. Strike inbound, ETA 3 minutes."

"Acknowledged. Sullivan out." He flashed a thought to the AI. *Put me on unit-wide com.*

The AI responded immediately. "You are on the unit-wide channel."

"Attention all personnel, we have inbound drones, ETA approximately two minutes forty five. Take position behind the crest of the ridgeline and maintain fire on retiring enemy forces. No one is to advance past the ridge without my express order."

He flashed another thought to the AI—to cut the line and reopen the one to his heavy weapons teams. "Why the hell don't I hear those things firing?" he snapped.

"Ten seconds, sir," the first response came, followed by similar answers from the others.

It was almost ten seconds exactly when he heard the familiar sound of autocannons firing. Within twenty, all six of the guns were active, sweeping the broad plateau with six hundred rounds a second. Sullivan looked over the tiny ridge, watching as several dozen Gold Spear soldiers went down under the heavy fire.

"Cease small arms fire," he roared on the unit-wide com. "Autocannons continue firing." The enemy was almost out of effective assault rifle range. His people had fought long and hard to take the position, and he wasn't looking to waste ammunition, not until he had a clearer idea of the supply situation.

"Drone strike incoming." The AI's warning was automatic, matter-of-fact. He glanced up at his display, and he could see the fast-moving formation moving onto the rear edge of the projection. It looked like two recon units and half a dozen anti-personnel drones.

Sullivan tried to imagine what warfare had been like before the Fall on Earth, where the need to move equipment across lightyears of space hadn't been a concern. Those battles had involved tanks and planes and all sorts of heavy ordnance—artillery, hovercraft, gunships. But thirty years after the Fall—and fifteen after the Second Incursion—war had become a much more economical endeavor. The great battleships that had fought man's wars years before were all gone, the last of them lost facing the First Imperium. The Black Eagles were the wealthiest and most technologically advanced military force in Occupied Space, yet they only fielded a fraction of the numbers that had fought in man's Frontier struggles and the Shadow War. And they had little capacity in their vessels for anything but their armor and a few drones. Planes, tanks, trucks—they were from a past age, before 99% of man's industrial capacity was turned into radioactive slag.

Sullivan watched the flight of drones zip overhead and fan out across the plateau. He knew the recon units were gathering information, counting the enemy, both casualties and remaining effectives. They were transmitting everything to HQ, and when they finished their sweep they would continue on, over the next ridgeline, scouting out the enemy positions beyond until they were taken out. The drones were one-shot tools.

The anti-personnel units were more interesting to watch. They networked with the recon units, and the AIs onboard each of them instantly used the realtime intel to generate optimal coverage patterns for their extensive ordnance. The drones each launched half a dozen rockets, targeted to specific groups of enemy troops. Sullivan could see the fiery trails as the weapons streaked to their targets and erupted into massive fireballs. The rockets were the longest-ranged weapons carried by the drones, and the units fired their entire complements immediately, to ensure they wouldn't be lost if the drone was shot down as it approached the enemy position.

The units then swooped lower, their thrusters firing to change trajectories as they angled toward more enemy troop concentrations, dropping spreads of cluster bombs as they passed over. The packages of small explosives cut fifty meter wide swaths through the enemy formations, hundreds of tiny shells carpeting the area with destruction and wiping away even the fully-armored troops in their paths.

The soldiers on the ground were retreating, but they were veterans, and they maintained their discipline. They fired at the drones, taking out three of the deadly devices as they dropped their cluster-bombs. But the others swung around and came back across the plateau, their dual autocannons raining death on those who had survived the initial attacks. Dozens of enemy soldiers went down under the barrage, but the survivors maintained their AA fire and, one at a time, each of the remaining three drones was blasted out of the sky.

The air attack was over, but at least 200 of the enemy lay dead on the plateau, almost half the number who had initially pulled back from the ridge. The drones had earned their keep, and the added attrition helped justify the losses the Eagles had suffered taking the position. The enemy force that had held so grimly was all but destroyed.

Sullivan felt a wave of elation, and he was overcome with the urge to order his troops forward. The enemy hadn't routed, and they were still moving back with some semblance of order. But they were a hell of a lot shakier than they had been, and he knew an all-out attack would send them flying in disarray. But he was a Black Eagle, and if there was one thing Darius Cain pounded into his soldiers, it was discipline. He knew from his training, HQ had a better picture of the overall battlefield. When it was time to advance, he'd get the orders. And until then Sullivan would stay right where he was.

But that wouldn't stop him from enjoying the spectacle on the plateau. The Spears had made his men pay dearly for the ridge, and now it was motherfucking payback time.

*　　*　　*　　*　　*

"Lieutenant Sullivan and Captain Krieger both report the enemy forces in front of their companies have retreated beyond the next ridgelines. Both are requesting permission to pursue." Antonia Camerici's voice was soft, almost like a child's. But Cain knew better than to read anything into that. Camerici was barely taller than a meter and a half, and she weighed about 45 kilos, but he'd seen her put two loudmouthed trainees, each more than twice her size, in the hospital the day she'd arrived at the Nest's training facility. Her adversaries both eventually washed, but Camerici took everything her stunned drillmasters could throw at her, and they'd eventually had to concede that, against all initial indications, the tiny slip of a girl was in fact Eagle material.

Cain was crouched low, staring out over the very plateau his officers wanted to move across. It was quiet now. The survivors of the Spears' force had pulled back beyond a line of hills, leaving only the dead behind, littering the scorched field. A lull had descended, and he knew his people were using the time to evac the wounded.

He was watching his display as the recon drone data fed into his system. "Negative, Lieutenant. They are to maintain position until further notice." The snooper drones didn't get far past the ridgeline before they were both blown away. They'd gotten some data through, but not enough. Cain didn't like what he was seeing, and he was even less happy with what his gut was telling him. There were a few enemy formations in reserve behind the ridge, but not enough to stop a concerted attack. That seemed like good news, at least to someone less paranoid than Cain, but he wasn't buying it. There was more out there than met the eye. He was sure of it.

"Lieutenant," he said briskly, "Contact *Eagle One*. I want Vandeveer's regiment in the tubes and ready for launch as soon as I send them coordinates."

"Yes, sir."

He heard the click as Camerici closed the channel to

call the flagship. He also caught the disapproving tone in her voice. She, like just about every other Eagle, thought he should be back at headquarters, if not still up with the fleet—and certainly not running around along the front lines without even a proper escort.

He glanced behind him at the two bodyguards he'd allowed to accompany him. His people wanted to surround his with guards, but they missed the point. Prowling around in a huge, self-important group was only advertising his presence. The Spears would go to almost any lengths to pick him off if he gave them the chance. But right now he was just another Black Eagle, out on point and behind decent cover. A target, certainly, but not one that would draw down all the ordnance General Ling's people could muster.

The Eagles' commander had a number of defining characteristics, but there was one that reigned supreme above them all. He did whatever he wanted, whenever he wanted. Darius Cain did not like being told what to do, and he reacted very poorly to efforts to compel his compliance. He knew his people considered him irreplaceable, and he also knew that was nonsense. Erik Teller could run the Eagles if anything happened to him—and if Teller was lost too, someone else would step up. War was war. If he'd wanted a safe profession, he'd have learned accounting.

He flashed a thought to his AI to increase the magnification on his visor. He looked out across the plateau. The Spears had been hit hard. His best guess was barely a third of those who'd been on the line along the ridge had made it back. But he was still uncomfortable. There was something else out there. He had no real intel, but he'd learned to trust his instincts.

The Spears were already on the ground when his ships arrived in the system. Indeed, there wasn't a sign of their fleet anywhere. The enemy ships had even less chance against the Eagles than their ground forces did. But the whole thing was nagging at him. Without their ships—and with no realistic prospect of getting them past the Eagles' fleet, the Spears were 100% committed to the battle. It was victory or utter destruction for them. Cain knew General Ling was a pompous, insufferable ass, but he wasn't stupid. Nor was he reckless with the mercenary company he'd taken ten years to build.

There's something I don't know. Ling's got some sort of surprise in store. He thinks he can win this battle. But what is it? What?

He activated the com unit. "Antonia, cancel my order for Vandeveer's people. They are to remain embarked and on alert for rapid deployment."

"Yes, sir," she replied crisply.

I need to keep something up my sleeve. At least until I know what the hell is going on.

He stared out across the plateau again. *What are you planning, Ling? What are you hiding out there?*

*   *   *   *   *

"They are just sitting there!" General Ling Jin stared at the display, his frustration clear in his posture. The commander of the Gold Spears was angry, frustrated that Darius Cain had so far refused to fall into trap he'd so carefully set for him.

"General Cain is a cautious man, General." Colonel Jiang Li stood two meters behind Ling, watching the general nervously. Ling was a gifted tactician, but he was prone to outbursts of anger, and his senior officers tended to handle him with considerable care.

"He is my curse!" Ling turned abruptly, staring at Jiang. "There is no valid tactical reason for him not to advance. None!" When he was upset, Ling tended to spit when he spoke, and Jiang stood firm, ignoring the blast of saliva that came his way. "Yet he just sits there on that ridge!"

Jiang had been less confident that Cain would barge right into the trap. It was true, every tactical indication suggested it was the right move, but it was no secret that Cain was a careful man—and a military genius no one on the Spears' command staff could match. Not that Jiang wasn't about to admit that in from of Ling.

"We will have to be patient, General Ling." The voice came from across the room. The man walking toward Ling was not one of the Spears. He was tall, with sandy brown hair and a muscular build. He was clad in a brown uniform, with a pair of black boots and a rank insignia on his collar that Ling had never seen before. "General Cain may yet take the bait."

Ling turned to face his guest. No, he reminded himself, ally. The whole thing was still difficult to accept. He couldn't argue with the discipline and skill of the troops his supposed new friend had brought with him, nor the fact that they presented him with his only real chance of destroying Darius Cain and his Black Eagles. But it still nagged at him. Where did Diomedes come from? How did such a force exist without the Spears knowing anything about it?

"That is true, General Diomedes, but have you considered what we will do if he does not?" Ling had been skeptical when Diomedes had first contacted him, but the mysterious commander had followed through on every promise. Not only did he bring 3,000 of his own superbly-equipped troops to Lysandria, but Ling suspected the sudden and mysterious ability of the locals to pay the Gold Spears' price had something to do with this new connection. There was clearly a significant power behind all of this, one that didn't seem to have any more good will toward the Eagles than he did. *The enemy of my enemy…*

"If we are unable to entice General Cain into making a mistake, we will have little choice but to attack his forces where they are." The mysterious general spoke calmly, his tone betraying almost no emotion at all.

"But can we defeat the Black Eagles if we attack them

on ground of their own choosing?" Ling's tone was edgy, showing signs of strain.

Diomedes returned Ling's gaze. "The Black Eagles are the most professional and the deadliest military unit in Occupied Space, General Ling. It is unlikely we will be able to defeat them in any scenario." He stared at Ling without an ounce of emotion on his face, as if he was reading from a script.

Ling went pale. "If you don't believe we can defeat the Eagles, why did you bring your forces to Lysandria?"

"It is my mission to inflict as much damage on the Black Eagles as possible."

"But how do you plan to get off Lysandria then?" Ling was confused, and he could feel the sweat pooling behind his neck.

"I do not plan to leave Lysandria, General Ling. My forces will fight until they are destroyed. And, as the Eagles have sworn not to take any of your people prisoner, you have little choice but to do the same. We will severely damage the Eagles, costing them soldiers it will take years to replace."

"I did not lead my soldiers here just to see them all slaughtered!" Ling's expression was a mix of fear and rage.

"No, I suspect your motivations were quite different, though your analysis of the situation was significantly flawed. You could not have reasonably determined that your forces could destroy the Black Eagles, not without allowing your own emotions and pride to supersede facts. Even my forces are inadequate to increase the odds of total victory in a fight to the finish above a few percentage points." He stared at Ling with a deadpan expression on his face. "In all likelihood, we will die here...you, me, and all of our soldiers. But we will kill many Black Eagles before we do." And still, there wasn't a trace of emotion in his voice.

*   *   *   *   *

"They're coming in again, General." Camerici turned to face Cain. "This is the third wave, sir, and it's at least 2,000 strong."

Cain nodded. He had smelled a trap and ordered his troops to stand fast and hold their positions. Now his fears had been confirmed. Wave after wave of enemy troops were assaulting him now, all from hidden positions beyond the ridge. If he'd allowed Kuragina's people to advance when they'd wanted to, they'd have been surrounded. It would have been a bloodbath.

He stared at the display. It was bad enough now. He had over 250 dead already, and at least that many wounded. It had been a long time since the Eagles had seen such a desperate fight, and they were acquitting themselves brilliantly. Estimating enemy losses in the middle of a battle was always a bit tricky, but he was sure his people had inflicted at least 3,000 casualties. They had the benefit of defending in most places, but still, that was a differential of six to one—and against supremely well-equipped forces.

All the fighting so far had been done by the Spears and their mysterious allies. The Lysandrian troops were woefully ill-equipped for the high tech war now going on, and they had remained in their forts and entrenchments around the capital city. Cain had sent a company to screen them, but he'd ordered them left alone as long as they stayed in place. The other forces he was facing were far more dangerous, and he wanted them neutralized before he even worried about seizing the planetary objectives. Once the Spears and their mysterious allies were destroyed, taking the Lysandrian cities would be child's play.

He was watching transmissions from some of the forward units, video of enemy formations as they attacked. He picked off the Gold Spears immediately. Their dark gray armor was immediately recognizable. But there were other forces mixed in with them, troops he'd never seen before. Their suits were dark brown, and based on his initial observations, they were superior to those worn by Ling's men. His best guess was they weren't quite on par with his own peoples' Mark VIII's, but they looked pretty close.

Who are these guys? Cain thought he knew every mercenary company in Occupied Space, especially forces as large and well-equipped as this one. *Why don't I have any intel on them?*

"Launch a double spread of snooper drones. I want to know where these troops are coming from. They've got a base out there somewhere, more than one maybe, and I want coordinates."

"Yes, sir." Camerici relayed Cain's orders. "Sir, I've got Colonel Kuragina for you."

"Put her through, Lieutenant."

"General, my people could use some backup. Any chance you could send some of Vandeveer's people down?"

Cain frowned. He hated turning a deaf ear to aid requests from his officers. And he knew for sure if Cyn Kuragina was calling him for help her people had been damned near overrun. But he still had no idea how large a force he was facing. He knew the strength of the Gold Spears—he'd have bet a hundred credits he knew their OB better than Ling did. But these new troops were a complete mystery.

"Sorry, Colonel, but I need to keep those reserves fresh until we have a better idea of what we're dealing with. You're just going to have to hold on somehow, Cyn." He paused. "I'm sending you a reserve company...and half a dozen Special Action Teams. But use them carefully, because it's all I've got to give you until we get some better intel."

"Thanks, sir. We'll manage somehow. Kuragina out."

Cain stared at the display, but he wasn't seeing anything. It had been a long time since so many of his troops were in such trouble. He trained them as ruthlessly as he did so they were always tougher than their opponents—so that victory was all but assured when they took the field. They were always most experienced, the best equipped. And they had the best intel too. But now he was standing around headquarters with no fucking clue what he was facing, and his troops were fighting strange enemies almost as well-trained and equipped as they were. He could feel the frustration building, the anger.

"Camerici, I want those snoopers launched, NOW!"

*   *   *   *   *

"Perretti, Horn…stay the fuck down. You want those pretty heads blown off? If I have to tell you again, I'm gonna shoot 'em off myself so you remember next time." Joseph "Bull" Trent was widely regarded as the toughest, most nasty-assed platoon sergeant in the Black Eagles. The stories about him were legion, and he did nothing to discourage them. By the time they'd reached the third or fourth retelling, he'd grown ten centimeter claws, and he spit fire. It was only a moderate exaggeration.

"Sorry, Sarge. Things are getting pretty damned hot around here. The Spears are a joke as usual. The shitheads were always overrated, but these guys in the brown suits are tough." Tony Perretti was one of those perennial privates, a longtime veteran and a hard-ass without compare. But he hated responsibility, and he didn't want to be in charge of anybody but himself—and he was a master of getting into enough petty trouble to get busted back down every time he earned a second stripe. It was a miracle Cain had never bounced him out of the Eagles—and a testament to his skills as a soldier too.

"No shit, Perretti. And there's a lot of 'em too. So pay fucking attention to what you're doing. I need ya at your best right now. Got it?" Bull's voice always had a caustic edge, but right then it sounded like something that could eat through metal.

"Yeah, Sarge, I got it." Tony Perretti was more than a match for most sergeants, but not Bull Trent, and his tone was almost pliant. There was a short pause then: "Sarge, I think we got another wave comin' on."

"I see it, Perretti." Bull was staring at the inside of his visor, watching a flood of new contacts pour onto the display. "And it looks like a big one." *Fuck. If was sittin' in HQ with the general's stars on my shoulder, I'd bet that was the big push. And if I'm right, we don't have enough to stop it.*

"Perretti, I need you and Horn to move forward. Scout the area and see if you can get a good read on where these guys are comin' from. They got a secret base out there someplace, and if we can get the coordinates to HQ, the general can give it to 'em. Straight up the ass."

"We're on it, Sarge."

"And Perretti…be careful. I want scouting info, not two dead assholes out there."

"I'm always careful, Sarge."

Bull sighed. Careful? He had to hold back a caustic laugh. Perretti was just about the craziest son of a bitch he knew.

*   *   *   *   *

Diomedes climbed the ladder to the surface. There were several dozen of the access tubes, and they were all filled with his soldiers. The underground base had been hastily constructed, but it had served its purpose well. But now it was time for the final push, and his place was on the surface with his forces. He knew victory was highly improbable, that they were all likely doomed. But that didn't matter. By the time the fighting was over on Lysandria, he would be dead, along with every one of his soldiers. He thought about that in a detached way, without fear, without even real regret.

Diomedes had memories of his past, but they were scattered, hazy, often unrelated to each other. Images of wandering the wasteland, scavenging for food. Of blasted, shattered buildings and poisoned waterways covered with the bloated corpses of dead fish. He remembered vague feelings—hunger, sickness, fear, though he didn't fully understand them. His earliest clear recollections were of his training, the months of drill and practice that had made him a soldier—and later an officer—in the Omega Force. And he remembered the long conditioning sessions, endless, almost brutal. On a level he couldn't entirely comprehend, he knew the conditioning had changed his persona, molded his emotions and his beliefs. But he didn't care. It had made him what he was, a part of the greater whole, and there was nothing more gratifying than to sacrifice oneself to the Plan. Anything that helped him to realize that was good, worth losing parts of who he had been.

"All battalion commanders, prepare to execute Plan Zed." He spoke evenly, calmly into the com unit. In a few moments, his remaining soldiers would launch an all-out attack. He didn't believe they would win the battle, but the Black Eagle units closest to their point of impact were exhausted and heavily depleted. His forces would inflict enormous casualties before Darius Cain was able to bring reinforcements forward from the other side of his lines. The Eagles would have their victory, but it would be a pyrrhic one. And that had been Diomedes' mission.

He had hoped the survivors of the Gold Spears would join his forces for the final attack, but General Ling was not part of the Plan, and he lacked the commitment to sacrifice all to degrade the Black Eagles. Despite his knowledge that Darius Cain had vowed not to take any prisoners, General Ling had decided to contact Cain and try to surrender. Such action was unthinkable. It would have been highly disruptive to the Plan, and Diomedes had been compelled to terminate Ling and his senior command staff to prevent it. His action had left the Spears' units were cut off and in complete disarray. Hopefully, they would continue to fight the Eagles—indeed, they would have little choice since their enemies would offer them no quarter.

Diomedes pulled himself up into the fading light of Lysandria's short winter afternoon. It would be dusk in less than an hour, and night in not much more than another. The attack would begin at nightfall, and it would continue as long as combatants remained in the field. He knew the Eagles would torture any of his people they captured; his pre-mission briefing had made that clear. And he had no intention of allowing that to happen. "Activate Alpha Omega protocols," he said grimly to his suit's AI."

"Alpha Omega confirmed." The artificial intelligence's voice had a grim sound to it.

His people were now safe from abuse at the hands of their enemies. If they were in danger of capture, their AIs would detonate the Alpha Omega charge in their suits, killing them instantly, and hopefully taking some of the enemy with them.

He moved forward, toward the area where his soldiers were forming up for the attack. In 90 minutes, the Black Eagles would suffer the worst losses in their storied history. The Plan would move inexorably forward, and Diomedes and his people would die as heroes, martyrs to the cause of saving humanity from chaos.

*   *   *   *   *

"General, I've got a Sergeant Trent on the com. He is insisting he needs to speak directly to you." Camerici sounded annoyed. She wasn't used to enlisted personnel arguing with her about talking with the general.

"Bull? Cain here. What's up?" Cain had no such hesitation. He was familiar with every soldier in his command, and he always had time for Bull Trent.

"I pushed a couple of my boys a little farther forward than your orders, sir." Bull Trent terrorized virtually everyone around him, but he was like a child speaking to a parent now. Darius Cain had a strange ability to turn even the deadliest warriors into quivering supplicants.

"And?" Cain knew Trent was half-expecting a dressing down, but there was no time for that. Bull was one of the best soldiers in the Black Eagles, and Darius wanted to hear anything the man had to say. Immediately.

"Sir, we've got enemy forces emerging from hidden positions, probably underground. Battalion strength at least, and probably more, sir. It looks like they're preparing to launch a major attack." A short pause. "Transmitting coordinates now, sir."

"Relay your data to Colonel Kuragina, Sergeant. And find a good place to dig in, because we're going to fight it out along your line. Nobody pulls back. Understood."

"Understood, sir!"

"And Sergeant…well done."

"Thank you, sir."

Cain cut the line. "Lieutenant, get me Colonel Vandeveer on Eagle One."

"On your line, sir."

"Ian, Cain here. Get your men into the launch bay. Now. I'm transmitting coordinates."

"On my way, sir. We'll be right down. Vandeveer out."

Hurry, Cain thought. Because Kuragina's people are going to get chewed to pieces if you don't get down here fast.

Chapter 8

Executive Habitat, Beneath the Ruins of the Ares Metroplex
Planet Mars, Sol IV
Earthdate: September, 2318 AD (33 Years After the Fall)

"Mr. Vance? I am sorry to wake you, sir." It was Bev, sticking her head cautiously through the open door. She had been Vance's assistant for almost thirty years, but she still acted like invading his inner sanctum was an almost unthinkable intrusion. His household staff had been under orders for decades to admit her to him at any time without question, but she was still hesitant to disturb him.

"What is it, Bev?" Vance didn't move, but his voice was clear, alert. He hadn't been asleep, not even close. He sat up, and looked over toward the rectangle of light coming through the doorway. He was naked except for a pair of shorts, but it didn't even occur to him. Bev was like an extension of himself, and he had no conception of modesty in front of her.

"Sir, we received a message from one of the settlements. They were under attack by an unidentified group." She also ignored the fact that he was sitting up in bed wearing a pair of shorts and nothing else, but her voice was still tentative, as if she was having second thoughts about disturbing him in the middle of the night. She knew he didn't get a lot of sleep, and she'd taken to treating him in a motherly way regarding his health and life, despite being nine years younger. Vance's duties had only grown in the aftermath of the final defeat of Gavin Stark and his Shadow Legions, and she had to continually remind him to eat and sleep. She suspected he would work continuously until he dropped if it wasn't for her.

Vance sighed. He'd given the com units to the biggest Earth settlements, as much because it seemed to make sense than for any specific purpose he could name. Indeed, there were many reasons the villages might call, but precious few things he could do to help them. The settlements were attacked all the time. They raided each other, fended off nomadic raiders. Earth was a desperate place, and anyone who had anything worthwhile—enough food to eat, a place to sleep, fuel for fire—had to defend it, or someone else would try to take it away.

He felt sorry for the inhabitants, but he barely had enough resources to send them food, medicine, and a few basic tools. Taking responsibility for their defense was out of the question. Thirty years after the devastating finish to the final series of wars between the Powers, Mars herself was still struggling to rebuild. He'd had a hard enough time getting the council to agree to the limited program of aid for the survivors on Earth. They wouldn't even consider military intervention.

"That is unfortunate, Bev, but you know there is nothing we can do…" He paused. "What settlement was it?"

"Jericho, sir." Her voice was somber. "That is why I decided to wake you."

Jericho was one of the biggest settlements on Earth, not that her own residents had any idea of that fact. Vance had selected the village, along with three others, for the second stage of his aid plan—assuming he ever managed to get the resolution through the council. Losing such a prime location would set things back. There just weren't many places on Earth that had achieved a level of development sufficient to serve as even a rudimentary base for reintroducing simple technology.

Vance sighed. "Any subsequent messages?"

"No, sir." Bev's voice was somber. "The supply drops are scheduled for tomorrow, so I asked Captain Clark to do a flyover." She looked at Vance tentatively, as if she was worried she'd overstepped her authority.

"Good thinking, Bev. I want that data the second we have it."

"Yes, sir. Will that be all?"

Vance took a deep breath. "Yes, Bev. But if there is another communication—or any news at all—I want to know immediately." He stared across the room at her. "Immediately…any time of the day or night. Understood?"

"Yes, sir. I understand." She nodded and slipped back through the still-open door. A few seconds later, it slid shut behind her.

Vance sat on the edge of his bed and put his face in his hands. *Jericho. I can't lose Jericho. They were the best positioned for stage two.* His mind drifted into darker thoughts. Losing the settlement was bad enough, but this was just another in a growing list of disturbing reports, mysterious raids and disappearances all over the planet. Someone had been attacking scattered bands of survivors and small villages for months now. *Years, probably.* At first Vance had written it off as an anomaly, an increase in fighting between settlements. But it had been getting worse—and if a target as big as Jericho was vulnerable, there was clearly something more dangerous at play than rival villages fighting over food.

He got up and walked toward his desk, grabbing the light sheet and wrapping it around his shoulders as he did. The room was cool—even thirty years after the devastating attack that had driven most of its population to the underground shelters, the Confederation was still on a strict conservation protocol. The decision to keep the massive terraforming reactors at the poles operating at full power virtually mandated major reductions in the standard of living. Mars' surface temperature was considerably higher than it had been when the first settlers had landed a century and a half before, but it still took enormous power to heat the colony—and to pump its air and produce its water.

Vance had always kept his quarters at the mandated temperatures, despite his status as one of the Confederation's wealthiest men and a member of the ruling council. He knew many of his colleagues exempted themselves from the regulations they imposed on the population. That made Vance uncomfortable. He couldn't stop his peers from indulging their personal comforts—there were far too many other battles to fight—but he'd resolved not to do it himself. It was too much like the behavior of the politicians on Earth, and it was only too obvious where that system eventually led. If an extra blanket could preserve his integrity, he'd decided long ago he could live with that.

He sat down and turned on his workstation. *Who the hell could take out Jericho? What is going on?* He'd been somewhat worried about the prior reports, but now he could feel the stress build in his stomach. Something was wrong, very wrong. The situation was much more serious than he'd imagined. And he had to find out what it was.

He moved his hand toward the com unit to contact General Astor, but he stopped himself. The council had been adamant, despite his repeated arguments. Mars had enough problems of its own, and they simply would not authorize the deployment of military units to Earth. They'd approved the aid program, a sop they threw to Vance, but that was all.

He sat quietly, feeling the frustration growing inside him. *Astor will do what I ask, and damned the council.* He stared at the com controls. *No, you can't.* Vance knew the council would eventually find out, and then they would expel him from his leadership position. He couldn't ignore the mandate. Not unless he was going to launch a coup and seize total power. But he was determined not to do that—not unless he had absolutely no choice.

But the council can't tell me what to do with my own resources. Vance had long been one of Mars' wealthiest men, the heir to a massive family fortune. He'd suffered crippling losses in Stark's attack on Mars and the subsequent economic collapse, but he'd managed to stabilize his remaining enterprises and, despite an 80% drop in the value of his holdings, he was still enormously wealthy.

Can I risk the family fortune? He had long kept his two roles separated, managing his investments and working as one of Mars' political leaders without unduly mixing the two. Vance had no children, but he did have a number of cousins and nieces and nephews. Did he have the right to risk their inheritance? It went against everything his father had taught him, all his ancestors had done. They had never risked the family businesses, despite their record of dedication to the effective governance of Mars.

But he couldn't put it out of his mind. If someone was attacking Earth settlements, there had to be a reason. Who could it be? None of the colony worlds had the resources to project their power to Earth and, even if they could, none would dare cross Mars. The Confederation had declared the entire Sol system as its protectorate. Mars was battered, struggling to get its own infrastructure and economy back to pre-war levels, but it was now the most powerful human-occupied world by a large margin.

Was there some power developing out there? Something Vance knew nothing about? The thought was extremely unsettling. He finally moved his hand and hit the com unit. "Bev, I'm sorry to jerk you around so late at night, but can you come back for a minute? I have something I want you to do, and I don't want to discuss it over the com."

"I'll be there in two minutes, sir." Her response was immediate and professional, as always. He suspected she'd just gotten back to her own quarters, but there wasn't a hint of annoyance in her voice. He realized how grateful he was to have an assistant like Bev.

He leaned back in his chair, his mind going over a short list of trusted colleagues. He needed someone smart and capable, someone he absolutely knew would be discrete. He considered a number of his operatives, but then he realized he'd known all along who he was going to send. Duncan Campbell.

If he'd go.

*   *   *   *   *

"Duncan, thank you for coming so late." Vance stood up and extended his hand to his guest. "Please, sit. I took the liberty of ordering us a late supper. I don't know if you ate, but I was tied up in council meetings all evening, and I confess, I'm starving."

Duncan Campbell grasped Vance's hand. "Of course, Roderick. I am always available to you. You know that." He glanced at the trays laid out before him. "I did eat, but that looks awfully good. Even post-Fall, your table has maintained its reputation. I might enjoy a bit of a snack at that." He walked over and sat opposite where Vance was standing, and his host followed suit.

Vance smiled and nodded. "You're probably wondering why I asked you to come on such short notice." Vance filled two glasses from an ancient looking bottle. "But first, share this with me. It is quite old...and very rare these days."

Campbell reached across the table and took the offered glass. He nodded his thanks and took a sip. His eyes widened. "A pre-Blight Burgundy? I didn't know there were any left." Campbell was no stranger to luxuries. His father had been a major Martian industrialist. The Campbell's hadn't been as wealthy as the Vance's but then almost no one was. Duncan had been his widowed father's last child, the illegitimate offspring of his housekeeper turned lover. The elder Campbell had been determined to force his older children to accept his youngest son, but they had resisted bitterly. Duncan had given up his claim to the business to maintain peace in the family, and he'd pursued a military career to further distance himself from any friction with his half-siblings.

Still, Arthur Campbell had seen his son well-provided for, leaving a very large trust in place when he died. And Duncan had excelled beyond anyone's wildest dreams, leading the ships that faced the last of Gavin Stark's Shadow fleet. Campbell and his naval personnel had performed with great distinction, and they'd returned to a Mars desperately in need of heroes to celebrate. He'd served another twenty-five years in the navy, the last fifteen as its commander-in-chief. He'd been retired five years now, and as far as Stark was aware, he'd spent most of that time catching up with his wife and playing with his grandchildren.

"Yes, it is very hard to find these days, though not quite extinct yet. I have a few bottles left, though not many, I'm afraid." Vance took a sip himself. "We move forward in time, but not always in other ways, I am afraid. Mankind has lost much."

"That is true. But there are things I find hard to mourn as well." He looked across the table. "The Superpowers deserved their fate, Roderick, if not the billions who died to cleanse away the stink of their governments. I know what they were like, in a way you could never, despite your decades of diplomatic—and other—experience." Vance had long been in the forefront of Mars' international relations, but it was a substantially smaller group of people who knew he'd led the Confederation's intelligence operation for four decades.

"The slums of Edinburgh were no joy to behold, my friend, a festering pit where most of the people went to bed hungry. The rats would have claimed the place, if the starving Cogs hadn't greedily scooped them up to supplement their meager diets."

He paused, a sad look taking over his face for a few seconds. "And if my father had not been the man he'd been, if he'd merely impregnated his housekeeper and cast her and her bastard child aside, as so many of Earth's elite would have done, I would no doubt have spent my life there in squalor... until the day the bombs came."

"I will not ask you to mourn the Superpowers, Duncan. Indeed, part of my daily struggle is an ongoing effort to ensure that Mars does not go down that path. And there are days I despair of success. It is man's nature to abuse what power and privilege is given to him, and those who resist such urges are few." He stared silently at his guest. "But you are one of those, my old friend...incorruptible. That is why I asked you to come here."

"So finally, we come to it. A last minute meeting, an almost extinct vintage to grease the gears. It must be serious, Roderick." Campbell took a deep breath. "So what is it you need?"

Vance nodded. "Long ago, you did a favor for me, a special mission."

"I remember. You sent me to Armstrong on one of those infernal Torch transports...with an encouragement to see if I could coax record speed from the thing, if I recall correctly."

Vance nodded. "You do. And you did. By a considerable margin, if I remember correctly."

"I also seem to remember burning the thing out and crash landing, almost killing myself in the process." He smiled. "Though I did get your message through, and there's a good chance it saved General Cain's life."

Vance nodded. "And Cain went on to kill Gavin Stark, doing more than any other single human being to end the Shadow Wars." He paused, his voice becoming somber. "And he was the hero of the second war with the First Imperium." Both men were silent for a moment. They knew all too well that Erik Cain had not come back from that last struggle.

Campbell broke the silence. "Erik Cain was a man who did more than his share, no one can ever argue that. He was a true hero, in every sense of the word." Changing the subject: "So what is it you want me to do, Roderick?"

Vance let out a soft breath, still remembering some of his encounters with Cain. The two had shared a cynicism, and also a determination, subconscious in Cain at least, not to allow their pessimism to interfere with duty. No man had ever fought harder and sacrificed more for mankind, while fundamentally believing in it so little. He'd spent his life at war to give people chances and freedoms he believed with all his heart they would squander and abuse. And Vance knew his own beliefs weren't far from what Cain's had been.

He pulled his thoughts back to the matter at hand. "There are raiding parties attacking settlements on Earth, Duncan. I don't know why or what is behind it all, but the situation is worsening." He paused, feeling uncomfortable even discussing the subject. "The council is adamant about not committing any Martian military assets, even just to investigate. They feel we have enough to do continuing to rebuild the Confederation, and they will not approve anything other than the basic food and medicine drops."

Campbell sighed softly. "I'm inclined to agree with you that such policy is short-sighted, but I'm not sure what I can do. Your influence is vastly greater than my own. If you can't sway them, I don't see how I…"

"I don't want you to sway them, Roderick. I want you to help me get around them. I have already accepted that committing Martian forces is out of the question, at least for the foreseeable future." He hesitated. "But I am prepared to fund a personal expedition, at least to investigate and get some idea of what is going on. I will pay for everything with Vance Interplanetary's assets."

Campbell stared back at his friend. "I know your holdings are vast, Roderick, but you suffered the effects of the Fall as badly as anyone. Your resources are not what they were, old friend, and military expeditions are extremely costly. You could risk your family's entire legacy."

Vance smiled. "The company is not so close to the edge as it was just after the attacks, Duncan. It can manage a small expedition. I'm not talking about funding a war. Just finding out what is going on—and doing it with a force large enough to take care of itself."

"You want to hire a mercenary company."

Vance nodded. "Not just any company. I want you to take a ship and go see Darius Cain for me."

Campbell stared back in shock. "You want to hire the Black Eagles? But Darius Cain and his people are…"

"Butchers? Barbarians? Come on, Duncan, you don't really believe any of that. The boy's got a healthy dose of his father's cynicism, no doubt, but if you ignore the spin and the tall tales, he's a professional soldier through and through. And he's as good as they come." He paused. "And I'm not trying to hire the entire company, just a detachment to do some investigating on Earth and to try to get some idea who is attacking settlements. That's all. We're not talking about a war."

"Do the Eagles even take small jobs like that? They're at the top of the food chain, Roderick, the best military force in Occupied Space. Planets mortgage their futures to hire them. What would they want with a piddling job like this?"

Vance nodded. "You're right. That is why I want to send you as my personal envoy. I'd go myself if I thought I could get away without drawing undue attention. I'm hoping Darius will do this for us…for me. I've met the boy a number of times, and he knows how closely his father and I worked together." He paused, his voice becoming sadder when he continued. "And whatever anyone says about Darius Cain, he loved his father without question. His whole life since Erik's disappearance, the Eagles and all the campaigns they have fought—it's all been his way of living up to Erik's legacy." He paused again. "I think he will do this for us."

Campbell nodded and sat quietly for a few seconds. "How far forward have you considered this? You may not be planning on funding a war, but what if your investigation leads to one?"

Vance took a deep breath then exhaled. "Well, I suppose that is a possibility. Perhaps solid evidence of external tampering on Earth will be enough to awaken the council to the danger and spur them to action. I guess I will cross that bridge when I come to it." He stared across the table, his eyes locked intently on Campbell's. "So will you go, old friend? Will you help me investigate what is going on?"

Campbell nodded slowly and offered his friend a faint smile. "Of course I will go." He smiled. "Retirement's a fucking bore anyway."

*   *   *   *   *

"Andre, thank you for meeting me down here." The sounds of heavy machinery almost drowned out Vance's words. The room was huge, the far wall barely visible in the distance. There were massive turbines all around, and a series of 20-meter high pumps along the far wall, connected to conduits taller than a man. The chamber was the very heart of the Ares Metroplex, pumping air and water and heat to the residences and commercial areas of the subterranean complex.

"Of course, Roderick. When have you called that I have not come?" Vance had known Andre Girard for seventy years. He'd been a teenager when they'd first met. Girard had been one of his father's brash young agents at the time. When the elder Vance was tragically killed, Girard had helped Roderick fill his father's chair far too early. Much of Vance's knowledge then, especially his tradecraft and understanding of the scope of Martian Intelligence's operations, had come right from Girard.

Vance smiled weakly. "You have been a loyal friend and companion, Andre, for more years than I care to count." His voice was halting. He'd called his friend to ask him to do something, but now he found it difficult to speak the words.

"I can't recall the last time I saw you so troubled. What is it, my old friend? There is no problem you cannot share with me." Girard stood tall and proud, and he looked decades years younger than his 107 years.

"It is not doubt about your trustworthiness that worries me, Andre. It is what I must ask of you that gives me pause. Your life has been one of service, most of it in secrecy. You have done as much as any man to guide the Confederation and to save if from the forces that might easily have destroyed it, but for you there have been no parades, no medals. Just the silent commendation of your spymasters. It is the bane of the successful spy, to live a life of such danger and to enjoy so little appreciation." He paused uncomfortably. "And now I must ask you to do something above and beyond all you have already done…and at great risk to yourself."

"Roderick," the old spy said, "parades and medals are meaningless to me. I've had all the accolades I could have wanted, from you and your father before you. Do I seem like a man who craves cheering crowds or little hunks of gold and silver on my chest? No…for me, the respect and admiration of men I admire is all I ever wanted." He reached out and put a weather-worn hand on Vance's arm. "Now tell me what is going on. And what you need of me. I am, as always, at your service."

Vance took a deep breath. "I may be overreacting about this. Indeed, this may be no more than my own paranoia."

"Save that for someone who knows you less well than I, Roderick. I have learned to trust your judgment without reservation. If you told me you expected a fire breathing dragon to attack the city, I'd get myself a flame-retardant suit."

Vance allowed himself a tiny smile, but it faded quickly from his lips. "Very well, Andre. You know, of course, that we have long been providing humanitarian supplies to settlements on Earth?"

Girard nodded.

"You are also aware that the council has expressly forbidden any expansion of the program? No provision of technology, no military units deployed to the surface?"

"Yes," Girard said softly. "At least my knowledge of the relief operation strongly suggests this. Though, my information pipeline in retirement is not what it was before." After a brief pause: "I hadn't been aware that you'd tried to obtain authorization for more."

"Indeed, I have. The population of Earth is less than 2% of what it was before the Fall, yet there are as many human beings still living on man's homeworld—in conditions of miserable squalor—than there are in the rest of Occupied Space combined. I understand caution, and I realize the Confederation has suffered greatly too and must focus its resources on its own recovery. But to do nothing—or as little as we have done—is a crime against humanity." The frustration of a dozen past arguments came out in Vance's tone. "I mean, the Superpowers aren't going to reappear if we give the survivors heaters and basic electrical generation. And those survivors were as much victims of the Powers they were compelled to live under as anyone else."

"They do not resist out of callous or selfish impulses, Roderick. They are afraid. The council is mostly civilian, industrialists and financiers. They saw most of their wealth evaporate in Stark's final assault and the Fall. They watched as the citizens of our four largest cities retreated underground, seeking safety from the destruction."

The sounds of the machinery almost drowned out their words, and Girard leaned in, closer to Vance's ear. "Even three decades later, they look inward...back, not ahead. They see most Martians still living below ground, in the tunnels beneath the shattered domes. They see how much weaker we are than we were before, how much of our old industry is gone. And the Second Incursion scared the hell out of them…it reminded them the First Imperium—and God knows what else—is still out there. And mankind is vastly weaker than he once was, far less able to face new threats."

"But that fear pushes them to make us weaker. It feeds on itself. Surely, they should understand."

"They should, Roderick. But they do not. And they will not." He paused and stared into his friend's eyes. "It is clear to me you need something done. Something not sanctioned by the council." He offered Vance a warm smile. "So, why don't you just tell me what it is and be done with it?"

Vance stood quietly for a few seconds, an expression of surprise on his face. "Now I remember why you were such a cornerstone of intelligence operations for 70 years." He hesitated a few more seconds. "I want to send someone to Earth, Andre. Someone reliable." Another pause. "In direct violation of council orders."

Girard stared back emotionlessly. If he was surprised by Vance's statement, he hid it completely. "Clearly there is a problem on Earth beyond a lack of portable heaters. What is happening, Roderick? What do you fear?"

"There have been reports, Andre…for several years now. People disappearing, rumors of kidnappers rounding up stragglers."

Girard's face was cold, expressionless. Mass kidnappings could be a number of things, but none of them were good. "Is it widespread?"

"I hadn't thought so." Vance's voice was grim. "But I was wrong. And that is why you are here."

Andre took a deep breath. "So what do you know? And what do you need me to go find out?"

"We had a list of settlements, big ones, places to start if we ever managed to get council approval for expanded operations. One of these was called Jericho. It was in the northeast of the old US section of the Alliance. Mostly refugees from New York and Boston."

"Was?""

"Yes. Was. That is the problem. There were over a thousand people in Jericho. It was one of the biggest settlements on Earth." Vance sighed. "I had given the larger villages radios—a borderline violation of council orders, but close enough to the gray area. They had instructions never to use them except in an emergency. The Jericho unit transmitted a distress call for 41 minutes...and then it went dead."

"You think someone attacked Jericho? I would have thought a settlement that big was strong enough to fend off any threats still existing on Earth."

Vance nodded. "You'd be right. There are no other villages or wandering bands capable of destroying something like Jericho. But it was nevertheless destroyed. I was able to confirm it with scanner readings from the observation satellites. It is completely abandoned, burned to the ground." He looked right into Girard's eyes. "It had to be a force from off-world. Jericho was just too big to be wiped out by anything else."

The two men stood staring at each other, silent except for the din of the machinery. It was obvious they had both known what they were talking about, but Vance had finally said it out loud. The Martian Confederation had declared the entire Sol system quarantined. But now, someone had violated that order. It was a direct challenge to the Confederation, though the council's shortsightedness masked it.

"But," Girard finally said, "that means they've been able to penetrate our scanning grid."

The Confederation tracked all traffic going through the Sol system's two warp gates. In theory, nothing should be able to get through without the Martian navy knowing everything about it. But the Martian Torches had partial stealth technology, and the ships Gavin Stark had used to attack Mars thirty years before had been even more proof against detection. Perhaps this enemy had something similar. Vance was about to say something to that effect when he realized his friend was already there.

Girard stared at Vance, a growing look of shock on his face. "You mean we are dealing with someone with stealth ships?" As far as anyone in Martian Intelligence knew, Stark's vessels had all been destroyed, the technology lost. And the other worlds in Occupied Space were too busy trying to become self-sufficient with food and basic industry to pour resources into staggeringly expensive R&D programs.

Vance nodded, exhaling hard as he did. "It would seem. So now you understand my concern. If we are dealing with an enemy with stealth technology, our potential dangers increase geometrically. It goes well beyond humanitarian concerns for the survivors on Earth."

"But the council...surely they..."

"They won't believe it, Andre. Not without some kind of proof. I've been trying to convince them to expand the Earth support efforts for too long. They will see it as an attempt on my part to stir up fears to win support for my programs. And the destruction we saw thirty years ago, the long, slow struggle to rebuild since then...it has made them insular and defensive in their thinking. They are convinced no one can threaten the Confederation if we put all our efforts into home defense and, as long as that is the case, they will resist all entreaties to divert resources to anything else."

"So," Girard said, "you want me to go to Earth." He spoke bluntly, without reservation. He knew they were alone. That's why Vance had chosen such an inconvenient spot to meet. "You want me to investigate, to find out what is going on." He paused. "To get you that proof."

"That is exactly what I need, Andre, but it is not that simple." He hesitated. "You would be violating the council's orders. You would be in danger not only on the mission, but upon your return as well if any word of this leaks out. You could lose everything. You could end up in prison. I am asking a great deal of you."

Girard nodded. "Bullshit. When have either of us let

personal risk get in the way of duty? Real duty, not pandering to a bunch of political hacks. Just tell me everything you know. And I'll need to get there without being noticed. Perhaps I could slip onto one of your relief ships."

Vance put his arm out, setting it on Girard's shoulder. "You are a true hero, Andre. And a patriot. A real one." He paused. "I don't know how to thank you."

"Then don't do it at all. I've served Mars since you were chasing schoolgirls, and I'll serve her until I die, in whatever manner I must."

Chapter 9

Dyracchium Plateau ("Dead Man's Ridge")
Planet Lysandria, Delta Sigma III
Earthdate: 2318 AD (33 Years After the Fall)

"All reserves forward now." Cyn Kuragina was standing just behind the front line, watching her troopers blaze away at the approaching enemy forces. They were outnumbered almost ten to one at the point of impact, and now ammunition was running low. She'd been steadily feeding in the last of her fresh reserves, but now she was down to the final two platoons. Once those 80 troopers were on the line, she'd have everything committed. Falstaff's people were moving around the flank, but there were enemy delaying forces holding them up every klick or so. And her people weren't going to last much longer.

She pulled her assault rifle from her back. She'd been doing a Colonel's job all day, but now that was done. Everybody was committed and fighting like hell, and they would stand or fall where they were. She could accomplish more as another rifle in the firing line than standing around playing commander. A single soldier might not seem like much, she thought, but one Black Eagle is a force to be reckoned with.

She moved up to the small lip of ground her people were using for cover, and she stared out over the plateau. The enemy was pounding her positions with rockets and mortars, trying to cut down on her people's fire while their infantry moved toward the ridge. The ground had been savaged by two days of constant battle, and the enemy soldiers were using the craters and mounds of disrupted earth as cover.

Half her autocannons were out of action, and the others were running low on ammunition. She had them firing aimed bursts now, trying to conserve. The soldiers moving forward were good, really good. They were maximizing the shattered ground, advancing in short bursts, leapfrogging while their heavier weapons tried to suppress her people along the defensive line.

The approaching soldiers were all the unidentified enemy, the ones with the brown armor. There were no Gold Spears anywhere. She'd gotten a dozen attempted communiques from various officers of the Spears—attempts to surrender, no doubt. But General Cain had issued his orders, and as far as Cyn Kuragina was concerned, that was like the word of God.

A wave of dirt and shattered stones pelted her armor, the result of an enemy shell that landed too close for comfort. Her eyes flitted up to her display. Another half dozen of her people were down since the last time she'd checked. She knew they were taking out more of the enemy, but this wasn't an even fight. They couldn't trade casualties, even at a 2-1 or 3-1 rate.

"Colonel Kuragina…" It was Cain, and there was something odd in his tone. A seething anger, malevolent, almost feral.

"Yes, General?"

"Colonel, you are to prepare to attack all across your line. I want everything committed, nothing held back."

She felt her stomach clench into a knot. There was no way her people could charge, not against what was coming at them. They'd been wiped out before they cleared the plateau. "Sir?"

"Look at your scanner, Colonel. The Blue Regiment is inbound. They'll be on the ground in three minutes. When they hit dirt, I want your people to advance immediately and pin the enemy between your forces."

She glanced at her display again, sending a thought to her AI to widen the scale. There they were, along the top edge. Waves of incoming troops, Ian Vandeveer and his 1,500 fresh Eagles.

The tactical situation had just changed. Dramatically. "Understood, sir," she snapped back. "It will be a pleasure." She *flipped her com to the unitwide channel. "White Regiment, we've got friendlies inbound. ETA two minutes forty-five seconds." Her tone was changing, becoming more determined with every word, until it was downright bloodthirsty. "And in two minutes thirty, we charge. It's time to end this, Eagles."*

*   *   *   *   *

"Stay on them…nobody escapes." Dan Sullivan flashed a thought to his AI, instructing it to administer another dose of stims. His own adrenalin was pumping hard, but after two days of almost constant fighting, it needed all the help it could get. "The general wants prisoners, so disable some of these guys and take them alive."

Sullivan's company was battered, down to roughly half strength. It was the worst he could remember an Eagles unit being hurt, and he was proud of those still in action, fighting hard despite the losses and fatigue. At least the others weren't all dead. Maybe 20% of his people were KIA, the rest wounded or disabled. And the Eagles' wounded got the best care in the history of war. From the leading edge trauma systems in their suits to the outstanding field hospitals Darius Cain maintained at enormous expense, if an Eagle could survive the first few minutes after being wounded, he had an 87% chance of returning to the colors. Suit damage and equipment failure also drained strength from a combat unit. You couldn't exactly keep fighting if your six ton suit developed a malfunction or power failure.

Still, it had been a brutal fight, and one that had looked for a while like it might turn into the first defeat they had suffered, at least to Sullivan and the rest of Kuragina's battered White Regiment. But then the Blues landed. Sullivan was still amazed at the magnificent accuracy of the drop. Vandeveer's people landed right on top of the stunned enemy forces, a level of precision almost unheard of. The pinpoint landing was a risk, leaving them potentially vulnerable while they extricated themselves from their gear. But then Kuragina's people struck, and the shocked enemy found themselves fighting a confused running battle with the Black Eagles.

Sullivan had to admire the foe, at least on one level. The battle was lost. Their lines were pierced in a dozen places, and they had no chance to reform and reorganize. But there hadn't been a single surrender attempt, nor even one confused rout. They simply continued to fight, wherever they were, at whatever disadvantage they found themselves. As General Cain's plan moved to fruition, it became a battle of annihilation, but still the enemy hadn't run. They just kept fighting until they went down.

He saw a cluster of the brown-armored troops caught in a crossfire between two of his squads. They all went down in a few seconds. "Kloster, Jing, move up there. If any of them are alive, take them prisoner." General Cain wanted captives from the mysterious enemy the Eagles were calling simply, "the browns." And since they didn't seem to surrender, the word had gone out to try and take them when they were wounded.

He watched his two troopers move forward, carefully, rifles in front of them. The Eagles were trained to be careful, methodical—and wounded men could still be dangerous. Sullivan moved up closer, watching his two soldiers.

"Looks like one's still alive, sir." Kloster was leaning down as he sent his report, pulling the rifle from the armored gloves of the wounded man. "He's hurt pretty bad, Lieutenant, but I think we can get him…"

A loud explosion cut him off. Sullivan lunged forward, but it was too late. Kloster had been blown several meters, and it was obvious from his twisted and blood-soaked armor he was dead. Jing was lying next to the obliterated remains of the enemy soldier. He looked badly hurt, but he was still alive.

"Medic!" Sullivan shouted as he ran up toward the cluster of enemy bodies. He held his rifle out in front of him, looking for any signs of life. He saw one of the figures move slightly, and he didn't hesitate. He opened up at full auto, riddling the soldier's body with hyper-velocity projectiles. He'd been driven half by rage, but he'd have done the same thing if he'd been totally calm. He'd lost one of his men, maybe two, and he'd be damned if he was going to allow that to happen again. He had no idea who these fanatics were, but he was more than ready to send them all to hell.

He opened a channel to headquarters. "This is Lieutenant Sullivan, commanding Third Company, 1st Battalion, White Regiment." His eyes were focused on the shattered remains of what had been Private Kloster a moment before. "I need to speak with Colonel Teller or General Cain. Now."

*   *   *   *   *

"General, we're getting reports from across the field." Teller was usually the epitome of cool during battle, but Cain could tell he was upset about something.

"What is it, Erik?"

"The enemy, the unidentified troops. They're booby-trapped, Darius. Every time one of our people tries to take a prisoner, some kind of charge detonates. We've got ten dead and two dozen wounded already."

"Cancel the order to take prisoners immediately. Terminate them on sight and at a distance, if possible." Cain's voice was harsh, angry. He wanted prisoners, but he wasn't willing to lose any more of his people to get them. Casualties had already been too high, and his first priority was ending the battle.

"Yes, Erik."

Cain walked across the command post, and the anger grew inside him. This was the second mission in a row where someone was fucking with his people. He had no idea where the unidentified enemy forces had come from, but his gut told him when he dumped a pile of debris from Lysandria on Tom Sparks' worktable, it was going to match the scraps he'd brought back from Karelia. And that would prove what he already knew. Someone was messing with the Black Eagles. And that meant someone was going to die.

"Get me an open line to the Lysandrian forces." His people had broken the enemy encryption and compromised their communications networks an hour into the fight, for the native forces, at least. Breaking the Gold Spears' security had been a lot tougher, and the unidentified "browns" used a security protocol that had so far defied the Eagles' best efforts to crack.

"You're live, General." Lieutenant Camerici's voice was sharp and alert, despite the fact that she'd been on duty 40 of the last 48 hours.

"Attention Lysandrian forces, this is General Darius Cain, commander of the Black Eagles." He knew the message would go out on every communications network on the planet—military, civilian, government. He suspected the authorities would scramble to try to block it, but to no avail. He had the best technology experts in Occupied Space on his team, and no group of locals was going to beat them.

"The Gold Spears have been defeated. They are reduced now to scattered bands of refugees begging my soldiers to accept their surrenders. General Ling, their commander is dead, as is their entire senior leadership. The unidentified force that fought alongside them has also been destroyed, and my soldiers are now hunting down and wiping out their last remnants." His voice dripped with venom, his tone evoking pure menace. Normally, it would be theatrics, intended to scare the civilians. But this time it was real. Darius Cain was livid about the losses his people had suffered. The Lysandrians had one chance. One. And then he would kill them all.

"You have not yet been attacked, but that is only by my order. Now, the moment of choice is upon you. My soldiers have suffered considerable losses facing your hired defenders, and at my word, they will fall upon you to claim their vengeance. Your laughable defenses will not stop my Eagles for an instant. Your pitiful weapons cannot match our armaments. You have but one chance to escape total annihilation, for if you spurn this offer, there will not be another. And your friends and families will share your bitter fates."

Teller was standing a few meters away, his armored form turned toward his friend as he listened. Everyone in the command post was doing the same. Darius Cain wasn't a man to be trifled with—they all knew that much. But the pure malevolence in his voice was intimidating on a new and terrifying level. The Eagles had not lost so many of their number in a fight in years, and their general was not a happy man. And he was determined to see someone pay. Preferably whoever was responsible, but if the people of Lysandria wouldn't help him track down the guilty parties then he would make them all pay.

"All Lysandrian military units will lay down their arms and surrender immediately. All civil and political leaders will surrender at once and cooperate fully, providing all information requested by my interrogators. All civilians will consider themselves under martial law and will remain in their homes, leaving only during hours to be posted and announced, and then only on vital business."

He paused for a few seconds, and when he continued his voice was even darker, more threatening. "Failure to comply at once and in full will result in the destruction of Lysandria's cities, the extermination of its armed forces, and incalculable suffering of its people. If I receive complete and total cooperation, my forces will leave your world intact. If I do not, I will turn Lysandria into a graveyard."

Cain turned toward Camerici and moved his hand across his throat. She hesitated, staring back at him for a few seconds before she turned with a start and closed the com line. Cain's people knew there was a toughness and an icy coldness in their leader, even beyond the normal professionalism that governed him, but they had never seen such pure and unrestrained menace.

Somebody was targeting Darius Cain's Black Eagles, trying to get his attention. *Well, whoever you are, you have it now. Let's see how much you like it.*

Chapter 10

Marine Headquarters
Planet Armstrong, Gamma Pavonis III
Earthdate: July, 2297 AD (12 Years After the Fall)

"I want to thank you all for coming. I know many of you had long and difficult journeys, but this matter will not wait any longer." Catherine Gilson stood at the podium looking out at the assembled representatives of the former Alliance colonies. She was wearing a perfectly-tailored, though old, uniform. She had left her medals behind, and her sidearm and sword as well. The planetary leaders tended to be prickly about anything that gave an impression of intimidation. They had all been part of the Alliance, lived under the yoke of the oppressive Earth government, but now they were independent, and they guarded that jealously. She knew part of that was the memory of the Alliance's heavy-handed tactics, and she understood that completely. She also suspected some of them were more interested in protecting their own power than in any altruism toward those they governed. A few of the colonies were beginning to remind her far too much of Alliance Gov.

"It has been ten years since the Fall, and there has been much discussion of what is to happen to the former Alliance colony worlds, how they will govern cooperation between themselves, and the manner in which they will be defended against external threats. Over that decade, the Marine Corps and the fleet have continued to serve their purposes, providing protection for all of your planets, with limited and extremely sporadic financial support. We have managed to fund—barely—our needs by selling surplus equipment and licensing technology. However, we have reached the end of our resources. Armstrong has long carried many times its share of the cost, and that is a burden its people can no longer sustain. It is time to forge a long term Confederation to see to the maintenance of the fleet and the Corps...or both services will be compelled to downsize and serve solely as Armstrong's planetary military force, leaving the rest of you to see to your own defense."

She looked out over the assembled representatives, most of them politicians and heads of state. Ten years of relative peace, enforced mostly by a general lack of resources sufficient to fight wars, had dulled their sensibilities to the need for long-term security. She could see it in their eyes, most of them, at least. They liked having the Corps and Garret's fleet out there, but they didn't want to pay for it. Their worlds needed investment to grow, and their governments were expanding, turning into rapacious bureaucracies, consuming resources at an ever-expanding rate.

"Before I open the floor to questions and debate, I would like to bring up a man who needs no introduction, a Marine who has been in the forefront of man's wars for thirty years. As he has been there whenever there was need, so has he come now, all the way from Atlantia." She glanced back to make sure he was ready. Then she looked out over the audience and said, "Please welcome General Erik Cain."

The room erupted into applause. Erik Cain was a genuine celebrity, a bonafide hero everywhere in former Alliance space. His reputation was more mixed on the colonies of the Corps' old enemies, but he was universally respected as one of the greatest military commanders of the modern age.

Cain walked up to the podium. His uniform was of an older style than Gilson's, and it was a bit snug. He'd added a few kilos over ten years of inactive status and nine of parenthood, though he was still in excellent shape by any measure. He moved with a hint of a limp and some stiffness. He'd had the rejuv treatments and the best medical care available, but he'd been wounded so many times, even cutting edge medical care couldn't undo everything. He carried the scars of his wars with him, in the soreness in his body and the sorrow in his mind.

He stared out at those seated before him, planetary presidents and other politicians. They were men and women who had become accustomed to being treated with exaggerated respect, but Cain was the wrong man for that. He made no attempt to hide his contempt. The very existence of this meeting, the need for Gilson to go hat in hand and beg the leaders to attend was proof enough of what he had always believed. These people didn't need the Corps now, and they behaved as if funding their own defense was an act of charity.

He knew when they were again threatened they would look to the Marines to save them, they would expect the armored warriors to come again, as they always had. They would forget their lack of support, the deaf ear they turned during peaceful times. What if there was no answer to their call next time? Cain knew that would be a disaster for humanity, but he couldn't help but believe that is what they all deserved.

"General Gilson has spoken to you in quite measured tones. She has respected your positions, and the offices and awards you have largely appointed for yourselves." His voice was caustic, an undisguised growl. "For those familiar with my reputation, you know you will get no such courtesy from me. You will hear the truth, and if that offends you, please understand this very clearly. *I do not give a damn.*"

Cain was a massive war hero, but his gruff manner and his unwillingness to pander to those around him had gradually chipped away at his popularity. The working people of the former Alliance worlds worshipped Cain, and they told and retold stories of his battles. His old veterans could count on parades in their home towns and free drinks wherever they went. But Cain was less popular with the emerging new leadership classes, mostly because he was far too willing to call them out for exactly what they were. Erik Cain did not offer false respect. If you wanted his admiration, you earned it; you didn't steal it with lies or crooked elections.

Cain didn't care what politicians thought of him. Indeed, the destruction of the Alliance and his subsequent retirement had removed the last needs for him to even pretend. But when Gilson called, he had come. Immediately, without question or delay. Whatever else he might do, however he might spend the rest of his life, he was a Marine. The Corps had his loyalty. Always. When it needed him, he would come.

"I have fought many wars, each one a desperate struggle with millions of lives in the balance. They were all different, save for one thing. Each was thought to be the last one. Every terrible battle, every war fought to the bitter end is believed to be the final struggle, the war that would finally cure mankind of the habit. And since the dawn of history, this belief has been wrong. No matter how horrific the struggle, no matter how many lay dead on the field and in blasted, ruined cities, men have found new reasons to fight, grievances to levy against fresh enemies. And, beyond men's fondness for killing each other, the memory is still fresh of our first, disastrous encounter with another race. There is always another war. The old flags will inevitably be removed from the place they were stowed, unfurled again to answer the renewed call to battle."

Cain paused and looked out again over his audience. They were silent, listening to his words, but he knew they weren't hearing them. Not really. As inevitable as the next war had always been, people never expected it. They ignored or ridiculed those who predicted it, those who warned against complacency. They convinced themselves peace would last, that they needn't devote resources to remain vigilant. When threats arose, they resorted to denial and appeasement before resistance. Cain knew he owed the words he was speaking to Gilson and to the Corps. But he also knew they would be ignored.

"The Alliance is gone. The billions on Earth whose work funded and sustained the Corps and the fleet are gone. It has fallen to you to take the full responsibility for your defense. Your economies, which were so heavily based on exports to Earth have suffered massive dislocations. You have scrambled and struggled to repurpose industry, to adjust to a post-Earth reality."

His eyes narrowed, and he brought a balled fist down on the podium. "Yet none of this changes the basic facts. If you would be defended against the next threat…one that will surely come…you must commit resources now. You must do your part. If you do not, in five years…or ten…or twenty, when the balloon again goes up, when some enemy comes to take what is yours, to enslave and kill your people, you will have no one to blame but yourselves when you stand alone. It will be a bitter reckoning, and as you fall, as you watch the fires of devastation sweep across your worlds, as they did across the Earth, you will know you allowed it to happen."

Cain stepped back a meter and allowed Gilson back to the podium. "Thank you, General Cain. I am sure our guests will give serious thought to your words, particularly since there are few human beings who have witnessed the reality of war the way you have." Her voice had a tone of surprise, as though she hadn't expected him to be quite so honest.

Cain nodded toward the audience, flashing Gilson a tentative smile before he turned away and walked from the stage. *They won't give serious thought to anything I said. They will say, 'they are so dramatic, the soldiers.' Then they will ask to pose for a photo with us, something they will take home and use on their campaign posters. But they will not commit the funding that is required. They will shirk their responsibility, until danger comes. Then they will be whining, begging for help, as if we can manufacture armored Marines and battleships out of thin air.*

He could hear Gilson's voice in the background, through his thoughts. "So, now let us move to debate. Who would like to begin?"

*   *   *   *   *

"So, just as I expected." Cain's voice was raw, angry. He'd expected exactly what happened, but it still hurt to see it. He was bitter. How many brave men and women had died protecting these people, defeating the forces that would have enslaved or massacred them all?"

The meeting had ended with all kinds of accolades and expressions of gratitude, but no promises of support. There had been a litany of excuses, but in the end, only Jarrod Tyler had argued forcefully for the planetary leaders to step up and provide the support the Corps and the fleet needed. Tyler was the famous commander of Columbia's planetary military, a man who had assumed temporary dictatorial powers and led his world through the Shadow Legion war before voluntarily resigning that position. He'd remained the commander of the armed forces over the intervening decade, fighting a gradually deteriorating struggle against the political forces demanding disarmament and the diversion of military spending to social programs.

Tyler's wife, Lucia, had been Columbia's longtime president, and she had been forced to remain home because of an election, one she was expected to lose, largely over the same issues. Columbia was a world with a difficult past, having been invaded multiple times, but in the aftermath of the Shadow War, there was a feeling that a long period of peace would ensue, a theme that had been exploited by Lucia's political opponents. It had taken ten years of relentless assaults in the press and elsewhere, but finally they were on the verge of ousting the once enormously popular president.

Tyler had warmly embraced General Gilson, who had led the force twelve years before that liberated Columbia, but he had no power to promise support to the Corps. He was angry and ashamed of his own people, and he'd left immediately after the meeting, bound for Columbia where he intended to resign his commission right after the election and retire to private life with Lucia.

Cate Gilson sighed, looking across the table. "Well, we did everything we could at least." She glanced over at Cain. "Even though things didn't work out, I want to thank you for coming, Erik."

"You couldn't have kept me away, Cate. I'm still a Marine, even if a retired one. Sarah wanted to come too, but the boys were just too young for so long a trip."

Gilson nodded. "I'd have loved to see her, but I understand. Maybe someday I will get to Atlantia and meet these young Cain men." When Erik and Sarah had left Armstrong for Atlantia, they had all promised to travel frequently and see each other often. But as things usually go, old comrades had drifted apart. Cain had come to Armstrong to support the Corps, certainly, but he'd also welcomed the chance to see old friends, regardless of the reason.

"I would like that too." Augustus Garret had been sitting quietly in the corner. He hadn't said much. He didn't seem surprised by the lack of support offered by the planets. He wasn't quite as cynical as Cain, perhaps, but those who knew him well understood he was close. He had aged considerably in ten years. The rejuv treatments were a medical marvel, adding decades to a healthy person's life expectancy, but at a certain age, the effects began to wane quickly, and aging resumed at an accelerated rate. "It has been a long time since I've seen the twins and Sarah." Garret had been to Atlantia twice since the Cain's made it their home, but the last time had been almost seven years before.

Cain smiled. "You are both welcome anytime...but only if you promise not to try to recruit them. My life has been my life...but I don't want it to be theirs."

Gilson nodded. "I understand, Erik. I think I'd feel the same. The Corps has been my existence. My friends, my loved ones, almost all the people I've truly known have been Marines. I am proud of what we have done, but if I had children, I would wish something else for them. An easier life. One where losing friends wasn't so commonplace a part of the routine."

Cain bowed his head slightly. He knew the Corps was in trouble, and the fleet as well, and his heart was heavy. "So what are we going to do?" Cain was on inactive status, but when the future of the Corps was at stake, he intended to be involved.

"There's nothing else we can do, Erik." Gilson's voice was soft, sad. "I couldn't bear to disband the Corps entirely, but we're going to have to come close." She sighed and continued, "I was counting on Jarrod Tyler, at least, but it never occurred to me that Lucia could be voted out of power. The two of them were enormous heroes when I went back there after the war. It is hard to believe things could change so much in ten years."

"That is what people are like, Cate." Cain's voice was fatigued, but the fiery anger he'd once felt about things like this was gone, replaced my exhausted acceptance. "It used to enrage me, but they are what they are. They are shortsighted, and few are willing to put in enough effort to truly understand things. That is why they become the playthings of political manipulators. That has always been the way of things, and I see no reason to expect anything different."

"Well, it doesn't matter now. I'll issue the orders tomorrow. Without a source of sufficient funding, the Corps will have to downsize dramatically. We will transition into Armstrong's planetary armed forces." The world of Armstrong had been the headquarters of the Alliance's interplanetary military since the rebellions twenty years before. The population was largely military and ex-military, or support services for the Corps and the fleet. In the years since the Fall, the planet had transitioned from almost entirely military-industrial to an export-based high tech economy. Its position as the home world for the Corps and the fleet ensured that its technology was the most advanced of any former colony, and within just a few short years, it was exporting microprocessors and sophisticated AIs to planets all across Occupied Space. Armstrong could afford a significant military of its own, but nothing like either the Corps or the fleet had been.

"What are you planning?" Cain asked, without providing any input of his own. Gilson had stood watch while he'd enjoyed retirement and fatherhood. He cared deeply about the future of the Corps, but he didn't feel it was his place to second-guess his colleague.

"I have a proposed organizational chart you can look at for specifics, but essentially, it calls for two regiments, each of two battalions, with a small cadre for a third battalion."

Cain exhaled softly. "So, three thousand combat troops, give or take?" He knew an armored Marine cost at least ten times what a normal planetary army soldier did, and he realized the expenses of even Gilson's tiny force would be staggering for a world like Armstrong. But hearing it spoken out loud hit him like a hammer. The Corps had fielded 375,000 at its peak at the end of the Third Frontier War. He understood what was happening, but part of him couldn't quite accept it.

"Yes…about. Plus support personnel. Roughly 5,000 in total." Gilson was trying to stay positive, but Cain could tell she was as hurt by all this as he was." We're going to turn the Marine and Naval Academies over to the new Armstrong University—most of them, at least. We'll be maintaining a small officer training facility, enough for an annual cadet class of about twenty Marines."

Cain turned toward Garret. "What about the fleet? What are you planning?"

Garret looked across the room at Cain, his face almost devoid of emotion. "I'm afraid the fleet is in even worse shape. Armstrong is building a strong economy, but maintaining a large fleet is out of the question. We're going to convert six fast attack ships for patrol duty. They will become Armstrong's navy, along with two light cruisers."

"Eight ships?" Cain was stunned, though he realized he shouldn't be. None of the colony worlds had the capacity to support significant navies. "What about the others?"

"I spoke with Roderick Vance, and he agreed to add them to the mothballed reserve on Phobos." Cain could see the pain on the admiral's face. Augustus Garret had been a naval officer for eighty years. He had sacrificed everything to the service. Cain had faced a difficult time imagining himself living a life outside the Corps, but he failed utterly to picture Garret anywhere but on the bridge of his flagship.

"There is something else we could consider." The words just blurted out. Cain had been thinking about it for days, but he'd discounted it again and again. Still, it kept coming back into his mind."

"What, Erik?" Garret's voice was soft, inquisitive. "What do you have in mind?" He paused, but when Erik remained silent, he added, "You're among friends here, Erik. By God, there's nothing you couldn't say to us."

"Well, Occupied Space is in complete disarray right now." He spoke slowly, uncomfortable with what he was about to suggest. "Instead of downsizing so severely, we could..." He hesitated again. "...we could be a bit more...insistent about it."

"You mean impose our will on the independent worlds?" Gilson's tone was odd, not exactly disapproving, as if she herself had considered what Cain was suggesting. "Force them at gunpoint?"

Garret was sitting in the corner, silently watching the exchange. His expression was deadpan, not giving away an inkling of what he was thinking.

"No, of course not. I don't mean park a battleship in orbit around Columbia or take control of any large worlds. But there are resource planets too, with very small populations, and incredibly valuable mineral deposits. If a few of those worlds were dedicated to supporting the Corps and the fleet, we could continue to protect everyone, at least at some level."

"And only oppress a few miners and their families? And the companies that own those mines?" Gilson's voice had no edge to it, no condemnation of what Cain had proposed, just a strange sense of fatigue. "I understand the thought, Erik. I've had it myself. But is that what the Corps stands for? Is that what you want our legacy to be?"

Cain sighed. "No, of course not. But we all know those worlds will eventually come under the control of the stronger planets anyway. All the colonies were declared independent after the Fall, but do you think over 1,000 worlds, with cultures from eight different Superpowers, will respect each other's sovereignty forever? When some are strong and others weak, with enormously valuable resources?"

"No, probably not," Gilson replied. "But think about it, Erik, do you want history to show the Corps was the first to impose its rule on a colony world? That we set up a military dictatorship so we could confiscate a planet's resources?"

"No, of course not." Cain's voice was strained. He knew he agreed with Gilson, but there was something else nagging at him. "But you know what will happen," he said, his voice becoming more agitated. "The Corps and the fleet will be virtually gone. What will we do when the next crisis hits, because you know it will. And all those puffed up heads of state who were here for the meeting will be yelling in fear, begging us for help. And they will be shit out of luck. When all these newly independent worlds are facing a deadly danger, and the Corps and the fleet are gone, what then?"

"I don't know, Erik. I went through all of this with myself." She looked across the room at Cain. "But we can't make ourselves what we want to be by ignoring who we are.

The Alliance was rotten, but for a century, the Corps managed to keep itself from being used as an instrument of oppression. When the rebellions came, we resisted the pressure to crush the freedom fighters, and we navigated an honorable path through the crisis. Would you see that legacy thrown away on your watch? Or mine?"

Cain didn't answer. He understood what she was saying, and he agreed. But he'd always been a realist, not one to fool himself and believe what he wanted to believe, pushing facts aside to do it. The thought of the Corps being used to conquer former Alliance worlds, to impose rule on their people—it was anathema to him. But he knew the alternative was allowing the colonies to behave irresponsibly. And if they did that, a lot of those people would die the next time war came. They would be almost defenseless, and the fleet and Corps that had always come wouldn't be there anymore. Those resource worlds the Corps didn't seize would be conquered by someone else, their wealth stripped with a brutal efficiency the Marines would never have matched. The cost of the next war would be vastly higher than it should be.

"Erik, I understand your frustration." Garret leaned forward in his chair. "My whole life, I have chosen duty first. You, more than anyone, know what that has cost me."

Cain and Garret had sat long one night long ago, talking about their pasts, and the admiral had spoken of the guilt he carried, the pain that consumed him every waking hour. Admiral Garret, even more than Cain, was credited with saving the human race from the First Imperium, and for countless other victories. But very few people knew what that record of success had cost Augustus Garret, the man.

"But life can't be all duty," Garret continued. "Men are not robots. Sometimes, you simply have to do what is right, even though you know there may be a price to pay one day." He paused. "I, too, am tempted to go down the road you suggest. But I will not do it. Whatever the consequences."

"Nor will I," Gilson added, though Cain could hear the

doubt in her voice. He suspected he just might convince her if he really tried. But he didn't have the drive to do it.

Cain nodded. "I am with you both. I thought it was something we had to discuss." He felt relieved—but there was still a nagging doubt, a certainty they would all one day regret their principled position. He wondered what he would have done on his own, if it had been his decision. Would he have lashed out, imposed military rule? He didn't know, and he suspected he never would. It was the kind of thing a man could never understand fully, not until he faced it.

Chapter 11

Mining Camp Delta
Planet Kalte, Beta Scorpii VI
Earthdate: 2318 AD (33 Years After the Fall)

"The pressure on the main pump is a little high, Fritzie." Dolph's voice was almost drowned out by static, and Fritz Ludendorf turned up the volume on his receiver so he could hear. "I think I should get down there and check it out."

Ludendorf was sitting in the command shed staring down at the panel. The gauge read 875. That was high, but not critically so. Still, if his nearly two years on this miserable hellhole had taught him anything it was that Dolph Gerhard could sniff out a problem in the equipment like a bloodhound.

"Go ahead, Dolph, but be careful. The rig's running full out. It's fucking dangerous in there."

"You know me, Fritzie. I'm the soul of caution." Ludendorf could hear his field engineer laughing. They both knew Gerhard was a crazy son of a bitch who'd take almost any chance to squeeze a little extra production out of the mine. When your product sold for 500 credits a gram, you tried hard not to waste anything.

Extracting stable super-heavy metals from the few planetary environments where they occurred naturally was not work for the faint of heart. The trans-uranian isotopes were extremely rare, and they were almost always found on planets that seemed otherwise designed to kill men. Kalte fit that bill nicely. Its atmosphere was toxic, and fairly corrosive to boot, except at night, when most of it liquefied into a hazardous mess that pooled all around, making even a slow walk back from the mine a hazardous adventure.

The frigid cold could kill an unprotected man in a two or three minutes, running a close race with asphyxiation as the cause of death. The radiation was deadly too, but while a lethal dose was almost instantaneous to an unprotected man, it actually took a few hours to die—time the victim didn't generally have. No matter how you categorized the dangers, Kalte was a nightmare world, one of the unlikeliest places one would expect to find human habitation. But it also had rich veins of the ultra-rare metals so vital in the construction of spaceship drives. So men were here battling the deadly environment for the most prosaic of reasons. To become extremely wealthy.

A two-year stint on Kalte could earn an engineer enough to retire to any colony world in Occupied Space and spend the rest of his life in considerable luxury without ever working another day. Ludendorf's crew had managed to beat the record for production during their tour, which meant when they left in three weeks, they were all rich men.

"OK, Fritzie, I'm down in the main shaft. Everything looks fine, but I don't like the way it feels." It was an open question if a man—especially one wrapped up head to toe in a Suit—could "feel" whether a mining pump was running properly. Of course, if there was anyone who could, it was Gerhard. "Can you back off to 80% for a few seconds?" Shutting down the pump would bring the whole mining operation to a halt. It would take at least half a day to restart everything, costing a king's ransom in lost production. But throttling back for a few minutes was no big deal.

"Down to 80%...now." Ludendorf stayed silent for a few seconds, letting his friend focus on the pump mechanism. He was about to ask how things were going when his com unit activated.

"Engineer Ludendorf, this is Heinrich in the control room." Otto Heinrich was the youngest member of the control room crew, barely twenty years old. His voice was cracking. Ludendorf could tell immediately something was wrong.

"What is it, Heinrich?"

"We're tracking incoming ships, sir." Ludendorf could tell Heinrich was scared shitless. "We have no ID, and they have failed to answer any of our communications."

"Alert the security team, Heinrich." It was some kind of raid, Ludendorf decided immediately. The Kalte team was sitting on a fortune in super-heavy metals, waiting for the transports due in three weeks. That made them a target. For pirates, for other worlds, for anyone.

"Yes, sir."

Ludendorf flipped his com unit back to Gerhard's channel. "Get the hell out of there, Dolph. Right now. We've got uninvited company. Unidentified ships coming in."

"I can't pinpoint any malfunction down here, but I'm sure this pump isn't right." Gerhard was distracted, focused on his analysis of the equipment.

"Fuck it, Dolph. We may be under attack in a few minutes. Get the hell out of the mine!"

"Attack...who?" He was paying attention now.

"No idea. Some kind of ships coming in now. We need to get to the bunkers. Now get the hell out of there, because I'm shutting the mine down in one minute."

"On my way, Fritzie."

Ludendorf cut the line, and began punching in the shutdown sequence. *Fuck*, he thought. *Whoever this is had to pull this shit now? They couldn't wait a month?*

*   *   *   *   *

"We're in position, Engineer Ludendorf." Dave Vanik was standing in a trench looking out across the rugged plateau. The high plain extended out from the narrow mountain range that housed the company mines, stretching a hundred kilometers into the distance. The ground was barren, covered with shattered stone and gray, powdery dust.

Vanik was an ex-Marine who'd bounced around for a number of years after the Corps disbanded most of its field forces twenty years earlier. He'd taken a number of training positions with planetary militias until the Kalte Ownership Combine offered him a 1,000% raise for organizing and training its security units.

"All the incoming ships appear to be on the surface. If this is an attack, I expect they'll be coming at you soon." Ludendorf was trying to sound calm, but Vanik knew the engineer was no soldier. He was probably halfway to shitting himself down there in the bunker.

Vanik was cool, calm. That didn't mean he wasn't afraid, but his training and experience helped keep things in perspective. He'd served under Erik Cain on Sandoval, fighting against the robots of the First Imperium, and later on Columbia with General Gilson. No pack of claim-jumping raiders was going to get inside his head.

Whoever was coming, they had to be reasonably well-funded. A planet like Kalte was no joke, and it would kill a poorly equipped force, saving Vanik and his defenders the trouble. But that didn't mean whoever was coming could beat his hand-picked and drilled warriors. There were half a dozen other Marines among his 120 troops, and four ex-Janissaries. And the rest had been trained with all the ferocity and thoroughness a veteran Marine sergeant had been able to muster. Vanik was cautious, as he always was on the eve of battle, but he was confident his people would prevail.

"Have you been able to make contact, sir?" Ludendorf's

tone had already told him what he needed to know, but he wanted express permission before he opened fire.

"Negative, Captain Vanik. We have issued multiple warnings. You are authorized to fire at your discretion. Your only consideration is the safety of the operation."

"Understood, sir. I suggest all non-combat personnel remain in the bunker until further notice." He stared out through the dusky light of late afternoon. The battlefield was going to be a nightmare. The atmosphere would begin to condense in another hour, making movement dangerous and slowing it to a crawl. He didn't know who it was out there thinking they were going to sweep away his dug in forces in less than an hour, but as far as he was concerned, they were in for a rude shock.

He stared at the display inside his helmet. His scanner array was crude, but he could see the enemy formations approaching. He didn't have exact numbers, but from the looks of things there were a lot of them. Two hundred at least.

His force was equipped with fighting suits, but they were sixty year old surplus units, poor substitutes for the top of the line armor he'd worn in the Corps. They lacked the portable nuclear power plants of the old Mark VII units, and that severely limited their capabilities. His people had standard assault rifles instead of the hyper-velocity electro-magnetic weapons the Marines had used. The servo-mechanical systems were powerful enough to move the suits around, but they lacked the enormous strength magnification of the Marine units. Perhaps the most telling difference in an environment like Kalte, the suits could only operate in hostile conditions for a day without a recharge, even less under full battle conditions. That was something to keep in mind on a world where a loss of air or heating meant almost instant death.

Still, they would do the job. He couldn't imagine any enemy having better equipment. Since the Corps retired its last combat units, few forces in Occupied Space could match the standards of the old armies that had fought the wars of the Superpowers. The Black Eagles, of course. Darius Cain's famous unit had even better armor, based on the Mark VIII designs that had never gone into full-scale production for the Corps. And a few of the other elite Companies had quality fighting suits too. But no one else. There wasn't a single world in human space that could afford to field its own army so equipped, at least not beyond a tiny elite group of Special Forces. Certainly no pack of raiders looking to pillage a mining world.

"Mortar teams, prepare to fire at 5,000 meters." Vanik's troops didn't have the grenade launchers that had been built into Marine armor, but they did have two mortar teams. With any luck, the enemy would panic as soon as his people opened up and started dropping shells in their ranks.

His eyes darted back to the display. He didn't like what he was seeing. The enemy was too ordered, their formations too perfect. They looked more like Marines than a pack of raiders. He had a cold feeling in his gut. He tried to ignore it, but it kept nagging at him. Was it possible someone had hired one of the top-tier merc companies to attack Kalte? *No, it couldn't be. There's no way.* The elite Companies considered themselves legitimate enterprises. Their clients were worlds with real political conflicts; they didn't take contracts for pirate raids on mining colonies. *At least not openly.*

Vanik glanced at his display. Just over 5,500 meters. His mortar teams would open up in…"

He saw a series of flashes on the small projected screen inside his visor. Then the ground shook hard, and the sounds of explosions reverberated in his helmet.

His head snapped around, watching the plumes of flame rising into the sky. *Rockets,* he thought immediately. *Hyper-velocity rockets. What the hell are these raiders doing with HVRs?*

"HVRs incoming," he shouted into the com, realizing the futility of the announcement as he opened his mouth. The ground shook again as another volley hit all around. He could feel a wave of dirt and crushed stone smacking into his armor, and he dove to the ground. "Get down," he yelled, his voice raw and scratchy.

He felt his heart pounding in his ears. *Keep it together, Marine. You're facing an enemy with HVRs.* "All units, form consecutive skirmish lines now." Extending the order of his troops would make them that much weaker against a direct assault, but there was no choice. The enemy outranged him. He had to minimize the effects of the incoming rockets or his force would be gutted before it could even return fire.

He looked up slowly, trying to get a view toward the enemy lines. According to his display, they were all hidden just behind the next ridge, but he couldn't get a decent view of any of them. *We have to advance. They've got better cover and longer-ranged weapons. We're fucked if we stay here.*

He stared down at the display. His troops were in three long lines, each one hundred meters behind the last. His troopers were 20 meters apart, making his overall position a little over 800 meters in frontage. "All units, advance. Fire at will with all weapons, as soon as you come into range." He wasn't about to sit there and let the enemy pick his people off with rockets.

He moved forward himself, trying to angle his path to take advantage of whatever cover the terrain offered. There were a few dips and folds in the ground, but he was forced to move across a lot of open country. He ducked behind a small ridgeline about 4,000 meters from the enemy positions. "Mortars….deploy and open fire." It was time to flush the enemy out from behind that hill. The rocket launchers were still firing, but they were hitting mostly behind his advancing troops. He knew that wouldn't last—the enemy would adjust their targeting. He had to do something now.

"Other units, continue to advance." *We'll drop a couple mortar rounds on their heads, and then the rest of the line will be on them.*

He'd just lunged forward when he saw the entire enemy

line advance from the cover of the hillside. They came over the crest, 150 of them, in a single perfect line. "Fire!" he screamed, just as the entire attacking force opened up.

His line was riddled with hyper-velocity rounds, virtually identical to the ones he'd used in the Corps. The deadly weapons overwhelmed his own peoples' return fire by a factor of at least ten. He leapt to the ground, feeling an impact in his leg as he went down. He screamed in pain, reaching around, trying to activate the pharmakit inside his armor. The old fighting suits didn't have AI-controlled trauma systems like Marine armor. He had to flip a switch and swing his hip into the now-exposed needle to give himself a cocktail of painkillers and stims.

His eyes drifted up to his display. It looked like two-thirds of his people were already down, and the enemy was advancing. He scrambled around, grabbing his dropped assault rifle and bringing it to bear, just as four enemy soldiers leapt up over the small hill in front of him.

His old Marine reflexes took over, and he ignored the pain and fired, as much by instinct as deliberation, and he dropped the first enemy he saw. But the others were on him. He felt the impacts, round after round slamming into his body, tearing through his armor. There was pain, but only for an instant. Then it was gone, and he slipped into blackness, his final thought on the absurdity of dying here after so many desperate battles as a Marine.

*   *   *   *   *

"Captain?" Ludendorf was sitting at the bunker's com station, frantically tuning the channel. He'd been trying to reach Captain Vanik—indeed, anyone at all on the surface—for fifteen minutes, but all he'd gotten was static. He turned toward Gerhard. The others were all gathered behind, most of them on the verge of panic. There were no cowards in Ludendorf's crew. It took a certain amount of courage just to agree to a rotation on a planet like Kalte. But dealing with a deadly environment wasn't the same thing as facing attacking enemy soldiers, and it was starting to look like these particular invaders had obliterated the entire defense force in a matter of minutes.

Vanik had been an Alliance Marine, like a dozen of his men, veterans of mankind's most devastating wars. The thought that whatever was approaching had blown his people away like they were nothing was almost beyond comprehension.

"I can't raise anyone." He turned and looked around the bunker, looking for anything to use as a weapon. "Grab whatever you can...tools, even a club. Anything."

"You mean fight?" They were all looking at Ludendorf with shocked expressions. One of the junior technicians was the first to speak. "They just blew away over a hundred trained guards. What the hell are we going to do?"

"Whatever we have to." Ludendorf turned his head, looking across the room. "You think these people are going to leave you alive? They just killed 120 of our people. You want to make it out of here, you better be ready to fight for it, because I don't see another way home." Ludendorf didn't think they had any chance either, but he preferred the idea of dying on his feet. Besides, it gave him something to think about instead of just waiting around for the end.

A loud bang reverberated through the room. It had come from above, from the surface entry. A few seconds later there was another sound, and then about twenty seconds after that an explosion.

"Make sure your suits are sealed," Ludendorf shouted. The bunker had a limited life support system, but that wouldn't last more than a minute once the armored hatch was breached.

He ran to the control panel, staring down at the display screens. There were monitors in the shaft leading down to the bunker. There was smoke everywhere, probably from the charge that blew the outer doors. It was hard to see anything, but he could make out a few shadowy forms climbing down.

"Here they come. Everybody get ready." His hand tightened around the plasma torch he was carrying. It wasn't a weapon, but he knew it would fuck up anyone he got close enough to, armor or no armor. About half the others had some kind of makeshift weapon. The rest were standing around, paralyzed by fear.

There was a rapping sound on the metal, just on the other side of the hatch. Ludendorf crept toward the door, moving cautiously, hesitant to get too close in case it blew.

He could hear someone working on the other side. It went on for a few minutes, and then it stopped. Ludendorf turned toward the display and saw the enemy troopers climbing back up a few meters. He turned and yelled, "Get down…"

The explosion blasted the heavy armored door into the room, twisted into an unrecognizable hunk of wreckage. Ludendorf had propelled himself to the side, and the door missed him completely, but a quick glance told him a good third of his people hadn't been so lucky.

He saw the shadowy figures pushing through the smoke into the room, firing at the panicking miners and engineers. He watched his people trying to flee, throwing themselves on the ground and begging for mercy.

The soldiers pushed forward, sweeping the room with their deadly rifles. There was no pause, no demand for surrender—they were just butchering everyone. Ludendorf was off to the side, out of the initial line of fire. He saw his people dying, and he felt an energy in his body, a searing rage that took him. He flexed his legs and threw himself forward, flipping the switch on the plasma torch as he lunged.

He held the torch's cutting edge in front of him as he fell into one of the enemy troopers. The exposed plasma cut through the osmium-iridium alloy of the man's armor, slicing his arm clean off. Ludendorf fell to the ground, his survival suit splattered with the soft white foam from his enemy's armor's repair systems. The soldier's suit was trying to seal the breach on the arm before the cold and deadly atmosphere did their work.

But Ludendorf wasn't about to allow it. He knew he had seconds left to live, and there was nothing more important to him than taking this soldier with him. A single wounded raider had become the proxy for his rage. He didn't have a chance to get to anyone else, but he reached out with the torch, pushing toward the stricken soldier even as he felt the bullets impacting on his body.

He was focused, determined. He didn't even feel the pain as the two of the enemy troopers raked him with fire. He could feel himself slipping away. There was weakness, and cold. His vision was failing. But his momentum carried him forward, and with the last of his strength, he held the plasma torch in front of him, plunging the blazing hot tip through the back of his target's armor before he fell to the ground and slipped into the darkness.

Chapter 12

Old Marine Hospital
Planet Armstrong, Gamma Pavonis III
Earthdate: September, 2318 AD (33 Years After the Fall)

Sarah Cain sat in her office, quietly scanning reports. At a fast glance, she appeared almost unchanged over the past thirty years, a strikingly beautiful woman who seemed immune to the passage of time. A closer inspection revealed a few lines on her face and streaks of gray in her hair, but nothing that made her seem remotely close to her age. It was her eyes that came closest to giving her away. A deep sadness had dulled their former blue sparkle. She felt her age more than she showed it, and a sense of fatigue had been growing on her.

She was two years shy of her ninetieth birthday, but a lifetime of rejuv treatments had left her the physical equivalent of a healthy fifty year old woman. She knew the effects of the drug therapies would begin to fade more quickly in the years ahead, eventually causing her to age the equivalent of two or three years for each one that passed. She could easily live to her 120th or 130th birthday, but she also realized she would be an old woman long before that. In many ways she already felt that way, as if she was simply waiting for her remaining years to pass.

Sarah's life had been a difficult one in many ways. She had served for years as the chief surgeon of the Alliance Marine Corps, and she had seen more horror and death than any man or woman should witness. When the final war between the Superpowers was over, she'd finally had a chance at peace, and for fifteen years she'd been happier than she'd ever imagined possible. But, like all good things, her joy had come to an end—and as usual, it was the trumpet of war that had shattered her bliss.

When the First Imperium struck again, Erik had answered the call, as he had all his life. It had been more difficult for him to take up the sword again this last time, for he too, Sarah was certain, had finally found a happy life with her and their teenaged twin sons. But in the end, he'd had to go. The First Imperium was a threat to all mankind. The Superpowers were gone, and the young colony worlds possessed a fraction of the strength that had been wielded in the first war against the alien menace. If the robotic invaders weren't defeated, eventually they would come to Atlantia. They would destroy that magnificent world, and kill every human being living there. Including Sarah and her sons. Even if Cain could leave the rest of mankind to its fate, he could never allow such an inhuman enemy to reach his family.

This war had been different from all the countless others he'd fought, however. He'd led his warriors as well as he ever had, winning a series of costly victories that stopped the First Imperium invasion in its tracks. Indeed, there were those who said history would call his innovative campaigns in this last struggle his most brilliant. But they were also his most costly, and there was one tragic difference from his earlier battles. This time Erik Cain didn't return. War had finally claimed him, and just like that, after forty years at her side, he was gone.

The struggle had been a brutal one, and many colonies, still striving toward self-sufficiency after the destruction of the Superpowers, were devastated before the fighting was over. Cain and his old comrades—Augustus Garret, James Teller,

Cate Gilson—had rallied the tiny remnant of the old Corps and fleet, and taken command of the hundreds of planetary militias. It was an array far weaker than the ones they had led in the first war with their alien enemy, but the First Imperium invaders were themselves a splinter force, the garrison of one ancient base that, for unexplained reasons, had responded twenty years late to the Regent's call.

Sarah hadn't felt anything at all when they'd first told her. She was a creature of duty, and she had two sixteen year old boys who needed her. Indeed, Darius and Elias had saved her, and she'd buried her sorrow in motherhood. But that was a short respite from despair. Darius never got over his father's death, and he became deeply troubled, running afoul of more than one of Atlantia's increasingly onerous slate of laws. He left home four months before his 19th birthday, running from his grief and anger—and destined for a life of war like his father's. Elias had remained home, but a year later he enrolled in the nascent Atlantian Patrol Service, joining its inaugural academy class. He embraced the stern laws and structured society his brother had repudiated, and he buried himself in his studies. Over time, he became more and more strident, almost a martinet, seeking to fill the void in his life with rules and regulations.

Just like that, Sarah was alone. Darius disappeared entirely for two years, and she hadn't known where he had gone or if he was even still alive. The boy had always been emotionally cold—cynical and hard in his assessment of others and the universe in general. He'd inherited those traits from his father, but he was colder, more robotic than Erik Cain had ever been. For all his caustic disregard for rules and his distaste for politicians, Erik Cain had always had an empathetic streak, one even he had been hesitant to acknowledge. It fueled the guilt that had kept him up nights, and he carried it his entire life. But Darius was relentless, immovable, imbued with a fire even more intense than the one that had driven his father.

Sarah knew he'd left to take out his grief on the universe,

and she'd been deathly afraid she would never see him again, that his rage would drive him to a tragic death in some misadventure. But two years to the day after he'd left, he sent her a message. He was fine. Indeed, he was an officer in one of the new mercenary companies, a warrior just like his father. The one thing Erik Cain hadn't wanted.

She'd seen him several times over the next decade, while he was founding the Black Eagles and building his reputation—and his infamy. She pretended not to hear later, after his reputation had spread, when people called him a savage, a butcher. She knew her son wasn't an evil man. Better than most people, she understood the seeming inevitability of conflict. Blaming the soldiers who fought the wars, while absolving the politicians who created them, was unjust. But it still hurt her to realize that most of the people in Occupied Space feared her son.

She often wondered what Erik would have said to Darius. Would he have approved of his son's steadfast resolution, been proud of his martial brilliance? Yes, probably, she had decided more than once. But would he also have spoken to the boy, tried to instill more tolerance in him, to help him to see people in less entirely absolute ways? Yes, again, she thought, though with a bit less conviction. Erik Cain had been the love of her life, but he'd been a hard man, forged by bitter experiences. He tended to think the worst of people all his life, unless they proved him wrong. She didn't know how he would have reacted to seeing the extent to which his son took that disdain for humanity.

Elias was just as steadfast—pigheaded would be a better word, she thought. He plunged into his career with the patrol, rising quickly in its burgeoning ranks. Atlantia hadn't been one of the richer colony worlds, but it was growing rapidly and beginning to exploit the resources of the other planets of its solar system. The exploitation of previously undiscovered resources kicked off an economic boom that put the planet on a trajectory toward the top tier of colonies.

Atlantia's colonists had created an old-fashioned, traditional society, and they strove to maintain it in the face of rapid expansion and population growth. Politicians ran on law and order platforms, and layers of new rules and regulations followed every election. The patrol took on the task of enforcing Atlantia's ever-growing body of law throughout the new mining colonies and trading posts.

Sarah had seen Elias more often than Darius, at least in the earlier years, and she'd watched him grow harder, more aggressive and pitiless in his inflexible enforcement of the edicts of the Atlantian government. She knew Erik would have respected his son's work ethic and his devotion to duty, but he would have been disturbed by Elias' robotic—and increasingly mindless—dedication to imposing a seemingly endless series of new dictats, without so much as a thought to whether he agreed with them in principle. Erik Cain had never allowed himself to become the unfettered tool of those in the halls of power, despite his long career in the military. He had always remained his own man, with his own thoughts and beliefs, and it would have hurt him to see his son behave differently. Erik—and Sarah—had seen where such mindless obedience led, to the stratified societies of the Superpowers, which had seen the vast majority of mankind living in appalling conditions, completely stripped of their freedoms.

Sarah had remained on Atlantia for a few years after Erik was lost, rambling alone through the waterfront home they had built two decades before. But the sorrow and loneliness grew on her. Time did nothing to diminish the pain she felt for her loss, and she reached the point where she couldn't bear the endless, empty hours. Her surroundings were a constant reminder of what she had lost, of the life she had waited decades to achieve, only to see it slip away. She finally returned to Armstrong, where at least a few old friends and comrades remained—and where she could spend her hours doing something truly productive.

She'd resumed her post running the Old Marine hospital.

The massive facility had transitioned into Armstrong's primary care facility, for both military and civilian patients. The leading edge capabilities, built over years of handling vast numbers of Marine and naval casualties, made the hospital a revenue source for the vastly-shrunken Corps. It was the premier medical center in Occupied Space, and wealthy individuals flocked to Armstrong for treatment of serious illnesses and injuries, pumping large amounts of money into the local economy.

It took Sarah a considerable time to get used to dealing with non-military patients. Her new position required a significantly more nuanced approach than had been required when the hospital was full of recovering Marines. Still, the Corps owned the facility, and she'd officially come out of retirement to assume the top job. She'd been a colonel when she'd elected to retire, but the Corps had bumped her up to brigadier general just before moving her to inactive status, and now she had a single star on each collar. When she wore a uniform, which was rarely. Most of the time when she wasn't in scrubs, she dressed in civilian clothes.

The com unit on her desk buzzed. "Yes?" she said as she pushed the button to activate the device.

"General Cain, you asked to be alerted when the patient regained consciousness."

She leapt up out of her chair. "On my way," she snapped, and flipped the com unit off.

She walked across her large—uncomfortably so, she'd always thought—office and slipped out into the reception area. "I'll be down in the ICU," she said as she trotted out into the hallway.

Her stomach was tight. Anderson didn't have much time left, and she knew each time he woke from his near-coma could be the last. Anderson-45 was, to the best of her knowledge, the last of Gavin Stark's Shadow Legion warriors still alive. He'd been created, as they all had, to fight the Marines and conquer mankind for the psychopathic Stark, but he had been captured in one of the early battles, and by the end of the war Sarah had broken his conditioning and Anderson-45 had become an ally of the Marines. He'd helped rehabilitate the few clones who survived the war, but now they were all gone, and only he remained.

The clone soldiers had been the work of a brilliant scientist, whose name was lost in the devastation of the climactic war. Likely, he was murdered by Stark as soon as he'd served his purpose. The cloning technology was perfect, and the hundreds of thousands of soldiers created were identical copies of their parent beings. Anderson-45 had been one of the senior officer class, the 45th quickened from the DNA of a kidnapped Marine colonel whose name had also been Anderson.

The Shadow clones had indeed been perfect, but with one complication. They began their existence as embryos, and they developed in their mechanical crèches until they were normal human infants. But Gavin Stark need adult soldiers, and he hadn't been prepared to wait almost two decades for his clones to mature naturally. The Shadow project developed the answer, an accelerated growth process along with a program of direct neural input, capable of creating a fully-grown and totally trained soldier in less than five years.

It had been an amazing leap forward, but it had not come without cost. The enhanced growth caused chromosomal damage, dramatically reducing the natural lifespans of the clones. And despite three decades of medical research, no way to significantly reverse the damage had ever been found. Anderson-45 was 38 years old, but he was the physical equivalent of a 130 year-old man.

Sarah put her palm on the access panel for the ICU, pausing for a second as the system confirmed her ID and cleared her for entry. The outer door slid open, allowing her access to the airlock entry. It slid shut behind her and, an instant later, the inner hatch opened. She walked inside and down the hall to Anderson's small room.

"If it isn't my favorite doctor," he said slowly, with great difficulty. It was clear that every word caused him pain, but he managed a reasonable facsimile of a smile for her.

She forced herself to return the smile, but it was difficult. She'd become very fond of the clone over the years, and she counted him among her few true friends. Watching him wither away was enormously painful. "And my favorite patient...and the one I've had longest too."

Anderson had been a strong and intelligent man, possessed of the DNA of one of the Corps' finest. Once she'd freed him of his conditioning, he'd made the most of his short life, doing his best to help his brethren. The Shadow Legion soldiers had been the Marines' enemy, but they had been tools, victims themselves, created to fight and die and controlled with experimental brain surgery and psychological conditioning. When Sarah had removed the conditioning, many of the survivors were wracked with guilt at the things they had done under Stark's control, driven to the edge of insanity. Many committed suicide, others turned to alcohol and drugs to block the pain. Anderson had worked with many of them, helping them to adapt and become productive members of society.

When the First Imperium returned, the old Shadow soldiers flocked to the Marine standards, despite the fact that they were already beginning to show signs of accelerating physical deterioration. They served with great distinction in that war, many of them fighting under Erik Cain in his last battles.

He shifted, trying to get comfortable, apparently without success. "It just hurts everywhere," he finally said, sinking back again. "Might as well accept it." His speech was slow and labored, but that was all physical, the best he could manage between his rasping breaths. But Anderson had kept his wits about him, and his mental state was as strong as that of any man in his late thirties. Sarah didn't wish that her friend suffered from dementia, but it somehow made it worse to watch such a young and strong mind trapped in a decaying body.

"Sarah," he said, looking up at her, "I want to thank you for everything you've done for me all these years." There was a sadness in his voice, and a weakness that made her eyes watery.

"Anderson…"

"No, Sarah," he croaked softly. "Please, let me say this. I remember how hard you worked to break that terrible conditioning, to allow me to live as a human being and not a slave. My life may have been a short one, but it wouldn't have been mine at all without you."

He reached out a trembling hand and put it on her arm. "I know how much sadness you have endured. Don't give up on the rest of your life, Sarah. You have more time, and where there is time, there is always hope."

"Thank you, Anderson. But you have already given me your gratitude…in how you have lived your life. You have shown me that every bit of effort was worthwhile. You may have begun life in a laboratory, but you are more of a human being than most I have known."

She sighed softly, and sat in the chair next to the bed. Her eyes were on his chest heaving up and down, her ears listening to the raspy, liquid sound of his breath. She had seen far too many men and women die in her years in the field hospitals, and she knew in her gut her friend Anderson wouldn't wake again when he slipped back into unconsciousness.

The clone lay still, silent, drawing increasingly shallow breaths. Sarah laid her hand on his and sat with him quietly. The minutes slipped into an hour then two. Anderson's breathing was becoming increasingly difficult, and he'd slipped back into a gentle delirium. Sarah sat and listened as his labored breathing became quiet, slow. A few minutes later she stood up and looked down at him, reaching out and gently closing his eyes. Anderson-45 was dead.

"General Cain? I am sorry to disturb you…"

Sarah always felt a pang when someone called her that. To her, General Cain would always mean Erik. But she was

General Cain now as well. She had decided to change her name when they'd gotten married. It was old-fashioned to be sure, but that had been the trend on colonies like Atlantia then, and Sarah had wanted nothing more than to fit in and live a normal life. And she'd lived that life, if only for a short while.

"Yes?" She turned and looked back toward the door. One of the ICU techs was standing there.

"There is a messenger waiting in your office, General."

That's strange. Who would be visiting me? "Did they say who it was?"

"No, General." A short pause. "Only that he was sent by a Roderick Vance."

Chapter 13

Just Outside the Ruins of Jericho
Planet Earth, Sol III
Earthdate: September, 2317 AD

Axe was adrift, floating in darkness. He knew it was over. Everything was lost—Ellie, Jericho, all of it. He was dying, or was he already dead? He didn't know. Nothing seemed real.

Then he felt something different. Pressure. On his shoulder, his leg. It was firm, not like the gauzy sensations he'd been feeling. Then pain. Terrible pain, agony. His whole body hurt. His arms, his gut, his legs—and his tortured lungs. Then he saw light, dim at first, spotty, cutting slowly through the blackness. Brighter. Sunlight. Shining through hazy eyes. *I'm alive, at least for a few moments more.*

But there shouldn't be light. He'd been shot. He remembered now. He'd been lying on the ground, watching one of the raiders raise his gun to finish him. But it had been the middle of the night. What was this light? Had he been lying here for all those hours?

"Axe?" He heard his name, softly, far away. He felt the pressure again, harder this time. Hands gripping his shoulders, shaking him. "Axe, you awake?"

Axe heard a sound, a groan. He realized it had come from his lips. His throat felt like fire as he tried to force words out. "What…" The pain was almost unbearable.

"Axe, come on, man. You're going to be OK. I got you out."

He turned his head slowly, so slowly he wasn't even sure it was moving at first. The light was brighter, his vision beginning to clear. He was in the woods, not Jericho.

"I managed to get the emergency message off before we left. To the Martians. I don't know if they received anything, but there's a chance at least."

Axe moved his head toward the voice. It was familiar. He forced a word through his agonized throat. "Where?"

"Axe, we're about half a klick from Jericho."

Jack. Jack Lompoc.

"I managed to get you out. They left you for dead."

"Jack?"

"Yes, Axe. It's Jack."

"What happened?" Memories were coming back. *I was fighting, the shot in the leg, falling back—that face staring down at me. Raising a pistol…*

"The town is gone, Axe. Whoever they were, they took almost everybody." Jack's voice was firm. There was a commanding sound there, a calmness in the face of disaster. "It was some kind of knockout gas. I'd say about 200 are dead, but the rest were dragged out, still alive. At least I think they were. They brought in a bunch of transports and loaded them all up." He paused. "Axe, they didn't take anything else. The grain, the equipment in the shed, none of it. They just burned it all. They didn't come to steal. They came for the people."

Axe looked up at Lompoc. His thoughts were still fuzzy. "The people?" he repeated, half question, half statement. He coughed hard, spraying blood all over himself as he did.

Lompoc dropped to a knee right next to him. "My God, Axe, what is that? Are you shot somewhere else?"

Axe stared down at himself, confused for a second. "Oh, the blood," he said, coughing again. His chin was covered with red, and it was splattered all over his shirt. "No, not a wound."

He felt terrible, but his head was starting to clear. And he damned sure wasn't dead. Not yet, at least. "No, it's not a wound. I haven't told anybody, but…"

Jack nodded. "I got it, Axe." His voice was somber. No one survived thirty years after the Fall without watching friends and loved ones die from the long-term effects of radiation. "How long?"

"A while. It's been getting worse. But we don't have time for that now. We have to do something." He stared up at Lompoc. "Ellie?"

"I don't know, Axe. I really don't. I searched for survivors, and I didn't see her with the…" He paused for a second. "…bodies. My best guess is they took her. And they didn't come for a pile of corpses, so I'd bet she's still alive."

Axe struggled to sit up, and Lompoc reached over and helped him. "We have to do something." What, he had no idea.

"Once I got you out and set you down, I went back and followed them. It took them a few hours to get everybody loaded up, and then they drove about three kilometers to some spot that looked like a makeshift base. They're still there, I think."

"Anybody else make it?"

Lompoc sighed. "I'm not sure, Axe. I think a few must have gotten out and run to the north. Tommie's with us. I sent him to get some water. He got clipped in the leg, but he's OK." He paused, and his voice became darker. "Reg was helping me search for survivors, but then I lost him. I don't know if he's dead or if they captured him."

Axe let out a deep breath. "You said you sent the distress call?"

"Yeah, Axe, but I'm not sure what that's going to do for us. The Martians send us food and meds, and that's great, but I've never seen a Confederation soldier down here, have you? That message won't accomplish anything. Probably just let them know they can scratch one drop from their schedule."

There was frustration in Lompoc's voice. Axe figured he'd been trying to decide what to do over the last ten hours, and he'd come up with almost nothing.

"We need to track them when they leave, Jack. We need to stay on their heels until we figure out what to do." Axe sat up. He felt like death, but he didn't have time for that now, and he pushed himself by sheer force of will. He looked up at Lompoc. "Give me a hand." He reached out.

Lompoc stared back doubtfully for a few seconds, but he didn't argue. He grabbed Axe's hand and helped pull him to his feet.

Axe stood still. He was a little dizzy, but he could feel his balance returning slowly. "OK, as soon as Tommie gets back, we'll head down to that camp."

Lompoc nodded, but he had a frown on his face. "And do what, Axe?" He sighed hard. "There are at least 40 men down there, and they're well-armed. There are three of us... and you and Tommie are wounded."

"I don't know what we're going to do, Jack, but we're damned sure not going to lose them. I don't know what these invaders want with our people, but it can't be good."

And it's probably downright unthinkable.

*　　*　　*　　*　　*

"Final headcount is 849. I'd estimate about 200 dead in the raid." Barkley was holding a small tablet. It was an old unit, crude and outdated. But on Earth 32 years after the Fall, it might as well have been witchcraft. And it was more than enough to do the job of tallying and sorting the captives.

Grax nodded. "I'd have liked a lower death count, but the target was just too big. We couldn't take any chances." And not taking chances meant shooting first and asking questions later. "Still, that's a damned good haul, my friend. How's the sorting going?"

"Good. Like any group of Earthers, there's a fair amount of them that are half-rotten. Too much radiation and contaminated food. But I'd say half of them are in good shape. And maybe 80 are prime." Barkley turned and glanced over his shoulder, where most of the crew were moving unconscious prisoners around. The initial sort had been done roughly, based on a cursory examination, and the captives were divided into four groups. Then the expedition's two doctors scanned them all more closely, moving a few up or down a category.

The primes were the first group, men and women sixteen to thirty years old, with no signs of long-term radiation sickness and in good physical condition. Eighty was by far the largest number Grax's people had ever bagged in one place.

"Eighty? Nice." Grax allowed himself a smile. "The Buyers will pay a top price for them, and a bonus for so many in one group. That alone will guarantee us a healthy profit on this run. All the rest are just gravy."

"I'd say we've got 250 As. They'll fetch a decent price." The A rated captives were basically healthy and strong enough to have a life expectancy of five years or longer at hard labor. Some of them had minor impairments that knocked them from the highest level, or they were out of the designated age range. Most of the As were destined for agricultural or factory work.

Grax nodded. "The As alone would be a strong payday, even without the primes. You were right, Pete. It was worth the risk of hitting that settlement."

Barkley nodded. "Of the rest, I culled out about 200. Too old, too weak. Or ones the doc flagged as sick—mostly cancers and other long term effects of radiation. I detached Waters and a team to put them down."

"So that leaves about 300 Bs then." The B class were older and weaker candidates, mostly destined for work in mines and other dangerous activities. Bs had a life expectancy of a couple years at best, which made them considerably less valuable than the As. Still, with the expedition already paid for, the proceeds from the 300 Bs was all profit. And 600 projected man-years of labor had a value, even deducting the costs of transit.

"Yeah. Looks like 309 total." Barkley smiled. "A damned good haul by any measure."

Grax returned the smile. "Maybe we'll recruit some more men after we get paid, and we'll try to find some other big targets. A couple more like this one, and we'll retire to some tropical planet and spend our days in a hammock with a couple girls each."

"Sounds good to me, boss." There was something in his voice, a hint of nervousness. Barkley had long ago overcome the moral issues of rounding up humans and selling them into servitude. There were enough mercenaries out there killing people for money, after all. But he still had reservations about the Buyers. The strange group ran an efficient operation, and they'd come through on every payment they had promised. But Barkley still didn't trust them. For one thing, he wondered where their human cargo was taken after he delivered them.

Society throughout Occupied Space was becoming harsher, the lofty ethics and optimism of the immediate post-Fall era rapidly fading away, but there still weren't many worlds that openly allowed human beings to be held as slaves. And the few that did generally restricted it to convicted criminals and indentured servants paying for transit with a set labor period. Kidnapped people stolen from another world were completely different. Perhaps there were a few small fringe worlds that might welcome such cargoes, but not many. And he knew there were other teams working Earth, sending hundreds, no thousands, of people to whatever world or worlds the mysterious Buyers represented.

Technically, it didn't matter where the captives went after he and Grax were paid, but there was still something about it that nagged at him.

*   *   *   *   *

Andre Girard crept through the heavy woods, moving slowly, cautiously. He was anxious, impatient, but decades of field service had taught him you could be quiet, or you could be fast, but not both. And he had no idea who else might be prowling around in these woods.

He'd checked out the village. Vance's information was correct. The place had been attacked and burned. He'd scoured the wreckage for clues, but he'd come up with very little. He was fairly certain some of the population was still alive somewhere—or at least that they'd been taken someplace else before they'd been killed. He'd found bodies—and ashes and bits of bones where others had been consumed by the flames—but nowhere near enough to account for the population of the settlement.

It didn't look like Jericho's meager wealth had been plundered. The village didn't have much, but Girard imagined that farming tools and stored grain would be valuable to any group wandering around post-Fall Earth. Yet it was clear the storehouses had been well-stocked before the fires took them. *Why would raiders from another settlement leave so much food behind? And why would they take the people instead of slaughtering them? It was just more mouths to feed.*

Girard never underestimated Roderick Vance, but when his friend had asked him to come to Earth and investigate the distress call he'd received, he'd wondered if Martian Intelligence's long time master had finally become a touch too paranoid. But now he was thinking differently. He had no idea what had happened here, but there was definitely something wrong. This was more than just warfare between rival settlements.

He crept along, following the trails leading south, and

he stopped dead in his tracks. There were footsteps, and disturbed earth where bodies had been dragged. And there were trails left by heavy tracked vehicles. As far as he knew, none of the surviving settlements on Earth had any trucks or transports left, and even if they did, they didn't have fuel to run them. Now Girard was sure Vance was right. Something very strange was going on here.

He slipped off to the side, back into the cover of the woods. He was dealing with something different now, and he had to be careful. Anyone who had a dozen or more transports could have other equipment too—binoculars, scanning devices, even drones.

He continued south, following the trail slowly, making sure to keep hidden as he did. It took him an hour to cover a kilometer, but Andre Girard had a lifetime of discipline, and he made certain each step was silent. There were dozens of ways to give a position away—a broken twig under foot, stepping on dried leaves, rustling branches as you passed. But Girard moved like a phantom, silent, invisible.

Another kilometer, another hour. The tracks continued in the same direction. Whoever he was following, they'd made no effort to hide their trail. *Why would they? Who would they be hiding from down here?* Still, he had a disapproving smile on his face. Girard believed in strong tradecraft, even when you didn't think you needed it. Especially when you didn't think you needed it. That's usually when you got in trouble.

He stopped suddenly. He'd caught a sound, something off in the distance. He couldn't tell what it was, but it didn't sound like something from the forest. He crouched down, still, listening. Yes, there was something ahead. He moved forward, his pace even slower than before, creeping toward the faint noise.

It became louder and more frequent. There was definitely something ahead, and whoever was there, they weren't trying to stay hidden. He swung off to the side, giving a wider berth to the camp as he moved around it. He found a good spot to hide, and he stayed there, motionless, listening. It was dusk already, and he decided to wait for dark to investigate further. He'd done his homework as always. It was overcast, and the moon would only be a sliver. A dark night. Perfect for scouting.

*   *   *   *   *

Axe was sitting against a tree, looking toward Jack and Tommie. The three of them had been hiding on the outskirts of the enemy camp for three days now. There had been a lot of activity, but the raiders had stayed in place. They appeared to be keeping the captives sedated, but Axe was pretty sure his people were still alive. The raiders were carrying still bodies around with a lot more care than they would have put into corpses.

He closed his eyes for a minute. Jack had cleaned out his wounds with a gusto that almost brought tears to his eyes. Axe considered himself fairly tough, but his friend had dug into him like an interrogator hard at work. But when he was done, the projectiles were both removed, and the wounds were thoroughly washed and neatly bound. They still hurt like hell, but Axe couldn't argue with Jack's skills. There wasn't a sign of infection, and he was beginning to heal.

"What are we going to do?" Axe's voice was heavy with frustration. For three days they had managed to stay undetected, but they were no closer to figuring a way to liberate their people. Indeed, it seemed more hopeless than ever. "They're not going to stay here indefinitely, Jack. We've got to make some kind of move. Soon."

"What?" Lompoc stared back at his friend. "I feel the same way you do, Axe, but what the hell can we do? Taking a risk is one thing. But if we make one move on that camp, the three of us will be dead or captured in seconds." He paused.

"There's just no way."

"I can't let them just take her, Jack." Axe shifted uncomfortably. Lompoc's work had passed medical muster, but Goddamnned if it still didn't hurt.

"Ellie wouldn't want you to get yourself killed for no reason, Axe. You know that." He paused. "A risk is one thing, even if it's a crazy one. But suicide is something else. And you know we have no chance to break our people out. None. And they're still unconscious, which means even if we got to them, they can't help us. How could we get them out? Unless you think the three of us can kill 40 heavily-armed men."

"I'm expendable, Jack." He stifled a cough. "What have I got left? Six months? At most? But I can't let them just take Ellie…all our people…away."

"But you're still…" Lompoc stopped abruptly and swung around, reaching for the machete hanging from his belt.

"Now don't do that," a voice said from the thick brush. Girard moved slowly out of the dense foliage. He was barely visible in the darkness, but they could see the pistol in his hand, pointing at Lompoc. "I've been listening to you boys for a while, and I think we can get along very well." He moved out into the open, off to the side where he had a good view of all three of his new acquaintances.

"Who are you?" Lompoc's voice was calm, disciplined.

"Let's just say I'm a friend. One you guys sorely need." His eyes darted to the blade at Lompoc's side. "But until we know each other better, what do you say you put that down."

Jack's hand was still on the machete's handle. He moved slowly, unhooking the belt that held the weapon and letting it slip to the ground. He was staring at the new arrival, as if scanning for weakness.

"Now, I take it you three are survivors from Jericho." Girard sat down slowly, his gun still in his hand.

"How do you know about Jericho?" Axe felt his stomach tense. *Is this guy one of the raiders?*

"I know about it because you sent us a message. I'm

from Martian Intelligence. My name is Girard. Andre Girard." His eyes focused on Lompoc. "And, if I'm not mistaken, you've got some tradecraft."

"I was an agent before the Fall." Jack glanced at his two companions, a nervous expression on his face.

"Alliance Intelligence?" Girard nodded without waiting for an answer. "Of course...one of Gavin Stark's people."

Lompoc turned and looked over at Axe. "Hardly that. Stark was well above my pay grade. I was just a junior agent." He took a breath and turned to face his friend. "Axe, I'm sorry I never told you. I...I was just..."

"Forget it, Jack." Axe's voice was warm, with no hint of condemnation. "It's been thirty years, and we've all struggled to survive together. That's all that matters now. Besides, I already had you pegged as Manhattan Police which, trust me, would have been just as bad to me. And I was a gang leader. I killed a lot of people. We're all living new lives now, so let's leave the old baggage where it belongs. In the past."

Lompoc smiled. "Thank you, Axe." There was relief in his voice. He turned toward Tommie, who just nodded with his own smile.

"I'm glad everyone has decided to stay friends," Girard said, "because I just scouted out that camp down the way, and we've all got a problem. It looks to me like your people have fallen into the hands of a group of slavers." He paused, taking a quick breath. "You ever run into any locals with trucks and equipment like that?"

"No, never." Axe answered first. "I haven't seen an operational truck in twenty years, and they've got at least a dozen. And weapons like none I've ever run into."

"They've got military-grade hardware," Lompoc added.

"Yes, I saw some myself," Girard said. "Not what I expected to find. This is a well-financed operation, not another band of wandering survivors."

"They've got our people, so we're stuck in this, but what do you have to do with it?" Axe's question was pointed.

"We received your distress call. Let's just say I was sent here to see what happened." He paused, glancing in the direction of the slavers' camp. "And I still don't know, at least not completely." He turned back toward the others. "But if you'll all work with me, I intend to find out everything. And maybe we can save your people in the process."

*   *   *   *   *

"Alright, let's move it. We lift off in two hours, and we need this cargo stowed for transit." Grax stood and watched as his men began placing the sedated captives on cargo sleds. Dragging them around was tedious, but it virtually eliminated security concerns. He just didn't have enough people to guard over 800 prisoners and still do everything else that had to be done. "Get the Primes loaded first."

"The last of the Primes will be secure in a few minutes." Peter Barkley was walking down the lowered hatch of one of the landers. He'd been running around all morning preparing. As soon as the two big ships hit ground, he got his crews moving. Barkley was second-in-command after Grax, and he was in charge of the loading operation.

"The sooner we lift off the better." Grax knew his people were strong enough to deal with any wanderers who happened by their camp, but the ships had been visible for hundreds of kilometers, and he would be happy to be in the air and bound for Eris before the spectacle attracted too much attention. The stealth ships were an amazing development, but even their advanced technology couldn't mask the massive output of the landing engines.

"Couldn't agree more." Barkley looked back over his shoulder. "Another five or six hours should do it, Boss. Then we can get the hell out of here and sell this load." He paused. "You know, Rufus, I've been wanting to talk with you." He sounded a little uncomfortable.

"What is it, Pete?" The two had run a dozen missions together, and Grax always expected his number two to discuss anything with him.

"It's the boys. Some of them, at least. They know we're looking at a huge score here, and I've heard a lot of talk… grumbling. A lot of them want to get their shares and take a break. They've got money burning holes in their pockets, and taverns and whorehouses on their minds."

Grax sighed. "How bad is it, Pete? Really?"

"I think we'll lose over half."

"That bad?" Grax sighed. "Any ideas?" He knew crews like his were temporary by nature, ragtag groups of society's castoffs, like pirates of the old wooden ships era on Earth. But Grax could feel the increasing pressure for more captives from their mysterious employers. He could see the bounties increasing. It was time to make as many big scores as possible—enough to disappear and retire in luxury somewhere, for good, not just for a wild, drunken blow off. He understood that, and he knew Barkley did too. But how many of the crew couldn't think beyond a six month blowout of drinking and getting laid—that was another question.

"We can try to bribe them with bigger shares if they stay." Barkley's tone was hesitant. Men drawn to professions like slaving didn't tend to part with their profits easily. "I know it'll come out of our end, but it'll cost us more if we're laid up for half a year recruiting a new team."

Grax exhaled hard, staring at the ground for half a minute. Finally, he looked up at Barkley. "Alright, Pete. Do it. Talk to the ones you think have the most influence, the ones that can convince others to stay. Anybody who signs on for another years' service gets a double share." His face was twisted into a scowl. That was going to cost him a ton. But it was still better than being out of business right now.

"I'm on it, Boss." He looked around. "We wouldn't want to miss another trip to this little slice of paradise, would we?"

*   *   *   *   *

"There is a way, at least a chance. But it's risky." Girard's eyes panned across his new companions, but they settled on Lompoc.

The three Jericho refugees had gone into a near panic when the landing ships put down. They'd been worried about keeping up with the raiders if they took off in their trucks—they hadn't imagined their enemies' destination was in space. They'd just about despaired of saving their people when Girard spoke up.

"What can we do?" Axe stepped toward Girard, wincing with each step.

"I have something. This." Girard held up a small capsule. It looked like some sort of pharmaceutical.

"What is that?"

"It's a tracking device. It will connect with the Martian scanning network in the solar system." He paused. "It might let us follow this vessel...or at least trace where it goes."

"Follow it? How?"

"I have a small ship hidden. It's how I got here. I can connect to the network and track them."

"But how do we get the tracker on one of their ships?" Tommie had been silent, but now he spoke up. "Sneak into their camp somehow?"

Lompoc was staring at Girard. "No, Tommie." He paused. "One of us swallows it." He turned toward his friend. "And he gets captured...and hopefully added to the cargo." His eyes darted to Girard. "Am I right?"

Girard nodded. "Yes, you are right. That is the only way we have a hope to track where they go. Otherwise, they'll slip away, and we won't have a chance in a million of finding your people."

"I'll do it." Axe's voice was calm, determined.

Girard sighed. "I'm sorry, Axe, but that won't work." He paused. "Look at yourself. These are slavers. They're only going to take captives they can sell at a profit." His tone was sympathetic, but firm. "And you're sick and wounded." Axe hadn't told Girard about his illness, but it was obvious. The stress of the past few days had made his symptoms worse— and impossible to hide.

"Girard is right, Axe." Lompoc's voice was grim. "They'd just put you down." He glanced to the side. "And you too, Tommie. They're not going to take anyone who is injured. Too much effort. Too much risk you'll just die in transit. They killed all the wounded in Jericho before they left. They'll certainly do the same to any unfit straggler that wanders into their camp."

"I'm afraid your friend is right, Axe." Girard's gaze fell on Lompoc. "If we're going to do this, it has to be Jack. And it has to be now." He paused. "But you need to know the risks first. You're certainly fit, but that's no guarantee they just don't shoot you on sight. It might be too much trouble to squeeze in another prisoner. Or they might get suspicious. Or you might get blasted without a second thought by a trigger-happy guard."

His eyes flashed to the small capsule in his hand. "This is a high tech device, very reliable. But that's no certainty we'll be able to maintain contact. We've got a good shot, but we could lose them too." He hesitated. "And if that happens, you'll be on your way to a life of slavery, Jack."

Lompoc stood still, staring wordlessly at Girard as the Martian continued. "Even if we manage to track you, there's no way to know we'll be able to mount a rescue operation. I'm here as a personal favor to Minister Vance, but official Martian policy is non-interference. If we can track these ships, and I can prove to the council that someone is running a slavery ring on Earth, Vance might convince them to take action. But they may still refuse to intervene." He stared at Lompoc with harsh eyes. "So consider all that before you decide."

Lompoc sighed hard and then stood silently, staring off into the woods, in the direction of the enemy camp. Girard was standing next to him, waiting, saying nothing. The only sound was Axe's rasping breath.

Finally, Lompoc looked over at his friend for a few seconds. He sighed again and said, "I will do it." Then he fixed his gaze on Girard. "So, how do I get myself captured?"

Chapter 14

Mining Complex
Planet Glaciem, Epsilon Indi XI
Earthdate: 2318 AD (33 Years After the Fall)

"I want every one of these habitats checked for survivors. Every centimeter." Elias Cain stood on a small rock outcropping, staring over the ruined structures. He knew they were unlikely to find survivors, but he was going to be damned sure before he called off the search. "And be careful. There's nitrogen ice all around here. One wrong step, and you could scrag yourself."

He stared at the settlement, a neat row of opaque white domes, connected by a two meter wide umbilical. It was holed in a dozen places now, and Cain doubted anyone could have survived for the 38 hours since headquarters had received the distress call. Not on Glaciem. The planet's temperature was remarkably stable, but that was in a range between 34 and 35 degrees Kelvin, a level of frigidity Cain would have characterized as substantially more than brisk.

Glaciem had been a barely noticed block of ice and rock for 96 of the 104 years since Atlantia had first been colonized. But the unexpected discovery of stable trans-uranian isotopes had set off a rush to build a mining facility. Atlantia was a beautiful world, by some accounts the most remarkable planet men have ever found, Earth included. But it wasn't a particularly wealthy colony. It had a wide variety of products derived from its vast seas, including some rare pharmaceuticals, but it had very little industry and, while it had enough mundane metals for its own needs, it didn't produce any minerals valuable enough for export. Until the barren and icy planet on the edge of the solar system yielded up its secrets.

Now someone had attacked Glaciem and, unless Elias was dead wrong, killed or captured the miners. It was a horrible crime, and Cain intended to see justice done. Indeed, he hoped it was just a crime. If this was something more than pirates or criminals—if another colony world was behind this, it was an act of war. And Atlantia was poorly prepared for a fight.

"Captain Cain, can you come over here, sir? I think we found something."

Cain looked down at the small tablet in his hand. Silvers. He was on the other side of the closest row of structures. He turned and walked around the outside of the end building. "On my way."

He moved slowly, methodically. The insulation on his boots was nearly perfect, but it didn't take much heat transfer to melt the top layer of the mostly-oxygen ice into a nearly frictionless surface. Glaciem was not the kind of place you wanted to take a fall. It was a deadly dangerous environment where one false step could be your last.

"What is it, Silvers?" He came around the corner, and he saw his deputy down on one knee, digging at a patch of frozen oxygen and nitrogen.

"This patch of ice over here...it looks like it got melted and then refroze. Probably an explosion when the colony was attacked." He picked up a small scrap of metal. "There are bits and pieces of equipment here, sir. And it doesn't look like anything the minors would have had."

Elias stepped forward and reached out. "Let me see." He held the chunk of metal up to the sky, taking a look in the faint light of the distant primary. "This looks like..." He paused.

He wasn't sure, but if his hunch was right, there had been a hell of a lot more at work on Glaciem than normal outlaws.

He activated his open com channel. "Attention all patrol officers. I want everyone to search the area thoroughly. You are looking for any kind of small wreckage or debris...bits of metal, anything. Look for patches of the ice that look like they've been melted and refrozen recently. Check near the breaches in the shelter units, and inside the buildings."

He stared down at the small piece of metal in his hand. "Check this whole area out, Silvers. Get me every scrap you can find."

"Yes, sir."

Elias walked back around the end of the structure, slowly, deep in thought. He looked down at his hand again. He remembered years back, when his father was leaving to fight against the First Imperium...the last time he'd seen him. He'd only seen his father in armor once, but he remembered the look of the fighting suit...and the chunk of metal in his hand looked a lot like the same material.

Who the hell attacked Glaciem wearing osmium-iridium alloy armor?

*   *   *   *   *

"Your initial guess was correct, Captain Cain." Josh Kilner was the Patrol's chief scientist and researcher. "I have inspected the samples you brought back, and a number of them are small chunks of osmium-iridium alloy."

"So, whoever attacked the mining colony on Glaciem was equipped with powered armor?" Cain had been suspicious all along, but even with validation, it still seemed unreal. Certainly no one on Atlantia or anywhere in its system had equipment like that. Armor of that nature was enormously expensive, and only the most well-equipped military organizations could afford to field even a small number of elite troops so outfitted.

"I wouldn't jump to any risky conclusions, Elias. Not based on what we have here. But that is certainly a possibility." He paused, thinking. "Though, I'm afraid a likely alternate scenario eludes me at the moment." He turned and looked at Cain. "Indeed, the spectral analysis of the samples suggests a manufacturing quality that is almost off the charts. It is not something I would expect to see anywhere post-Fall. Except perhaps on Armstrong, in its local Marine units. If even they have material of that quality anymore."

Elias returned the scientist's gaze. The Corps still existed, technically at least, but it didn't field more than two rump battalions, and those served solely on Armstrong, as part of the planet's defensive military. No Marine unit had left Armstrong since the battles against the First Imperium thirteen years before, and Cain couldn't imagine the Corps launching an attack like this against any colony world. The Corps had lost much since the days when his father had been one of its leaders, but it had kept its honor, declining to turn into outlawry and intimidation, even at the cost of shrinking away into insignificance.

"Who besides the Corps could have armor like that? Columbia?" Jarrod Tyler ruled that world with an iron fist, and his military was preeminent among the colonies. But Tyler's regime wasn't expansionist, or at least it never had been. And there were dozens of rich systems closer to Columbia than Atlantia's if he had suddenly developed a taste for empire.

"Tyler's army fields powered units, but if they have any armor like this, it is limited to a small guard or Special Forces unit. Equipping an army with this material would bankrupt Columbia."

"The Companies?" Elias sounded like he'd bitten into something sour. The idea of military operations existing outside the bounds of duly-constituted national authority was anathema to him. He considered the Companies to be little more than pirates, brigands, killers for hire. *And my brother is the worst of them all.*

"Few of the Companies could afford armor of this quality, Captain Cain. Only the very top tier."

Elias' expression hardened. "Like the Black Eagles?"

Kilner hesitated. "Yes," he finally said. "And a few of the other Great Companies."

Elias stood stone still, his face an angry mask.

Yes, but my brother doesn't command the other companies. And the commanders of the other companies aren't Atlantian citizens who'd been outlawed and banished from their homeworld.

Elias knew his brother considered himself above petty emotions, but he also knew in spite of that, Darius resented Atlantia for the edicts that had branded him a criminal—along with all the other mercenary companies. Darius Cain had been banished from the world of his birth, and he wasn't a man to take things like that well. And the Eagles could afford the most expensive osmium-iridium alloys for their armor.

Have you become such a monster, brother? Did you massacre these miners because you are angry at the Atlantian government? The nascent mining operation on Glaciem had promised a considerable boost to the economy. Destroying it was probably the easiest way to strike a serious blow against Atlantia.

He sighed and stared down at his boots. Elias Cain had become very estranged from his twin, but it still hurt him to think of Darius as some kind of terrorist, killing innocent people to vent his anger or strike back against the government he felt had wronged him.

Was it you, brother?

*   *   *   *   *

"Captain Cain, I appreciate your seeing me on such short notice. Minister Vance dispatched me with little warning. I'm afraid there wasn't time to send word ahead." The man was exquisitely dressed and flawlessly polite. He carried himself like a diplomat, but he had a nasty scar along the side of his face that suggested a military background. "Perhaps it is just as well that we speak confidentially for now."

"No apologies necessary, Mr. Coulette, though you should understand that regulations require me to submit a report on anything we discuss...other than purely personal matters, of course. Atlantian citizens are not allowed to have private dealings with foreign nationals, I'm afraid."

The visitor nodded. "Of course. I will do us both a favor and come right to the point. Minister Vance sends his best regards, Captain Cain, and he wishes me to request that you come to Mars to participate in a meeting he believes to be of the utmost importance." Coulette paused for a few seconds. He had indeed gotten to the point very quickly, and he seemed to be giving Cain a chance to absorb it. "He understands this is an extreme imposition, and I can assure you he would not ask if he didn't feel it was of vital import."

Elias was silent. He had no idea why Roderick Vance had sent an emissary to him personally, and not to the Atlantian government. Vance had been one of his father's closest allies, but that had been years before. Elias had met the Martian spymaster, but only as a child. *What could Vance want with me now?*

"I have the greatest respect for Mr. Vance, of course. My father always spoke highly of him, and I know they worked very closely together. But I'm at a loss to understand what Mr. Vance could want from me. Perhaps you could enlighten me."

Coulette shook his head slowly. "I wish I could, Captain Cain. But I believe the matters Minister Vance wishes to discuss are highly sensitive...and best discussed in person, directly with him." He saw the doubt in Cain's expression, and he added, "However, I can tell you that if you come to Mars, you may gain some insight regarding the recent attack on your mining facilities on Glaciem."

Cain felt a flush of anger. "How do you even know about that? The entire episode is still classified." He tried to keep his voice professional, but his suspicion was obvious.

"Please, Captain, I certainly didn't mean to suggest that Mars or Minister Vance had anything to do with that terrible tragedy. I am simply saying that such things do not usually happen in a vacuum, and it is often helpful to pool resources and share information with others."

Cain stared across the table. He had calmed down a bit, but there was still doubt in his expression. "I do not understand why Mr. Vance would not simply send what information he had. He could have transmitted it under Patrol Seal if it was sensitive."

Coulette looked across at Cain. "Captain, I am most uncomfortable speculating too broadly on Minister Vance's motivations, but let me say this. The minister held a position of almost crushing responsibility during the past several wars. I am privileged to know him quite well, and I can tell you he is more prone to trust individuals than institutions. Your Atlantian Patrol is a fine service, though it is also young. But in matters of security, an organization is only as trustworthy as its weakest member."

"I can assure you, Mr. Coulette, the Patrol is incorruptible." Cain's voice was brittle.

Coulette sighed softly. "Please, Captain…it was not my intention to denigrate your patrol in any way. But no entity is utterly trustworthy. Even the Alliance Marine Corps your father served for so many years had its own crisis…a traitor who almost took it down." He paused. "Minister Vance is not suggesting your Patrol isn't a worthy institution. But, for now, he is only prepared to extend this invitation to you personally."

Cain looked across the table. It wasn't normal procedure. The representative of a foreign government should deal directly with the Atlantian State Department. His first instinct was to contact his superiors and ask their guidance. Elias Cain's career had been spotless, and every step of the way he had followed the rules explicitly, gone by the book. He could take leave, he supposed, and go see what Vance wanted. But he was worried it would violate regulations somehow. He would have to disclose his destination at the very least to obtain an exit visa. That would entail the appearance of irregularity if nothing more. It was highly unusual for a member of the patrol to take so long an interstellar trip. And post-Fall Mars wasn't exactly a common tourist destination, so there would be questions on why he had gone there.

"I would put my career at considerable risk if I were to travel to Mars with no stated reason." He took a deep breath. "But my father always spoke very highly of Mr. Vance." From what Erik Cain had said of the Martian spymaster, he was just about the least likely person to waste anyone's time. *If Vance wants this conference so badly, it must be important.*
"Very well, Mr. Coulette," Cain said tentatively, "I will come to Mars." His stomach tightened. He knew that Atlantian citizens—and especially members of the patrol—were bound by ever-tighter regulations, attempts to control the development of the planet and to maintain security in uncertain times. Implications of disloyalty were becoming more common, and those who came under suspicion were increasingly subject to preemptive legal action. But beneath the veneer of the obedient patrol officer there was the son of Erik Cain. He'd buried the side of him that held his father's defiance, the part his brother had allowed to run wild. But now that voice in his psyche was telling him one thing. Go to Mars. He owed it to his father, if nothing else.

Chapter 15

"The Nest" – Black Eagles Base
Second Moon of Eos, Eta Cassiopeiae VII
Earthdate: 2318 AD (33 Years After the Fall)

"I know it has only been a month, but I want answers."
Darius Cain's voice was like an elemental force, shaking the
very structural supports of the Eagles' massive underground
base. The Nest was an engineering accomplishment
unmatched anywhere since the Fall, a cavernous and well-
defended home for the Eagles and their spacefleet. The moon
held training facilities, living quarters, laboratories, storage
areas, armories, and hangers. It had cost an incalculable
fortune, and it had been paid for with the proceeds of a decade
of unceasing combat operations.

"I've checked with everyone in our information network,
Darius, and I've instructed them all to spread around some
wealth and try to loosen some tongues. But nobody seems to
know anything." Teller was standing on the opposite side of
the room, looking across the long table at his friend. They'd
been in the conference room for ten minutes, but neither of
them had taken a seat yet. And that meant the others in the
room were still standing as well.

"I want to go see Jarrod Tyler." Cain's voice was cold,
decisive. It wasn't a question, and he clearly wasn't asking for

anyone's opinion.

Tyler was the military dictator of Columbia, the second planet of the system. The Eagles had an agreement with Tyler, granting them possession of one of the moons of Eos. The system's seventh planet was a massive gas giant, and its moons had both been valueless rocks. But now, the second one housed the greatest mercenary company in Occupied Space, and Cain's band of warriors had signed a pact with Tyler to come to his defense if Columbia was attacked. It was a symbiotic relationship. The Eagles found a home, paying for it only with the promise of future action, a service that was unlikely ever to be needed. Columbia was one of the most powerful worlds in Occupied Space, and it was heavily militarized. With the guaranteed intervention of the Eagles in support of the Columbians, it was almost inconceivable anyone would make a move against the planet. Cain's people benefited as well. Anyone attacking the Black Eagles had to violate Columbian space to do it. And no one in Occupied Space wanted to fight both the Eagles and the Columbians.

Cain had intentionally sought out Tyler when he was searching for a home for his growing band of mercenaries. Columbia had been one of the most invaded worlds in human space, and he'd suspected the two parties could make a deal that made sense for both. Tyler immediately agreed to the treaty, ceding Eos' moon to the Eagles in return for a defensive alliance.

"You think he knows something we don't?"

"I don't know, Erik, but if someone is making a move against us, my guess is they'd have personnel on Columbia. The Nest's security is impenetrable, but even with Tyler's secret police monitoring immigrants and visitors, it would be a lot easier to get someone on Columbia. And if there's even a chance that another power had infiltrated his world, Jarrod Tyler will want to know."

"Do you think that's a good idea? You know what Tyler is like. Do you really want to start this with him?"

Cain glared across the table. "Over ten percent of our people were killed or wounded on Lysandria, Erik." His hands were clenched into fists. "And we have no idea who was behind it...who those soldiers in the brown armor were. They fought to the death, and they didn't leave behind so much as a clue or a shadowy trail back where they came from. They didn't break and rout, no matter how dire the situation was. They just kept fighting until we killed every last one of them. This force is no joke."

He turned away and stared at the wall. "That is what we are facing. And they started this, they targeted us. I will not rest while there is an enemy out there, one that knows everything about us while we know almost nothing about them." He spun back around. "I don't care if Jarrod Tyler kicks down every door on Columbia or interrogates a million of his people. One way or another, we are going to find out who this is...and then they are going to pay for every Black Eagle who died on Lysandria."

He tapped the com unit on his collar. "Control, General Cain here. I want my speeder readied for immediate launch."

Teller took a few steps toward Cain. "Erik, if you insist on doing this, at least take *Eagle One*. If someone is after us, you wandering out of here in a tiny ship with no guard would be playing right into their hands.

Cain looked over at his executive officer and grudgingly nodded. "Control," he said into the com unit, "cancel that order. I want *Eagle One* readied for liftoff in one hour."

There was a short pause. "Yes, sir," the tenuous voice finally responded. An hour was woefully inadequate to scramble the flagship's crew and ready her for launch. But it was common knowledge in the Black Eagles that Darius Cain meant what he said. They were the scourge of human-inhabited space, but there were few among the great mercenary company who had what it took to stand up to their leader.

"I'm going with you." Erik Teller was one of the few who did.

"I don't need a babysitter, Erik." Cain was shaking his head. "You're in command while I'm gone."

"Those Eagles who died were my friends too." Teller's voice was grim, determined. "And Falstaff can hold down the fort while we blast across the system and back."

Cain didn't respond immediately. He just stood staring back at Teller. Finally, he nodded. "Alright, Erik. You've got as much right as me to hunt down whoever this is." He looked around the room. "The rest of you, I want all investigations proceeding full speed ahead." His eyes fixed on Sparks. "Tom, I want you to redo all your analysis. We've confirmed the debris from Karelia and Lysandria are the same, but we need some idea where it came from. No limit on resources. None at all. Just requisition whatever you need."

Sparks nodded. "I'll try, Darius, but I don't see what else we're going to be able to find. The materials have a vague similarity to those we use…and also the Corps. I tried to match the materials to all known major sources and mines. Such procedures are not entirely accurate, but my best guess is the source of these metals is a previously unknown planet. But that's all I have."

Thomas Sparks was over 100 years old, having served as the Corps' lead scientist for almost 40 years, until General Gilson had been compelled to disband the research division. Darius Cain had tracked him down a few years later and enticed him to join the Eagles, and to bring his technical wizardry to the mercenary company.

"Do what you can, Tom." He turned and faced Teller. "Alright, Erik. Grab your kit and meet me at the *Eagle One* berth." He paused an instant. "I'm going to head down there now and see if I can get them to shave a few minutes off the launch sequence."

*   *   *   *   *

"Welcome, General Cain. It is always a pleasure to see you. One we enjoy all too infrequently considering we are such close neighbors." General Jarrod Tyler was the absolute and unchallenged ruler of Columbia.

"Indeed, General Tyler. I am equally gratified to see you." Darius moved toward the table, taking a chair when Tyler gestured for him to sit.

"And Colonel Teller, I am pleased to see you as well."

"And you, General." Teller slid into the chair next to Cain.

Jarrod Tyler wore the gray uniform of Columbia's army, as he did at all times. He wasn't a politician, and he left no doubt that his power came from the army. His rule over the planet was total, but there was no cruelty, no abuse of his enormous power, save of course from denying the population any political authority.   Columbia had no pretenses of democracy, no assembly or senate, no phony elections— none of the window dressing that so often accompanied dictatorships.

Tyler had seized power in the aftermath of the Second Incursion. Columbia had entered that war completely unprepared, the result of the massive disarmament programs of the government that had taken power in a series of elections five years before. Tyler had come out of retirement and rallied his old veterans, and when the robots of the First Imperium landed, they grimly took the field. Without equipment, without supplies, they were massacred. Thousands died, some of Columbia's best, and the rest fled into the wilderness, escaping the genocidal invaders and holding a thin defensive line for the refugee camps where the civilians had fled from First Imperium genocide.

The war, like all those that had preceded it, ended—in this case, with the arrival of Erik Cain and his Marines. But the cost of Columbia's lack of vigilance had been enormous. And this time, the toll had been especially personal to Tyler. Among the hundreds of thousands dead was Lucia Collins, Columbia's former president—and Jarrod Tyler's wife.

The general flew into an inconsolable rage, and he blamed the politicians, branding their pursuit of power as the cause of Columbia unreadiness. He led the remnants of his armies, fanatically loyal after their seemingly hopeless victory and ready to follow him anywhere, against the civilian politicians who had so poorly led the planet. He seized control of every aspect of government, becoming Columbia's absolute ruler. Driven by rage and the pain of his loss, he had all the surviving politicians rounded up and executed without pity, without mercy. Tyler had been driven past the point of restraint, even sanity, and he vowed never again would he trust the people to choose their own leaders. And for fourteen years he had been true to his word.

Tyler had become cold, ruthless, and utterly unwilling to cede even the remotest shred of control over the planet. It wasn't lust for power—he simply didn't trust the people to make responsible decisions for themselves. Apart from his iron grip, he was just and rational, and in the most unlikely of developments, Columbia rapidly returned to prosperity, and within a few years the planet had the highest GPP of any of Earth's former colonies. As long as her citizens didn't challenge their leader's authority, they enjoyed a stunning amount of personal freedom in their day-to-day lives. Columbia was a military dictatorship like few that had ever existed, and the people had come to accept Tyler's rule and even to love the man who had brought them such wealth and security. There were hushed whispers, worries about what would happen when Tyler was gone, when a successor might exhibit less wisdom and greater brutality, but there was virtually no opposition to the current regime. And Tyler's secret police were expert at rooting out what little dissent did exist.

"Can I offer you any refreshment?" Tyler asked.

"No, thank you, General. We came to ask for your help and your counsel."

Tyler nodded. "I assumed as much. So what can I do for

you, gentlemen?"

Cain reached down and scooped a small sack from the ground, setting it on the table. "Someone is targeting my people, General." He pulled a small pile of metal bits from the bag and laid them on the table. "They've intervened in our last two jobs, most recently with over 3,000 troops, all equipped with first rate powered armor." He paused and stared across the table. "And we have no idea who they are. Or what they are trying to achieve."

"But you think they may have people on Columbia." Tyler's voice was soft, thoughtful.

"Yes," Cain replied. "It makes sense. I'm confident they couldn't infiltrate the Nest, at least not in any meaningful way." Darius Cain believed completely in the loyalty of his people. And he tended to doubt anyone who had seen his own merciless brand of justice would be quick to betray him, even if that loyalty had failed. There were many dangerous enemies in Occupied Space, but none that instilled fear like the Black Eagles.

"Our economy has continued to grow rapidly. We add new trading partners almost weekly." Tyler nodded back to Cain. "Inevitably, security has suffered. I regret to admit, it is entirely possible that agents of your enemy may have infiltrated Columbia."

"That is why we have come, General. To request your assistance in investigating this. If we truly have an enemy capable of mounting an attack on the Nest, Columbia may be at risk as well." Cain pushed the small pile of metal debris forward a few centimeters. "This material is from the armor. It is a high quality alloy, similar to that my people and the Corps use."

Tyler stood up and walked across the room, reaching down and picking up one of the small pieces. "I always forget how heavy this alloy is. It's no wonder you need those nuclear reactors to move your suits around." The osmium-iridium combination used in the best powered armor was almost three times as heavy as steel.

"Yes, it is a very expensive material as well," Cain said. "And that means whoever fielded those 3,000 troops is well funded. Very well-funded indeed."

Tyler exhaled slowly. "I couldn't hope to finance a force so equipped, even with all of Columbia's military budget." He paused. "And if they could afford to lose 3,000 troops just to weaken you, I hesitate to estimate at their total strength and resources. This is a very disturbing development when considered from a strategic perspective." His eyes locked on Cain's. "Darius, this might be more than a threat to the Black Eagles. This could be a force with designs on Occupied Space."

Cain nodded slowly. He knew Tyler tended to be paranoid, occasionally seeing exaggerated threats where none existed. But now he thought about what the dictator had said, and he found himself agreeing. "What you say makes sense." Cain stared at Tyler intently. "Which makes it even more imperative to root out any enemy presence on Columbia."

"I am inclined to agree." Tyler was focused, attentive. "I would have aided you at your request, simply as a friend and an ally, but what you describe sounds like a threat to all of us." He pressed a small button on the table, activating a com unit. "Barria, I am declaring a level two security alert. I want all senior command staff assembled in one hour."

"Yes, sir."

Cain forced back a smile. The officer's response had been crisp and immediate. He knew Jarrod Tyler ran a tight ship, and he was getting confirmation of that now.

"I am sure you gentlemen are anxious to return to the Nest, but I would be pleased to have you attend the strategy meeting if you can spare the time."

Cain nodded. "Of course, General. We would be pleased to attend."

Tyler returned the nod. "Very well. Can I offer you both some lunch before? I'm afraid sandwiches are all we have time for." He pressed the com button before either of his guests could respond. "Lunch for three in the conference room."

"Yes, sir," came the instant response.

Cain couldn't hold back the grin this time. Apparently, Jarrod Tyler's stewards were as disciplined as his military staff.

*   *   *   *   *

"I understand why you are so upset, but you need to stop making yourself so crazy. You have a lot of responsibilities. So much stress. And whatever else you may believe, you are still a man. You can only take so much." Ana was lying next to him, her hand moving slowly across his chest. The room was dark, just a hint of light coming from the glowing screen of the workstation on his desk. "I'm worried about you."

He looked at her, and he managed a smile, though he didn't suspect it was very convincing. He'd been tense for weeks now, and he'd been growing increasingly frustrated with the lack of progress in investigating the mysterious enemy stalking his people.

Ana had been sharing his bed since the night he'd returned from Lysandria. At first he told himself she was a pleasant diversion, something to distract him from the worries that consumed him day and night. But he knew that wasn't the truth. He'd been strangely drawn to Ana Bazarov since the day he'd first set eyes on her outside the burning hell of Petersburg. And once she'd gotten past her initial anger and suspicion, he knew she felt the same thing. He still refused to admit she was anything more than another mistress, albeit a new one that piqued his interest with greater intensity, but he hadn't seen any of his other concubines since the first night with her.

"I am fine, Ana." He sighed softly. "I am always fine."

"You can save that for your soldiers, who might believe at least some of it. But you are wasting your efforts on me." She put her hand on his face. "I know you are not fine."

"So you think you know me now?" His voice was soft, gentle, not prickly, as it might have been.

"I'm getting there." She slid onto her side, so she could face him more directly. "I know you never show weakness to anyone. Not even Erik." She paused. "That must be difficult. To be strong all the time."

"There is no place in my life for weakness, Ana." His tone was more guarded now, defensive. "I have too many people counting on me. Including Erik. They may enjoy camaraderie with me, value my friendship or admiration—but the one thing they absolutely need from me is strength. If that falters, they die." He paused. "That is the burden of command. I know it is what my father carried all those years, and I know what it did to him. But as great a man as he was, he allowed himself to be human...and he paid the price for it."

He looked into her eyes, but his thoughts were distant. "He never slept, Ana. I remember waking up in the middle of the night many times, slipping out of my room and seeing my father sitting on the patio, looking off into the night. No matter how many nights I got up, there he was—or he was outside walking in the dark. Or standing at the window, gazing off into the blackness. I would hide and watch him—I don't know if he ever knew I was there. I could feel that he was in pain. At first, I didn't understand. I wanted to run to him, but something always held me back. When I got older, I began to realize he was tormented by memories, and by guilt. Sometimes he would speak softly to himself, and I would hear names. Jax. He was my father's closest friend. Like a brother." His tone soured. Darius and his own brother had anything but a close relationship.

"I found out years later that Jax was killed because of my father's mistake. He carried that guilt the rest of his life, Ana. I am named after him...after Darius Jax." He took a deep breath. "No, I saw what humanity did to my father. There is no room in our profession for weakness. None. Erik Teller is my friend, but he is also my second in command. What happens when he dies because of a mistake, as Jax did so long ago? Or when I must send him into deadly danger for the good of the unit? Do I hold him back because he is my friend, and put the entire force at risk? Or do I send a friend to his death?"

He sat quietly for a few seconds, breathing softly. "I will not allow myself the human weakness that so tormented my father. That is not my life, it was his. I must be strong. Always."

Ana looked back at Darius, and he could see tears welling up in her eyes. "No man can be a pillar of stone," she said, her voice barely a whisper. "Your father was a hero, Darius. His name is remembered with great reverence on hundreds of planets." She put her hand on his head, ran her fingers slowly through his hair. "Did you ever consider that the very traits that tormented him so were also responsible for his greatness? That he is as revered as he is for the very reason that he had human weaknesses?"

"While I am called a butcher, and my name is cursed? And people wonder how the great hero spawned such a cold-blooded monster?"

"That is not what I said, Darius."

"But it is the truth." He took a slow breath. "Which is another reason why I cannot afford myself the luxury of weakness. Let people say what they wish. Their adoration did my father no more good than their revulsion does me harm. Indeed, my reputation is of great value, more ever than my father's was to him. What did he get? Empty platitudes? Fear is far more useful. People will follow the herd, and they will adopt whatever viewpoints they are fed. But I don't care what they think. I make my own decisions, and I answer to no man. Let them hate me. Let them worry that one day my soldiers will come for them...for if they fear me enough, they will stay out of my way and not provoke my anger."

Ana was about to respond when the AI spoke. "General

Cain, there is a vessel approaching the Nest, requesting permission to land. The passenger states he is an envoy from Roderick Vance of the Martian Confederation."

"Confirm the identification," Cain snapped, swinging his legs over the side of the bed as he did. "And then authorize immediate landing in the VIP bay." He stood up and glanced back at Ana. "I've got to go see what this is about. But you go back to sleep. It's the middle of the night." He managed to flash her a quick smile, and then he turned, heading for the shower.

Chapter 16

Inner Sanctum of the Triumvirate
Planet Vali, Draconia Terminii IV
Earthdate: 2318 AD (33 Years After the Fall)

"The flow of captives from Earth has doubled over the last year. The increased bounties have proven to be extremely effective at accelerating production. Not only have we recruited more prospecting crews, but the ones already at work have shown improved productivity." One spoke slowly, softly, his aged voice struggling to maintain its volume. "We have also noticed a considerable uptick in the percentage of captives meeting Prime qualifications. As we increased the bounties for this group the most, it would appear that simple human greed has proven to be an extremely effective tool."

"This is fortunate," said Two, "as our most recent experiments into the artificial production of new specimens have failed across the board. Despite three decades of research and millions of credits in expenditures, we have been unable to replicate the procedures that were used to create us." He drew a long, raspy breath into his lungs. "The experimental clones have been plagued with a high rate of replicative degeneration issues, and the accelerated development process has failed entirely. All experimental subjects died within one month of the start of the procedure."

"Indeed, it is now apparent that we must rely entirely on captured subjects to meet our needs." Three moved his gnarled, aged fingers across a small 'pad. "I am sending you both projected data on industrial output and troop strengths. I propose that even after the recent increase in shipments from Earth, the implementation of the Plan requires still greater numbers, especially in the total absence of supplementation with cloned personnel. We require more Prime level candidates to attain target troop levels, and we must reach our quotas on an accelerated basis to allow sufficient time for conditioning and training before deployment."

He swiped his hand across the 'pad again. "Further, if you will review the figures I just highlighted, you will see that we have significant industrial capacity set to come online over the next year. We require additional labor to increase mining production to meet the raw material requirements of the new factories." He hesitated, taking another breath. "In summary, we require more manpower at every level of our operation, even beyond the projected numbers now in route."

The room's other two occupants looked down at their 'pads, scanning the tables Three had sent them. One looked up and said, "I concur with your analysis, Three." He turned and looked to his right. "Two?"

"I am also in agreement. I propose we further increase the bounties, with additional bonuses based on production levels. Let us reward the teams that strive to raid larger settlements." His eyes dropped back to the 'pad for a few seconds. "Extrapolating from the data on the previous increase, I submit that a further doubling of the bounties will allow us to hit our target levels within the next Earth year."

One said, "Are we agreed then? The bounties will be doubled from present levels, effective immediately."

"Agreed," said Two.

Three nodded. "Agreed."

"Very well." One slid his fingers across his 'pad. "It is done. What is the next order of business?"

Three looked down the table with a frown. "I would discuss another effect of our lack of progress with the cloning technology. Clearly, this has eliminated the last chance that we may reverse our own accelerated degeneration. We must now consider it a virtual certainty that the three of us will be dead within eighteen months, two years at most." His voice was strangely unemotional, even as he was speaking of his own imminent death. "We must take steps now to ensure that nothing interferes with the Plan, even after we are gone." He paused. "I submit that we must move forward with the final activation of the Intelligence."

The room was quiet for a few seconds, the three men all deep in thought. Finally, One broke the silence. "We have been working on that project for fifteen Earth years, yet I fear the risk involved in total activation remains very high. We have input the required data and the sum total of all our knowledge, yet we cannot be sure what will happen when it is fully activated. I remind you that we did not build the Intelligence, that it is not of our science and, indeed, is thousands of years beyond our technology. We have discovered how to reprogram it, at least after a fashion, but we cannot know what abilities and safeguards it has that we have not even discovered. Our testing has been necessarily limited, and despite all of our efforts, we must acknowledge the possibility that full commitment of the Intelligence could destroy the Plan in one fell swoop...or alter it beyond our own recognition. It may revert to its old directives, and seek to destroy mankind outright. Or it may behave in ways we cannot conceive."

"I cannot counter your concerns with facts, One, nor can I disagree with any of your assertions." Three stared across the table, holding his shaking hands in front of him. "I simply ask one question. What alternative do we have? When we conceived the Plan, in the aftermath of the Fall, we relied upon a number of assumptions. We anticipated rediscovering the secrets of the Shadow process. We expected to arrest our own accelerated physical deterioration and, indeed, extend our own lives almost indefinitely. Our failure to succeed on either of these fronts compelled us to radically alter the Plan.

"We can either depend on inherently unreliable, hand-chosen successors—who themselves will have to select the generation of leaders to follow them—or we can take a risk and, if we succeed, leave behind a device that will preserve our mentalities…and extend our rule in the distant future. Mankind has a poor record of creating states that are sustainable, largely because of the mortality of men. The firmest rulers, the most absolute and iron-willed dictators inevitably give way to those who follow…heirs, rivals, colleagues. The dynamism of those with the strength to seize power is slowly bled away with each passing generation. If we are successful with the Intelligence, we will end all that. We will create a state that will place all humanity under the rule of an entity that is, for all intents and purposes, immortal. Mankind will cease squandering resources on foolishness and wasteful conflicts. Humanity's efforts will be channeled toward growth, toward increasing the technological abilities of the race. We will prevent men from making foolish choices, directing their every activity toward the most productive uses."

He paused. "When next we encounter a threat like the First Imperium, we will be ready. And on a thousand worlds, mankind will be ready to accept our orders." Another pause, longer this time. "We simply cannot leave something as crucial as the Plan to the vagaries of generational successors.

Two spoke next. "I am inclined to agree with Three. Our unleashing of the Second Incursion was a mixed success. Fifteen years of our clandestine work, sowing distrust and discontent among the colonies, working to bring them to the brink of territorial conflicts and expanding warfare between them, was washed away, temporarily, at least, by the unifying effect of the First Imperium threat.

"In the end, however, the discovery of Zeta Omicron and our activation of the Intelligence we found there, was, in sum total, a positive to our efforts. The destruction unleashed upon

Occupied Space was extraordinary, and the colony worlds are far weaker now than they were…far more so than they would have been if they'd enjoyed thirty years of uninterrupted growth. Our ability to create overwhelming superiority at any point of conflict is almost assured, and if we are able to bring about the destruction of the Great Companies, the last forces capable of truly facing our Omega Force soldiers will be gone. We find ourselves now at a similar crossroads to the day we touched off the Second Incursion. We must decide. Do we trust in a decade and a half's tireless reprogramming efforts and reactivate the Intelligence? Or do we allow ourselves to be ruled by fear and choked by caution…and trust in normal men to succeed us, imperfect beings just as likely to fight each other for power as to steward the Plan?"

"Indeed," Three interjected, "the Second Incursion was certainly a net positive, increasing the likelihood of the Plan's ultimate success. Our audacity was rewarded, and I see no reason for us to shy away from the aggressive course now. The destruction of the First Imperium forces allowed us to deactivate the Intelligence and bring it back to Vali. For fifteen years we have labored to mold it to our needs, to program it with our plans…and our thoughts and memories. We have hoped it wouldn't be necessary, that our medical research would discover a means to reverse our physical deterioration and extend our human lives, but now we must accept that such hope had gone unfulfilled. Even if we were to attain some last minute advance, the likelihood of meaningfully reversing deterioration as advanced as that we have already suffered is vanishingly small. It is too late. We must now look to a future as part of the Intelligence."

He lifted his head, staring at each of his colleagues in turn. "I submit we have been over this before, that we have considered all of the risks. One's concerns have been duly noted and adequately debated. Indeed, I am inclined to agree with him almost in total, save for one overwhelming fact. We have no other realistic option." He paused, looking at One and Three again. "I therefore propose that we activate the Intelligence in six months, and we position it to continue with the Plan after the three of us are gone."

Three nodded. "Agreed."

One hesitated, an uncomfortable look on his face. But after a few seconds he, too, nodded. "Agreed."

"Very well, it is decided. The Plan will proceed…and when it is completed, mankind will be ruled for all time by the Intelligence. And we shall be immortal, the essence of our minds, at least, within the great sentient computer.

*   *   *   *   *

Ivan Maranov walked slowly down the corridor, admiring the sheer enormity of the complex. Vali was an amazing world, and thirty years of the Triumvirate's ceaseless efforts had turned it into an industrial powerhouse without compare. Its vast factories and assembly plants dwarfed those of any colony in Occupied Space. It was a testament to what legions of forced labor could accomplish. The vast majority of those who lived on Vali were there to work, and they toiled ceaselessly, with only enough rest to keep them alive. It was an existence that defied imagination, a living nightmare for the millions so enslaved.

The Draconis Terminii system was itself a natural marvel, with no less than three extremely habitable worlds—and another two ice planets that possessed remarkable mineral wealth. The small cluster of worlds, and the legion of massive farms and sprawling industrial plants upon them, were in constant operation. They produced everything the Triumvirate required to prepare for the day when they would launch the final stage of the Plan, a day Maranov knew had to be close when he'd received the summons.

For all the amazing characteristics of the Triumvirate's

home system, perhaps Draconis Terminii's greatest strength
was secrecy. The star lay beyond the Rim, through a secret
warp gate, the location of which was one of the most closely
guarded secrets in the galaxy. That single fact had made the
Triumvirate's efforts—indeed, its very existence—possible.

Maranov had served the Triumvirate for two decades,
but he had never laid eyes on the three beings who wielded
so much power in utter secrecy. He'd heard the rumors, of
course, that they were Gavin Stark clones that had survived
the Fall. Maybe, he had thought many times. From what he
had heard, the Shadow program had produced thousands
of clones, so it was certainly a possibility. Or perhaps they
were just deputies of Stark's who had escaped their master's
destruction. *I may never know. But I cannot argue with the success
they have achieved.*

Whoever they were, they had selected him to serve them,
and they had given him the means to accumulate power—and
so he had. He had been born with the name Maranov, but
no one called him that anymore. To all but a very few he was
known by his title only, the Tyrant of Eldaron.

He reached the end of the hallway and stopped. There
were two guards flanking the doorway, and they snapped
to attention as he approached. Maranov was impressed,
as he always was by the Omega Force soldiers. There was
something about them, a relentless quality, almost robotic. At
first he'd suspected they were clones, that the Triumvirate had
rediscovered the lost secret to the Shadow program. But then
he realized none of them resembled each other. Whatever
was done to them to turn them into such cold, unquestioning
warriors was a mystery, a secret the Triumvirs had not deigned
to share with him. His Eldari troops were normal conscripts,
motivated by a typical combination of pay and discipline. He
could only guess, but he suspected they wouldn't last an hour
in the field against the Omega forces.

He walked through the door, and it shut behind him. The
room was exactly the same. He'd been here twice before—

three times in twenty years that he'd come at the bidding of his masters. It felt different this time. There was an anger inside him, a resentment at being called halfway across Occupied Space at the whim of his puppetmasters. When they'd first selected him, he'd been an officer in the Eldari militia, and their offer of sponsorship and support had been enough to win his pledges of undying loyalty. He'd returned from his first trip to Vali with everything he needed to begin his ascent to power. His second pilgrimage had come shortly after he'd declared himself Tyrant, and he'd been enormously grateful to his benefactors for the power they had helped him attain.

But now he had been the ruler of Eldaron for almost twenty years, and his arrogance had grown with his power. On his world he was feared by all, and his slightest whim was law. Yet here he was, once again on Vali, called to attend his masters like a schoolboy summoned to the headmaster's office. He knew he couldn't match the power of the Triumvirate, and he was too smart to defy them. However powerful he was on Eldaron, he understood he was only a part of the Plan. His continued power depended on his good standing with the three beings who had given it in the beginning—and who could undoubtedly take it from him if they wished.

He walked to the chair in the middle of the room. It was plush leather, a large and comfortable seat—and the only bit of furniture in the room. He walked over and sat down, his mind filling with old memories. The room looked exactly the same as it had. Even the chair was identical. He knew it was twenty years older now, yet it still looked new, as it had that day long before.

The lights went down. *I can see the theatrics haven't changed.* There was an odd psychology to the way the Triumvirate operated. He suspected they analyzed every move they made, even the way they issued orders and communicated with minions. He couldn't argue with their effectiveness. The three unseen despots ruled a secret organization that controlled over 100 worlds, mostly discretely, through local leaders like

Maranov. And on hundreds of other planets, they wielded partial power. They operated through secret ownership of industrial concerns, shadowy underworld operations, well-placed bribes and blackmail to control politicians. For thirty years they had extended their tentacles throughout human-occupied space—and now they were almost ready to make their bid for total control.

"Greetings to you, Tyrant of Eldaron. And welcome to Vali. We have summoned you for a reason." The voice was strange, different than last time. When he'd been here twenty years before, he had sat in the same spot, but the voices he'd heard had been natural, as if those speaking were sitting in the room with him. Now, there was an artificiality to them, some kind of electronic enhancement. *I wonder what has changed. Why are they hiding behind artificial voices?*

"Greetings, noble Triumvirs."

"Congratulations are in order for the manner in which you have ruled Eldaron. Your world has become one of the leading powers in Occupied Space. You have very effectively deployed the resources we have provided, and to any observer, Eldaron's growth would appear organic. Your control is absolute, and you have avoided petty disputes with neighbors that would have brought unwanted attention to your activities."

"My thanks, noble Triumvirs. I strive only to serve."

"And that service will be rewarded. When the Plan is activated, we have decided that your rule will be expanded beyond your world. Eldaron is to be a sector capital, and you are to be the governor, with 100 planets to be conquered and placed under your control."

Maranov was stunned. "Thank you, noble Triumvirs," he stammered. He'd been worried the summons to Vali had come because of his growing discontent, that he had somehow given off signals that he resented the Triumvirs' control over him. He'd even had a flash of panic that he would never return. But now they were heaping praise on him—and offering him power beyond his wildest dreams.

"We would add to your responsibilities, even now, before the Plan's final stage."

"I am at your command, noble Triumvirs."

"Your loyalty is known and appreciated, Tyrant." The voice paused for an instant. "We have a number of programs underway designed to maximize disruption throughout Occupied Space prior to the activation of the final stage of the Plan. Among these initiatives are a number of attacks we have launched on various outposts and locations, designed to implicate the Black Eagles and the other Great Companies. We seek to spread discord, and to increase tensions, matching the companies against each other with the ultimate goal of destroying them, or at least weakening them before we release the Omega Forces."

The screen on the far wall shimmered to life. "This map summarizes the operations in your pending area of control... both those that have already begun and those that are in the planning stages. You will note that the largest of these was recently conducted at Lysandria, where we successfully manipulated the Gold Spears into facing off against the Black Eagles. We supplemented the Spears with 3,000 of our Omega forces in an attempt to attrit the Eagles as much as possible.

"The effort was marginally successful. Although the Black Eagles were hurt in the battle, the damage done to them was less than we had hoped—and extremely disproportional to the resources deployed. As the Gold Spears were effectively destroyed, and thus eliminated from the overall pool of mercenary units that could become potential adversaries, the operation must be accounted an overall success. But we must now consider the Black Eagles to be the greatest threat to the success of the Plan, even more so than before. The alliance of 3,000 of our Omega warriors with the Gold Spears was less far effective than we'd expected. Darius Cain is a military genius, perhaps the greatest mankind has ever produced. If he should attempt to rally support, and use his Eagles as the spearhead of a united resistance, the Plan could be in jeopardy."

"I understand, noble Triumvirs. What can I do?"

"You can help us set a trap for Darius Cain. You can destroy the Black Eagles."

Maranov felt as if he'd been hit by a sledgehammer. All his arrogance faded, and he felt a rush of fear. The Black Eagles had never lost a battle. And they had just proven their abilities again on Lysandria. Now he was supposed to entice them to attack his world? How could he possibly face them?

"You needn't be concerned," the voice continued. "You will be provided with ample forces to supplement your Eldari army, more than enough to destroy the Black Eagles. You will go now and return to Eldaron. Fortify the planet. Turn it into a death trap for an invader. Built fortresses, tunnels, bunkers. Put all of your weapons into a state of complete readiness. Turn your cities into traps for an enemy. We will begin sending you Omega forces shortly. They will be disguised, appearing as immigrants and foreign workers, and you will arrange to house them in total secrecy. No word of their presence must leak."

"Yes, noble Triumvirs." He swallowed hard. He hadn't known what to expect when he'd been summoned, but this certainly wasn't it. "But, if I may ask a question..."

"You may, Tyrant."

"I can prepare Eldaron, as you command, but how can I make the Black Eagles attack? I am sure I can provoke them, but there is no guarantee they will actually assault Eldaron."

"Do not concern yourself with that at present, Tyrant. You already have in your possession the means to lure General Cain into an ill-fated attack, and when it is time, you will receive further instructions on how to proceed. When you activate the final stage of the plan, the Black Eagles will come, all of them."

"But Darius Cain is a brilliant commander. What if he suspects a trap?"

"He will almost certainly suspect a trap, Tyrant. But when the bait is fully deployed, he will attack anyway."

Chapter 17

Cargo Hold – Unidentified Spaceship
Somewhere in the Sol System
Earthdate: 2318 AD (33 Years After the Fall)

He felt like he was floating. Thoughts were drifting through his head, vague, disconnected. He didn't understand, didn't know where he was, how he had gotten there. Even who he was. There was something…a thought? A sound? Reaching to him from the distance.

He ignored it at first, but it was still there. Stronger, more insistent. Then his thoughts began to fuse together, to take on clarity. The sound became louder, and now there was feeling too, something hitting him, poking at his side.

His eyes opened, the lids crusted together, peeling slowly apart. The light was bright, harsh. Memories were coming back. *Jack Lompoc, I am Jack Lompoc. I remember.* He winced as he felt another poke in his side. His eyes began to focus. There was someone standing over him, leaning down, hitting him.

He felt a rush of anger, an urge to leap up at the image, but now he remembered. Wandering into the enemy camp, surrendering, something in his arm…pain…an injection. Then nothing…now he was here. He had succeeded, gotten himself captured. *What the hell was I thinking?*

"Hey!" Another poke. "Wake the fuck up. This isn't a fucking vacation."

The voice was coarse, with an angry tone. He turned his head, looking up at the man standing over him. "I'm awake," he croaked, his parched voice barely managing a whisper.

"Yeah? Then get the fuck up. It's time to wash your filthy hide and get your classification confirmed." Another poke, harder than the others. "C'mon. Move!"

Lompoc forced himself to sit upright. The pain threatening to blow his head off gave him an idea just how powerful a sedative his captors had given him. He was stiff, barely able to force his limbs to move. He figured he'd been out for a while, days probably. He wondered where he was... and if Girard had managed to maintain contact. He knew that was his only hope. But had the ship transited one of Sol's two warp gates? Could the Martian spy still track him if they had left the system?

"Get on your feet!" The yell was angry, impatient. "That's the last time I'm going tell you."

Lompoc felt another impact, harder. Pain. He swung his feet around the edge of the small shelf he'd been lying upon. His head was spinning, and he closed his eyes for a few seconds, trying to regain his equilibrium. He slid himself slowly off the shelf, feeling his feet hit the ground. His legs almost buckled, but he managed to keep himself up.

"Where are we?" His throat was still dry, but his words were clearer, less slurred.

He heard harsh laughter. "We're someplace better than you're going to, I can tell you that much. Now move your ass." Another shove, this time in the back—and more caustic laughter.

Lompoc moved slowly, shuffling in the direction his captor pushed him. He was sore everywhere, but there was a sharp pain in his abdomen, worse than the rest. The tracker, he realized. *Of course, it would have to dig in somewhere or I'd just crap it out.* He wondered if Girard had left out that little detail deliberately. He wondered offhand how the thing came out when the mission was done. *That's the least of your worries now.*

He stumbled, reaching out, grabbing onto the wall.

"C'mon boy, we ain't got all day. You know how many of you stinking carcasses we gotta move?"

*   *   *   *   *

"Do you still have contact?" Axe's voice was weak, and there was a rattling sound in his chest. The last few days had been extremely difficult ones, and his first blast-off into space hadn't helped things. He'd gotten motion sickness that almost turned him inside out, until he was at a loss to even guess where all the bloody vomit was coming from.

"Yes, Axe. The signal is good. It's highly encrypted, so unless they're really looking for it, it should remain undetected. "And that means Jack is alive and onboard. The device works off body heat, so if the host dies, the signal will fade as the emergency battery is drained." Girard looked at the battered Earthlings and changed the subject. "You two really need some decent medical treatment. I'm going to set a course for Mars." There was an edge to his voice. His trip to Earth had been extremely unofficial. He wasn't exactly sure how he was going to explain two sick and injured passengers. But Axe was done for if he didn't get to a hospital soon, and Tommie's wound didn't look good either. It had been a long time since Girard had run into it last, but you never forgot the smell of gangrene.

"No." Axe's voice was weak, but there was certainty to his tone. "We have to follow them. We can't let them escape."

Girard shook his head. "The tracking device's signal will be picked up by the Commnet stations throughout the system. We don't need to follow them closely to track where they go." Axe was shaking his head. "No, Axe, you don't understand.

We can't follow them. They clearly have some sort of stealth system on their ships. We don't. If we pursue them now—and if their pilot isn't an imbecile—they'll know they're being followed. And since they were gathering slaves, and now they're slipping away in what have to be extremely expensive stealth ships, my guess is they wouldn't take well to having a tail."

He walked over and sat down next to Axe. "This ship is almost unarmed, so there's a good chance they'd just blow us away. Or, if they panicked, they might space their captives or throw them in the reactor core." He sighed. "No, we need to go to Mars. I need to tell Roderick Vance about all of this. He has the resources to do something about it. All we can do ourselves is blunder into getting caught...and that would just get us—and probably the prisoners—scragged."

Axe slumped a bit in his seat, but he didn't argue. Finally, he looked over at Girard and said, "I guess you're right, but what if they leave the system? What if they go through one of the warp gates and vanish?"

Girard sighed. "That tracker will link up with any Commnet relay, and there are well-developed networks on the other side of both of Sol's warp gates. If they leave the system, things will get more complicated, certainly. We'll have to deal with the governments of whatever systems they travel through, but we'll still have a good chance to track them."

The Martian spy knew "good chance" wasn't what Axe was looking for, though he'd rather exaggerated the prospects even to get to that. If the target ships left the system, there was some chance to track where they went, but if he was being honest, he wouldn't characterize it as good. Still, he figured massaging the truth was the right move at the moment. Axe didn't look happy by any means, but he wasn't arguing either.

Girard got up and walked across the small room, sliding into the pilot's chair. He activated the com unit, choosing a direct laser relay to Martian Control. "This is the Martian vessel Fortuna, requesting landing   clearance at Ares spaceport."

"*Fortuna*, why are you transmitting via direct laser contact? Are you under attack or being pursued by hostiles?"

Girard took a deep breath. *And so the questions begin.* "Negative, Martian Control." *Think fast, Girard.* "We are having problems with our communications. The emergency communications circuit is all that is functioning right now."

There was a short delay in the response. *I hope they buy that.*

"Very well, *Fortuna*, you are cleared to land. Approach coordinates are being transmitted now."

Girard sighed with relief. "Affirmative, Martian Control. *Fortuna* out."

So far so good, but they're going to be all over me with questions when we touch down. What the hell am I going to tell them? This should be fun.

He flipped a switch, activating another com line, a very secret one. "This is Girard, calling for Roderick Vance. Immediate reply requested." *Sorry, Roderick, but this is messier than either of us expected when you sent me out.*

*   *   *   *   *

Lompoc lay still, feeling the heaviness of 4g deceleration pressing against him. At least he thought it was deceleration. In truth, it was hard to tell if a ship was accelerating or decelerating. He was surrounded by other captives, and all of them were awake now. They were lying on shelves, three to a level. He was in the middle, with another prisoner on either side. They were all shackled at the wrists and ankles. The sanitation arrangements were rudimentary—just a hosing down of the shelves every few hours—and the place stank like nothing he'd experienced.

He'd been trying his best to pay attention, listening to the conversations of the guards and the activity all around. The g forces had been the same when he'd first awakened, but then there had been a brief period of free fall. When the heaviness returned, it felt slightly different. He was no expert on space travel, but he'd guessed the ship had begun decelerating—and that meant they were approaching their destination.

Lompoc had only been in space twice, and both of those trips had been to Earth's moon. But he'd known agents who'd gone on interstellar trips, and from the descriptions they'd given him of the experience, he was pretty sure they hadn't passed through a warp gate, at least not since he'd been conscious. His best guess was they were still in the Sol system. But he knew the Confederation maintained installations on most of the planets and major moons. And it was very unlikely they would welcome a band of slavers on any of them.

He turned his head to the left, trying to get a look past the man lying next to him. He could see some vague movement, but nothing he could place. He sighed hard and looked up at the shelf twenty centimeters above his head. *I hope you guys are following this ship*, he thought. *'Cause I'm fucked if you're not.*

He tried to move his arms, testing the strength of the shackles. He only had a few centimeters of slack, and when he tried to move his arms they didn't budge. Not a millimeter. He felt a surge of fear. The prospect of spending whatever was left of his life as a slave—or a guinea pig in some lab, or whatever else—was a hard one to take. He was no coward. He'd lived with danger in the years since the Fall, and even before as an agent stationed in New York. But nothing like this. The whole stupid plan had made sense when Girard suggested it, but now Lompoc realized how many things could go wrong. Or, perhaps more to the point, how many had to all go right for this escapade to end well for him.

They'll come, he thought to himself. But he wasn't sure he believed it.

*   *   *   *   *

Axe woke up in a hospital bed. He was tired—no, exhausted. He was sore in a dozen places, but he felt strangely better too. He turned to look across the room...and there was no pain! He moved his hand to his side, feeling for the crude bandages that had covered his wound. They were gone, replaced by a simple gauze pad. He threw the sheet down off of him and looked down. Both his wounds had healed considerably. Most of the pain was gone, and they were just a bit tender.

He took a breath—and he realized the pain was gone there too. He breathed again, deeply this time, deeper than he had dared in months. He felt a little flutter in his chest, but there was no coughing spasm, so spray of blood from his throat.

He leaned forward and turned his head, scanning his surroundings. He was alone in a small room. Most of the furniture and fixtures were bright white, and the place was lit by a pair of strip lights on the ceiling. He turned to try to get up, and he felt a sharp pain. He stopped and looked around. There were a pair of IVs connected to his left arm. One was still firmly in place, but he had pulled the other one partially loose. A fluid was leaking out and running down his arm. It was almost clear, with just a slight yellow tinge to it.

A few seconds later, a medical technician came in. She was dressed in spotless white scrubs, and when she saw he was awake, she smiled. "Good morning, Mr. Axe."

Axe almost laughed. His name sounded ridiculous with "Mr." before it. He hadn't been born Axe, of course, but for more years than he could count, way back to his days as a young boy hanging out around the gang, desperately trying to be accepted, he had been called simply Axe.

"Good morning," he stammered. "Where am I?"

"You are in Ares Hospital. Mr. Vance himself checked you in for treatment."

"Treatment?" He stared down at the dressing on his wound. "Oh, yes, the gunshots."

The tech looked down earnestly. "Yes, of course. And the cancer. If you had only had the gunshot injuries, you would have been released already. They have been thoroughly cleaned out and the wounds fused. They will be a bit sore for another day or two, but otherwise they are fine. But the cancer treatment was a bit more involved."

"Treatment? What did you do?" Axe had lived with a death sentence over his head for at least a year, along with the stress of trying to hide it—from Ellie, from the people of Jericho.

"Customized antibody treatment, of course."

"Customized antibody treatment?" Axe had been living for thirty years with the functional eighteenth century technology that had become the norm on Earth. And before that, he'd been a gang leader living outside the civilization of the Manhattan Protected Zone. He'd never in his life had access to modern medical care.

"Of course, Mr. Axe. We harvested some of your white blood cells along with a sample of the tumor, and customized a series of antibodies to seek out and destroy the cancer cells. It is usually a very simple procedure, often not even requiring an overnight stay. However, your cancer was quite advanced, and it had spread to multiple organs. We had to synthesize three rounds of antibodies to successfully cure your condition."

Axe's eyes widened. "Did you say cure?"

"Of course, Mr. Axe. I'm afraid you will have to stay in the hospital for at least another day, and you will be quite weak for considerably longer. However, the treatment will result in the complete eradication of your cancer." She sounded as if she was explaining how to tie his shoes. "We have also created some self-replicating killer cells, which will considerably reduce your risk of future cancers related to your radiation exposure."

"You cured me?" he repeated, still not completely accepting the answer.

"Indeed we did, Axe." The voice came from the doorway. He turned and saw a tall man walk into the room. "If I may call you Axe. Allow me to introduce myself. I am Roderick Vance. If you feel up to it, I would like to discuss the men who attacked your village."

*   *   *   *   *

"You exceeded your authority, Mr. Vance, in sending Agent Girard to Earth." Boris Vallen spoke harshly, angrily. He had been the council member most vocal against any form of intervention on Earth, and that had fed a growing rivalry with Vance.

Vance controlled his anger perfectly, as always. But he couldn't help but wish Boris' father was still alive. Sebastien Vallen had been a close friend of Vance's father, and he'd become a mentor to the young Roderick when he'd been orphaned suddenly and left to fill his father's very large shoes. Vance's parents had been killed in an 'accident' many still blamed on Alliance Intelligence's legendary agent, Jack Dutton. Vance had never been able to discover the truth, to confirm if Dutton had indeed murdered his mother and father, but it didn't matter anymore. His parents were long-dead, as was Dutton. And Alliance Intelligence had been destroyed along with its namesake Superpower. But he missed old Sebastien who, he suspected, would have been his ally on moving more aggressively with operations on Earth.

"Mr. Vallen, I did not exceed my authority because, by definition, I did not conduct anything that falls within that authority. I did not act as the head of Martian Intelligence in any of this. The expedition was conducted as a private venture by Vance Interplanetary. All costs were paid by my family's company, and no laws of the Confederation were violated."

"That is the basest technicality, and you know it!" Vallen

slammed his hand down on the table.

Keep it up, Vance thought. *Show everyone what a spoiled brat succeeded your great father. You only help my cause.* "There is nothing base about it. Vance Interplanetary has long had a philanthropic tradition. This council has refused to deploy Martian state assets to ease the suffering on Earth, but it has never expressly outlawed it."

"That would be politically impossible!" Vallen roared. "But you knew well the wishes of this council. And you have paid them no mind."

"I have behaved lawfully, as a member of this body, as the head of Martian Intelligence, and as a citizen of the Confederation at the head of a private concern." He knew that wasn't entirely true. The actual legal aspects of conducting private relief missions to Earth were quite complex. But he was hoping the gray area was big enough to save him. The Vance name still carried a lot of weight on the council—and even more with the people. He doubted his colleagues had the guts to remove him, even though he suspected some of them would be glad to be rid of him.

"This is a pointless waste of time. I understand why this council has been reluctant to commit resources to aid missions on Earth. Our people on Mars have suffered themselves, and this body has decided its first obligation is to them." He paused. He was about to turn the matter toward something he thought would spur more of his colleagues to action. "However, we are not speaking of humanitarian causes now. I have come to discuss a threat, my colleagues. A grave menace to our own security—and worse, one on which we have precious little concrete information."

"A threat?" Katarina Berchtold replied quickly, before Vallen could launch another pointless attack on Vance. Katarina had by no means been a reliable ally to Vance over the years, but she was perhaps the most hawkish member of the council, the one most anxious to hear intelligence on potential threats. In this, Vance dared to hope she would side with him.

"Yes, a threat. My agent's expedition to Earth uncovered something of great concern. Some force has been raiding settlements and abducting their residents. The village my agent visited had a population of over 1,000. He found three survivors. The rest of the occupants had been killed or taken away. I believe that some power is operating a massive slaving ring on Earth. If this is the case, it is a clear violation of the Martian Doctrine. All of the other worlds are aware that the Confederation claims control over the entire Sol system. Whoever is behind this has committed an aggression against Mars, possibly even an act of war."

"An act of war?" Vallen blurted out. "I believed you were reckless with the use of scarce Confederation resources, but I hadn't imagined you were seeking to provoke a war. Your service in the past has been of great value, but I fear that you have lost the perspective that made you so formidable years ago when you worked with my father."

"The Confederation can only mourn the loss of your great father...and lament that his successor is such a pale shadow of what he was." Vance knew he should have held his tongue, but he was sick of putting up with Vallen and treading so cautiously around the council. If, after all they'd lived through over the past thirty years, the fools couldn't see that there were still dangers in the galaxy, then to hell with them. He would do what had to be done himself, with his own resources. And if he had to do more...well, then they would find that he was not an adversary to be trifled with.

Vance was confident in his control over Martian Intelligence, and he had strong ties with several of the other magnates—as well as a number of senior military officers. If the council pushed him too far, they would provoke a power struggle he doubted they were ready to face. He didn't relish destroying Martian republican government, though he had to admit the Confederation had become more of a constitutional oligarchy than a true democracy. There had been a time when acting against his colleagues in the government would

have been unthinkable, but years had passed since then—
and billions of people had died. Roderick Vance had finally
admitted to himself he would do anything to prevent another
catastrophe like the Fall. Even if he had to seize total control
of the Confederation—and rule as a dictator.

Berchtold intervened before Vance and Vallen could take
their argument any further. "Please, gentlemen. Let us stop
this at once. We have differing opinions, but we all share the
same concern, the well-being of the Confederation. Let us
focus on that. Perhaps we should adjourn this meeting for
now." She turned to Vance. "Roderick, I suggest you send
each of us the full report you have compiled so we can review
it ourselves. Then we will reconvene tomorrow, with a better
perspective on the situation, one that may allow us to avoid any
unfortunate disagreements."

Vance nodded. "As you suggest, Katarina. You will all
have the information within the hour." He'd send them all
enough to give them fodder to debate endlessly, but he decided
then and there he would have to act alone.

"I propose we adjourn for 24 hours." Berchtold's voice
was sincere. He had no doubt she meant what she said.
What the others were thinking was a bit more of a puzzle,
but he knew too many of them were driven by fear, hesitant
to acknowledge a threat as if putting their heads in the sand
would make dangers disappear.

"Second," he said, his voice deadpan, disinterested. He'd
already moved past the council. He had work to do, and no
time to waste with endless, unproductive debates. He would
do what had to be done.

Chapter 18

Martian Intelligence HQ
Beneath the Ruins of the Ares Metroplex
Planet Mars, Sol IV
Earthdate: September, 2318 AD (33 Years
After the Fall)

Darius Cain unhooked his harness and got up. The flight in from the warp gate had been a bruising one, eight gees almost the entire way, accelerating half the time and decelerating the rest. But Roderick Vance had said it was important, and based on everything he knew of the brilliant Martian spy, he was inclined to take him at face value. His father had spoken of Vance many times, and he'd said more than once that he'd come to trust the spymaster almost completely.

Darius was his own man now, with his own accomplishments. He was one of the wealthiest and most powerful men in Occupied Space, not to mention one of the most feared. He had risen to the top of his profession and won the respect and admiration of his soldiers. But he still valued what he had left of his father's counsel and guidance. If Erik Cain had trusted Roderick Vance, Darius Cain did as well. It was that simple.

He moved toward the door, watching out of the corner of his eye as his guards pulled themselves painfully from their chairs and prepared to disembark. It occurred to Cain that protocol probably mandated a change into dress uniforms, but then he decided he had no more use for such nonsense than he'd ever had. He'd come halfway across the universe at Vance's bidding, and if that wasn't enough show of respect, then tough.

"You all ready?" He glanced at the ten guards forming in behind him. He'd sworn to Teller he'd take the escort with him everywhere he went and, and unnecessary as he thought it was, he intended to keep his promise.

"Yes, sir!" Captain Alcabedo was standing in front of the escort. Ernesto Alcabedo was a long-service veteran and an officer in the Special Action Teams. That made him one of the deadliest fighters in Occupied Space. Cain felt a rush of embarrassment that such an accomplished veteran had drawn babysitting duty, but he'd allowed Teller to designate his guard. They were all from the Teams. Teller hadn't been able to convince Cain he needed more than ten in his guard, but he'd made that force just about as powerful as any ten soldiers could be.

"Then let's go and see what Mr. Vance wants." He walked toward the hatch, but two of the guards rushed around and opened it first, looking outside and then leaping onto the deck before Cain. Darius held back a laugh. He was trying to imagine what Teller had said to Alcabedo and his detachment. He appreciated the concern, but he was visiting an ally, not hitting the dirt of an enemy planet. Cain knew Teller was a year younger than him, but sometimes his number two reminded him of an old lady.

He stepped down the ramp into the open hanger. The two guards that had preceded him were standing at attention. They were unarmored—something he'd had to insist on when Alcabedo suggested they all suit up—so they were carrying standard assault rifles instead of the nuclear-powered electro-

.

magnetic monsters they took into battle. Still, the ordnance was top of the line, built for the battlefield and not for ceremonial duty.

Cain looked across the deck. There was a line of Martian Marines at attention, and in front of them, a man who looked like he was in his mid-60s, but who Cain knew was over 100. He walked toward him and stopped about a meter away. "Minister Vance. It is good to see you again."

"Indeed, General Cain. Though I doubt you could remember me well. The last time I saw you I'm afraid you were only seven years old."

Cain smiled. "I remember. You particularly liked the rocky coastline, if I recall."

"Yes," Vance said with some surprise, pausing as if to savor a memory. "I was born a Martian, and I've lived my whole life here." He made a vague gesture to the area around him. "One day, I hope, Mars will have its own open seas, and windswept coastlines like Atlantia's, but that will be for another generation to enjoy, I am afraid."

"Indeed, Minister, one day." Cain paused. "Atlantia is a magnificent world. I've never seen a match of its physical beauty anywhere else." Another pause, and a frown. "I'm afraid I live underground now, as you do. I have been banished from my homeworld. Sadly, my fellow Atlantians have not shown the wisdom in choosing leaders that their ancestors did in selecting a new home world.

"Yes, I had heard of your troubles with the Atlantian government. Such foolishness. But those who select... controversial careers...must be willing to accept the consequences."

"That is true, Minister Vance. It would seem if I ever return to Atlantia it will be under far different circumstances than those in which I left. And the politicians who banished me will have much to consider." There was a flush of menace in Cain's voice, but it quickly faded.

Vance nodded. "Tomorrow's business, perhaps. For now,

you have my thanks for answering my call. I was surprised when I was told you were coming yourself. I had initially just hoped you would hire out several companies to me, however, in light of what I have learned since I sent my courier, I am greatly pleased that you have come. You may not consider what I have to tell you to be your problem, but you should know about it. I fear it represents a grave threat to all of Occupied Space."

"My father greatly respected you, Minister Vance. He considered you a man he could trust, and there were not many he so regarded. It is because of this that I have come. And because I, too, have a matter to discuss, and I would welcome your counsel in it.

Vance smiled. "You shall have all the thoughts and assistance I can give, General Cain, for whatever it is worth. And we shall discuss all of this in detail later today. I have requested the presence of several others, and if you are willing, I would have you join us in counsel this evening." Vance looked a bit edgy, but he didn't elaborate. "But for now, allow me to show you to your quarters so you may rest. You have had a long journey, and though it has been some years since I have traveled in space, I remember the soreness well."

*   *   *   *   *

"What is he doing here?" Darius' words were icy. He stood at the doorway, staring across the room at his twin. Elias Cain was on the other side of the table, flanked by a pair of officers wearing Atlantian Patrol uniforms. He looked just as surprised—and unhappy—to see his sibling.

Darius' eyes fixed on his brother's with a withering gaze. They had been close as children, but that compatibility had not survived the loss of their father. Erik Cain's two sons, had developed very different personalities despite their being identical twins brought up in the same household. And neither had taken his loss well, though they had faced their grief in vastly different ways.

"What are you doing here?" Darius said, voice grim as he redirected the inquiry to his brother. Darius hadn't seen Elias in almost a decade, and one look at his brother was enough to convince him that was far too short a time. He detested what Elias stood for now, and he knew Elias disapproved just as fiercely of him and the choices he had made. They shared the same DNA, but they'd developed almost opposite points of view, and each pitied the other for perceived foolishness.

"I was invited here, brother. I have come because our father always valued Roderick Vance's friendship, and because I wished to discuss a matter with him." Elias' tone dripped with anger that matched his brother's, and he stared at Darius suspiciously. "Now that I see you here, my doubts begin to fade. I suspect you know why I have come. Are you here to attempt to escape guilt for your actions? Because you have wasted a trip, brother. You have gone too far this time."

Darius felt a flush of rage, and he struggled to maintain control of himself. "I have no idea what nonsense you are talking about. But it is like you to find wrongdoing everywhere you go. I warn you, brother, I am not one of your powerless citizens, subject to the whims of your kangaroo courts. Try to take my freedom, and you will feel what it is like to face would-be victims who are not helpless and prostrate before your power."

Elias' eyes were wide, and he quivered with rage. "Why would I believe anything you say? Are you proud of what you have become, what you have done? Of the thousands you and your butchers have killed? And now, you direct your brutality toward your own people."

"I have no idea what insanity you are spewing," Darius spat. "And I have no interest in anything you have to say. You have become a servant of that which led to Earth's destruction, that which stole freedom from humanity. You are a part of a government growing out of control, strangling the people, just as the Superpowers did on Earth. Do you even see the difference between what Atlantia was when we were children and what it has become? Do you feel the loss of liberty, hear the death rattle of freedom as it draws its last rasping breaths? No, for it is your own boot grinding that freedom into the ground, your hands clasped firmly about its neck." Darius was angry, and his rage was increasing with each word.

"You assign a perceived reverence to laws, as if granting the very designation automatically implies some kind of wisdom or fairness. As though they were delivered from on high, instead of being the creations of fallible, and usually dishonest, men. Laws, brother, have no inherent justice to them...they are but words. Laws have held men in slavery, sent them to their deaths, controlled large groups for the enrichment of their masters. Governments have lied to their citizens since the dawn of history, and intimidated them, forcing compliance for its own sake and not in any pursuit of fairness. There must be justice first and foremost, and laws must flow from it, and respect the high ideal. But this rarely occurs. Men are weak, and they are easily led—and they fail to value their freedom. And those you serve take it from them, sending you and your thugs to crush any who stand against them and lament the long slide into servitude."

He stared at Elias with wild eyes, his fists clenched tightly. "You serve with mindless obedience, brother, never questioning the edicts you enforce, and you expect others to do the same. You brand them as criminals if they stand for their own, refuse to obey the dictats of those who would be their masters. Your politicians threaten, mislead, scare the population—whatever they must do, by means however foul, to control their needed 51%, and they use it to bludgeon the other 49%, to impose their own will, to serve their lust for power and their bottomless greed. Your leaders speak of right and wrong, but such are their own constructs, bent and twisted at will to serve their base needs."

His voice was caustic, his anger directed as much at the situation on Atlantia as at Elias personally. He had seen his home planet steadily embrace suffocating laws and regulations, moving ever farther away from the free and peace loving world his parents had chosen as their home. Still, though he knew there were many at fault, he felt a searing anger toward his twin. He expected better from his brother, and he believed in his heart, Elias' beliefs betrayed their father. He could forgive his twin any offense—save being part of the budding totalitarian establishment he despised.

"Your laws," he continued, "those you revere with such intensity, are made by men, brother, as often as not for evil and dishonest purposes. I am a grower of crops, and I give you money to buy the votes you need to gain your office. In return, you pass the laws I ask for, to make other growers less able to compete with me, to make my customers pay higher prices for my grain, to threaten my rivals with the power of the state if they resist. Then you lie, obfuscate your corruption and vilify those who challenge you. Where is there justice in that? Is that something men should support, fight for…die for? Indeed, what is it but the basest foulness—man at his dishonest best? Your laws masquerade as codified morality, but they are nothing more than power auctioned off to the highest bidder."

Elias stood firm and returned his brother's gaze, with no less intensity. "And you, brother? Are you so unspotted, so moral and true? Is there equity behind the might you employ for those who pay you? Do your causes acquire righteousness through the exchange of coin? Does your brutality procure the gleam of justice because those who retain you drown you in wealth? Indeed, do you not work for the same politicians you despise, those who gain control of a world's resources to hire your trained killers to expand their power?"

He was rigid, his body tense with anger. "It is just and fair that your soldiers are trained and experienced—and have powered armor and advanced weapons—while, as often as not, they face half-trained planetary levies, sweeping them away as a scythe does wheat? That they are able to impose their will on behalf of their paymaster? This is what you call justice? To be a mercenary…a hired killer with no nation, no home?"

Elias' voice was thick with disdain, and his hands shook as he gave Darius back his own venom in equal measure. "You criticize the laws I enforce, but do you believe in anything? It there no arbiter of human conduct you respect, save brutality and force? Is there no measure of right or wrong except whoever is able to pay your blood price? What are you but a cold-blooded killer, a hired thug, albeit a skilled and expensive one?"

Elias' face was flushed red. "You speak of laws, as if none were just. But what becomes of the worlds you conquer when your soldiers leave? Is there looting and rapine and plunder in their wake, even if your Black Eagles do not invoke such horrors themselves? Do your paymasters impose their own laws on the conquered? Are the mandates impressed upon the victims of your aggression somehow less corrupt and foul than the laws you accuse me of supporting? What becomes of the precious freedom you worship so profoundly, in the wake of war and conquest? You are a fool, my brother. You have imposed slavery on more millions than the laws of Atlantia, even if, as you say, many of those are corrupt and misguided. And you leave the dead behind you wherever you go, the grisly trail of a man who knows of nothing but butchery."

Darius stood stone still, anger pulsating throughout his body. If any man had spoken to him thusly, save his own brother, he would have killed him where he stood. But Darius Cain would not assault his brother, however much of a fool he was, whatever he said or did. He wanted to—he felt the urge to choke the life from the man standing opposite him, to silence his forked tongue forever. But Elias was his father's son, and his mother's. And that stayed his hand.

"Perhaps I am a butcher, brother, but I am an honest one.

And it was not I who created the ways of the universe nor the failings of men. Events will be dictated in some manner, and I proudly chose the road I have taken. If it is at times brutal, it is at least never based on lies and deceit. When my people come, it is because of a dispute, one that could have been resolved by the politicians long before, had they the time and the will to turn aside from their thievery and constant aggregation of personal power. The Black Eagles do not serve would-be despots, nor conquerors seeking empire. We contract only with those who have legitimate disputes, and we resolve those with greater speed and less bloodshed than any other means."

He stared right into Elias' eyes. "Can you say the same, brother? Are your laws honest? They restrict speech, movement, trade, worship, relationships. They intrude into the peoples' bank accounts and their bedrooms with equal aggressiveness. They control what people say, what they eat, how they raise their children. You defend them to people with simplistic examples, claiming that without law there would be anarchy and widespread violence. But does this justify the vast majority of what you enforce? Are Atlantia's courts and jails full of mass murderers and violent criminals, monsters all men would see prosecuted? I think not. For your political masters use the law to serve their own ends, and they jail their rivals and enemies—and those who resist them, and nary a thought goes toward anything that resembles true justice."

Elias stared back at Darius, not retreating a centimeter. "Tell yourself that brother, when your killers board their craft and depart a world, leaving behind despair and pestilence. Convince yourself you believe in freedom, when no one has brought servitude to more millions than you have. Say that your soldiers are not brigands and murderers, and forget that you serve no people, no world, no society, save your own overflowing coffers. You are a modern day alchemist, my brother, for you have learned to turn blood to gold. But in the end you have nothing but piles of wealth…and a human race that fears you and curses your name."

"Stop!" a voice roared from the corridor. "Enough. Both of you." There were footsteps echoing off the hard floor and, an instant later, a tall woman came in, her blond hair, streaked now with gray, flowing behind her. Roderick Vance had been walking beside her, but he paused at the entrance to the room, allowing her to deal with her sons alone.

Darius and Elias both fell silent, turning toward the hallway as their mother strode into the room. They wore neutral expressions, and they looked toward Sarah without saying a world.

"I heard enough of that exchange to feel a sorrow as deep as any I have experienced." Her voice was sad, but it was energized with her own, not inconsiderable, anger. "To hear my sons speak like this to each other breaks my heart. When I first saw the two of you, newborn and so small and red, screaming so loudly, the both of you, as if you were already competing, I knew I would love you forever, and so I do. But I don't *like* either of you much right now, and I am ashamed to my core of you both."

They both looked as if they were going to respond, but Sarah flashed them each a nasty glare, and they remained silent.

"Your father would be ashamed of you both too. He would have been hurt deeply listening to what I just heard." Tears welled up in her eyes when she mentioned Erik, but her voice remained steady and strong. "Erik Cain was a great man, and he deserves for his sons to live up to what he was. And neither of you have done that. You are both pale imitations."

She turned toward Elias. "Your father grew up in squalor you can't imagine, as did I. And that misery grew from generations of mindless obedience to authority, from people too weak to question the mandates heaped upon them year after year. From a population more concerned with its own petty indulgences than in the difficult task of regulating government. Atlantia is no longer the place Erik and I chose for our home, and I have left it behind, along with much sorrow and regret."

She paused for an instant, taking a breath, but neither Darius nor Elias dared to speak. "Your father would be ashamed of the way you have become so unquestioning of the laws you enforce and the will you impose on people. Erik Cain was a Marine all his adult life. He worked for the Alliance government in that capacity, but never once did he yield his free will and bow down unquestioningly before the bureaucrats who would have been his masters. It wasn't an easy path he trod. Indeed, it came close to costing him his career, his freedom…even his life…more than once. But he was a steadfast man, and through all his years he did what he thought was right."

She turned and stared at Darius next, and her eyes bored into him like lasers. "And you…your father would be ashamed of you as well. What lesson did you take from his life to justify spending yours as a paid mercenary? Whatever standards you think you apply in taking contracts, in the end, you kill people for money. Your father and I were Marines. We fought for good, to protect people, even when that required us to stand firm against our own government. Never in the history of the Corps could anyone buy a force of Marines…however legitimate their dispute, however large their purse. We fought for the colonies, to give them a chance to forge a better future than the fools on Earth who had preceded them. And we never justified aggression by blithely declaring it inevitable, as if that washed all the blood from our hands."

She stood between them, staring at one then the other. They stayed where they were, but both of them averted her gaze slightly. "I have spoken long with Roderick, and I believe mankind faces another threat now, one we know little about save for the great danger it represents. You have gone down different paths, and used oversimplified morality to justify what you have done. You have convinced yourselves your father would have approved. Well, he would not…he would have looked at both of you with shame and regret." She paused for a few seconds. Her words were brutal, and they cut deeply. "But there is always time to change your course. The two of you can work together, cooperate, help to face whatever danger is coming. You can stand against the darkness, fight for the good of the people, try to lead them by example, not by military force or suffocating laws."

She sighed, and for the first time it was apparent how much pain she was feeling. "You are both my sons, and I will love you until the day I die. Will you set aside your differences and work together, fight together if need be? If you do, it will be a gift to me, and I will not just love my sons, I will be proud of them. And that is something I have not felt in many years."

Darius slid his foot forward slightly, opening his mouth and closing it again. There was no one in Occupied Space who could impact him with such force, no one save the woman standing in the room facing him. Darius had run from the pain of his father's death, and since then he'd been drawn ever more deeply into his new life. He'd neglected his mother, abandoned her when she faced her own pain of loss. Indeed, he'd made it worse, depriving her of a son as well as her husband. Only now did he begin to realize how much guilt he had carried—and buried under his pride and arrogance.

"Come in, Roderick," he said softly. "Tell us what threat you have uncovered." He glanced uncomfortably toward his brother. Elias hesitated for a few seconds, and then he nodded silently. Darius walked toward the table, taking a seat. Vance sat at one end of the table, and Sarah at the other. Finally, Elias slipped into the chair opposite Darius.

The Cain brothers looked toward Vance, but the Martian just sat quietly, waiting. A few seconds later the sound of footsteps came from the hallway. Darius turned to see Augustus Garret and Catherine Gilson walk into the room.

Garret was the most revered hero in Occupied Space, widely considered to be the greatest naval commander in history. He'd retired after the final downsizing of the fleet, but he'd come back to preside over the activation of the mothballed reserve and the second struggle against the First Imperium. After the terrible enemy was again defeated, he'd supervised the decommissioning of the remnants of the fleet, now vastly smaller after the horrific losses sustained in the war. When he had seen to the last of his duties, he retired again, handing the reins of the tiny active fleet to his subordinates.

"Sarah, it is such a pleasure to see you again. It has been too long." Garret had attended the memorial service held for Erik Cain, but it had been thirteen years since he'd seen her. He had disappeared, faded from the public eye, returning to his family home of Terra Nova for a time. He put his arms around her, and gave her a long and warm hug before taking a seat next to her. "Darius, Elias." Garret nodded, turning his head toward each of the Cain boys in turn.

"It is good to see you, Admiral." Darius looked down the table and nodded. His eyes settled on Gilson. "And you as well, General."

"Yes, Admiral Garret. It has been too long." Elias glanced down the table with a motion almost identical to his brother's. "It is a pleasant surprise to see you, General Gilson."

"So, Minster Vance, you have gone to considerable trouble to assemble this counsel." Darius' tone was professional, polite. "It is my guess that many of us have come here with concerns, and I suggest we share these. Perhaps now you will begin, and tell us what caused you to call this meeting."

Vance shifted in his chair. "Very well, Darius." Vance took a deep breath and stared out across the table. "I want to thank you all again for coming. Some of you have been here before, when we faced the First Imperium and the Shadow Legions together. We successfully met those earlier threats, though not, as we all know, without cost." He glanced at Elias and then Darius. "Others are here for the first time."

He sat upright in his chair. "I must tell you that I have called you here as a private citizen and not on behalf of the Martian Confederation. I will not mislead you. What I have learned has come through unofficial channels, and I cannot guarantee the council will support any actions we discuss here." He looked around the room, gauging reactions. "However, I am prepared to utilize my own personal resources…" He paused uncomfortably. "…and do whatever is necessary to ensure that if there truly is a grave new threat we are prepared to meet it." Another pause. "It is my hope that when all of you hear what I am about to tell you—and share your own information with us—you will agree to join me in doing whatever must be done."

Vance glanced at Garret. "Some of us have stood at this crossroads before, been compelled to choose the course of action that was right, even at great risk. Without men and women willing to take such steps, it is my fervent belief none of us would be here. Mankind would be gone, extinct, with nothing but slowly decaying ruins to mark that we'd ever been here."

He stood silently for a few seconds, allowing his words to settle over his guests. "I do not know if this new threat is as dire as those which came before, but I fear it may be. And we will again need men and women to stand in the breach, to set aside personal concerns and face the darkness on behalf of the entire race." He looked around the table at each of them. "The people in this room are cut from that cloth. Sarah, Cate, Augustus…you have been there before, faced other crises. Darius, Elias…your father was a great man, always the first to answer the call. He fought the fight for humanity for decades…and he gave his life to it."

Vance took a deep breath. "As some of you know, the Confederation has operated a humanitarian relief program for a number of years, making drops of food, medicine, and tools to survivor settlements on Earth. It is through this operation that I first noticed something of concern, and I decided to investigate matters more closely. What I uncovered is horrifying. Someone has been running a slavery ring on Earth, rounding up survivors and shipping them off-world…

for purposes still unknown."

The room was silent. Whatever they'd expected to hear, that was certainly not it. Vance continued, "A short time ago, one of the settlements we had been monitoring sent out a distress signal. I sent one of my most trusted agents to investigate. He found the village burned, its people gone. He was able to track the raiders...and he discovered the terrible truth."

Vance reached down and pressed a small button on the table. "My agent also made contact with three villagers who escaped from the raid."

Everyone turned toward the entrance. There were footsteps coming from the hallway. A tall man in his mid-fifties walked into the room. His brown hair was neatly trimmed, and he was wearing a suit of Martian design.

Vance waited until the new arrival was halfway to the table. "Allow me to introduce one of my guests from Earth. This is Axe."

A wave of greetings and nods worked its way around the table. Axe stopped a few meters away and said, "It is a pleasure to meet all of you."

"Please, Axe, take a seat." Vance gestured to the chair next to him. "And then tell us about Jericho...and the events of the last several weeks."

*   *   *   *   *

"Are you insane, brother?" There was a ragged edge to Darius' voice, anger and disgust combined into one caustic tone. "If I had attacked Glaciem and wanted you to know, I'd have left a message far clearer than scraps of unidentified equipment. And if I didn't want you to know, you wouldn't. My people are not that sloppy."

Elias Cain glared across the room. "Then who could

it have been? Who else with such resources would attack Atlantia's interests? Who, except a mercenary angry at his homeworld for branding him the criminal he is?"

"Elias, listen carefully, because I am only going to say this once." Darius' voice had changed. It was cold now, unemotional. To most people, it sounded more reasonable than the previous angry growl, but those who knew him well understood that the coldness of this tone was far more dangerous than the fiery anger of the prior one. "If I cared about Atlantia enough to be angry at what they did to me, I wouldn't take it out on a few innocent miners. I would land directly on the planet and drag those lying, power-hungry politicians from their arrogant perches. I would wait until every communications network on the planet had their cameras in place, and then I would force them to their knees and execute them myself, one at a time. And then I would leave, for my grievances lie against Atlantia's government and not its people, save for their negligence in allowing such men and women to lead them."

"You think you could so easily invade Atlantia? That your band of cutthroats could destroy our military and take control so easily?" Elias was just as angry as his brother, and his body was shaking as he spoke.

Darius suppressed an angry laugh. "Elias, my people could sweep away Atlantia's pathetic excuse for an army like a hand brushing away flies at a picnic. You are the expert on suppressing thought and filling prisons. But this is my skillset."

"Oh my God, stop! Both of you!" Sarah had been on the other side of the room, speaking with Garret and Vance until the escalating confrontation between her sons brought all other conversation to a halt. She stared at Elias. "Whatever your quarrels with your brother, it is ridiculous to harbor the belief that he was behind the attack on Glaciem."

Darius smiled. "Thank you, moth…"

"And you," Sarah interrupted, "do you think you persuade anyone of your virtue by speaking of invading your homeworld for vengeance? Even in jest? Out of your own mouth, you reinforce the image so many have of you, as a ruthless, soulless conqueror. Does that make you proud, Darius? What of your father? Do you think he would be pleased if he was here?"

The two brothers stood silently, glaring at each other but exchanging no further barbs. Sarah continued, "Neither of you have lived through the kind of crises your father and I— and Roderick and Augustus—experienced. But for those of us who have, the situation now looks dangerously like those that came before." She turned toward Darius. "Your Black Eagles twice encountered a mysterious enemy, one equipped with extremely advanced armor and weaponry. And it is clear that, for all your resources and whatever vague suspicions you harbor, you have no real idea who it is."

She turned toward her other son. "And you...you have a destroyed settlement and evidence that you are facing a very advanced and well-equipped foe. Do you have any idea who attacked you, save your foolish suspicions feeding your petty anger toward your brother?"

She paused, shifting her gaze from one of them to the other. "Now, you learn that someone has been running a large scale kidnapping operation on Earth, and that thousands have been seized and shipped somewhere unknown, probably to spend the rest of their lives as slaves. These slave catchers are well-equipped..." She glared at each of her sons again. "... just like those who have attacked both of your people. And now, thanks to agent Girard's tracker, we know a group of these slavers have landed on Eris, deep in the nearly empty wastes of the outer solar system."

"Your mother speaks wisely." Vance was walking across the room, coming to Sarah's support with Garret close behind. "It would be highly coincidental if these were the acts of unrelated parties with such similar—and extraordinary— capabilities. Yet the alternative is we face an adversary with truly enormous reach, one that could pillage Earth right under the noses of the Confederation, set itself against the Black Eagles, and move against Glaciem. Not only those efforts indeed, for we have just received word of several other unexplained attacks. Resource worlds are being targeted, and on each one there is evidence of a highly-advanced combat force, one clearly intended to look like the Black Eagles."

He turned toward Darius. "Someone is attempting to frame your people, to spread outrage throughout Occupied Space...and hatred toward the Eagles."

Darius turned toward Vance. "Why would they want to do that? What purpose could it serve?"

"Because your people are the strongest force in Occupied Space, Darius. Though you have a different purpose and code, the Eagles occupy a position not unlike the Marine Corps did thirty years ago. You are the most capable, the most veteran military organization in existence. At least that we know about."

Vance's last words hung heavily in the room. Clearly there was another force out there—and they knew almost nothing about it.

Chapter 19

"The Cape"
Planet Atlantia, Epsilon Indi II
Earthdate: 2302 AD (17 Years After the Fall)

"Please, Erik, don't go. You have done your share. More. Let others carry the flag now." Sarah was standing behind Cain on the stone patio. It was almost dusk, and the sun was setting over the waves. It was a beautiful sight, the last light of day twinkling off the rippling waves. But she didn't even see it. Her mind was in darker places.

Erik Cain stood at the edge of the small stone wall staring out at the same scene but no more aware of it than Sarah. He wanted nothing so much as to stay on Atlantia with her, to enjoy the life they had built. Fifteen years. They had lived fifteen years in near bliss, and Cain had savored every day of it. He'd even begun to believe that the rest of his life would be the same, that after all the death and destruction, he would live his remaining days in peace and contentment. But deep down, where the dark side that would always be part of him dwelled, he'd known one day his joyful life would come crashing down. That the bugle would again call, and that his efforts to resist would be futile.

"I don't want to go, Sarah." His voice was gentle, sad. He knew how much this was hurting her. "But I have to."

He turned to face her. "You know I have to go. You read the communique." Every word of that fateful message was burned into his mind. There had been rumors for weeks, and then confirmed accounts. There was war again in Occupied Space, worlds burning, people dying. Cain had watched the accounts grimly, but he'd sworn to himself this time men could fight their wars without him. Then the message from Admiral Garret arrived, and it contained the two words Erik Cain knew he couldn't ignore. First Imperium.

Garret had confirmed it. The mysterious forces attacking colony worlds were the robot legions of that lost ancient empire. They still appeared to regard the worlds of humanity as being part of their imperium, and they refrained from orbital bombardments and nuclear attacks. But they remained as genocidal as ever, and they had methodically slaughtered the populations of the invaded planets.

As soon as Cain had read the message, he knew he had to go. Allowing human worlds to fight each other was one thing. But the First Imperium was a threat to all. The fighting was far from Atlantia now, almost on the other side of Occupied Space. But Cain knew, if the robot legions were not destroyed, they would continue their advance. If mankind didn't put forth all its ability to again defeat the nightmarish enemy, eventually they would reach his new home. And then they would kill everyone. Cain could stay behind, allow others to determine if his family lived or died, but that wasn't how he was wired. His mind flashed with waking nightmares, the deadly robot warriors, gunning down Sarah, the twins. It was more than he could bear.

Sarah sobbed softly, but she didn't say anything else. She just stepped forward and held on to him. He felt her warmth against him, inhaled the sweet scent of her hair. He wanted to stay on Atlantia with every fiber of his being. He might turn his back on his duty, allow his comrades to go into battle without him—but the images were still there, Sarah, his sons, lying in pools of blood, slaughtered by the deadly robots.

He stood there, forgetting the time, holding her close to him as dusk slipped into the blackness of night. Then, slowly, reluctantly, he pulled away. "I have to get ready. My ship leaves in the morning." He stood for a few seconds, looking into her moist blue eyes, and then he turned and walked into the house.

He slipped into a small room with a wall of windows looking out over the sea. His study had been a refuge for the last fifteen years, the place he'd gone when he had to be alone. On the days when the demons of the past burst out of their place deep in the recesses of his mind.

"It is late, General. Are you having difficulty sleeping again?" The voice was familiar. He'd heard it almost every day for the past fifteen years, but now it was taking him back farther, to the battlefields of his younger days.

"No sleep tonight, Hector." He'd been in his mid-twenties when he'd first named the AI. He'd just read the Iliad at the Academy, and he'd been drawn to the doomed Trojan hero. It had been an impulse then, but now he looked back and saw deeper meaning in his choice. He could have just as easily chosen Achilles. The two had both been doomed, neither fated to survive their life of war. "We're leaving tomorrow. Being recalled back to duty." It had been more than fifteen years since the AI had been downloaded into Cain's armor. Indeed, the fighting suit was down in the storage room, stowed in a box where it had sat undisturbed since he and Sarah had moved in. It wasn't normal procedure for a Marine to take his nuclear-powered suit of armor with him into retirement, but no one even tried to tell Erik Cain what to do—or not to do—anymore.

For years he wondered why he'd bothered to bring it, but now he knew he'd realized all along. War had given him a respite, a period of happiness beyond anything he could have imagined. But it hadn't let him go. It still owned him. His soul still belonged to the Corps, as it always would.

"Should I download myself into your armor, General?"

Hector had developed a prickly demeanor in Cain's younger days, part of its programming to adapt itself to the needs of its master. Cain had complained about Hector's quirks without ever realizing how effective the AI's efforts had been in maintaining his focus and controlling his stress. He still complained about it from time to time, though the AI had long ago evolved its behavior to match an older Cain. For the last fifteen years, Hector had done little but run the Cain household, answering the com unit, making coffee, running the heating system. It was almost as if the veteran AI had also retired. And now it too was going back to war.

"Yes, Hector. And run a partial power-up sequence and a diagnostic. The thing's been sitting there for fifteen years."

"Very well. I will proceed with caution." There was a brief silence. "Once more into the breach, General?"

Cain sighed softly. "Yes, Hector. Once more into the breach."

*   *   *   *   *

"We need these ships up and running now, Roderick." Augustus Garret stood in the hanger, looking through the clear hyper-polycarbonate wall out onto Phobos' rocky surface. The huge bulk of *Pershing* lay in the distance, held in place by a massive framework of steel brackets and surrounded by dozens of other vessels. It had been barely half a decade since she had been put in place along with the other ships of the Superpowers' fleets, and now there were crews working night and day to prepare her again for war.

"We're moving as quickly as possible, Augustus. We've virtually shut down Martian industry. Every worker with applicable experience, from engineers down to cleaning crew, have been assigned to fleet duty."

"I know, Roderick." Garret realized there had been an

edge to his voice, and he knew Vance didn't deserve that. Indeed, he doubted anyone could move the recommissioning any faster than the Martian. But Garret had been to the front already. He'd seen what the First Imperium forces had left in their wake. Gregoria, San Rafael, Yang-Tzon...all once-prosperous colonies, now silent graveyards, the bodies of the dead unburied, lying where they had fallen. Augustus Garret had fought the First Imperium before, and he knew, better than almost anyone, that those dead worlds were a look at mankind's future. Unless they could once again defeat the dreaded foe.

Vance moved closer to Garret and put his hand on his friend's shoulder. "I understand, Augustus." He sighed. "I knew we'd face trouble again one day, but I hadn't expected it so soon. And the First Imperium? Of everything that could have struck us, that is the most terrible." He stared out at the rows of mothballed ships for a few seconds. Then he turned and looked at Garret intently. "Do you think we have a chance to win this, Augustus? I mean a real chance?"

The initial war with the enemy had been a holocaust, which had been "won" only by exploding one of the enemy's massive, planet-killer bombs in the sole warp gate connecting the worlds of the First Imperium with those of Occupied Space. The perfectly-placed detonation had disrupted the gate, rendering transit impossible for an indeterminate time, generally projected to be measured in centuries—and buying time for humanity to prepare for its next showdown with the robot warriors of the long-dead civilization. But it had been less than twenty years, not several centuries, and mankind was weaker than it had been, not stronger.

Garret took a deep breath. "I don't know, Roderick." He turned from the windows and looked at Vance. "We were vastly stronger when we faced them before. The Superpowers and all their industry still existed. And the fleet was so much larger. We've lost so much. Terrance, and all his ships..." Garret's voice trailed off. When he'd disrupted the warp gate, he'd stranded his best friend, and half of humanity's ships, beyond the newly created Barrier—and in the midst of a massive First Imperium fleet. He'd had no choice, but he had still never forgiven himself.

He took another breath, deeper this time. "Indeed, by the standards of what we faced before, we are doomed. Militarily, we wouldn't stand a chance. But there is a hope. By all accounts, the forces attacking us are far smaller than those we faced before. Perhaps we are fighting some isolated group of First Imperium forces, activated by some unknown means. If so, we have a chance. If the vast forces of that terrible empire are still trapped behind the Barrier, we may be able to defeat what we now face." He sighed. "Though whatever happens, the cost, I am sure, will be very high indeed."

"It would seem that mankind again relies upon your skills, Augustus. Yours and those of your extraordinary companions. A mere five years after they denied you the resources to maintain your forces. There is irony in that, is there not?"

"I have come to agree with Erik Cain on this matter. I fear men will never become what they should be. They will always make poor choices, fail to look toward the future responsibly. And yet we must do what we can to save them, for they are all we have."

Vance didn't say anything. Indeed, neither of them did for a long while. They just stood, watching the tiny shapes of the work crews crawling over the superstructure holding *Pershing* in place. Soon she would take to space again, along with the other ships of the fleet. Another battle, one no less desperate than any that had come before.

*   *   *   *   *

"Now, James. Now is the time. Bring your forces around." Erik Cain stood on a rocky promontory looking out over the battlefield. His troops were deployed along a narrow frontage, falling back slowly, enticing the enemy forward. The

battle was not a typical one. Territory didn't matter. Normal
military tactics didn't apply. The robot warriors of the First
Imperium didn't know fear, and they would never yield. There
was only one way to defeat them—total annihilation. And
Cain had planned this battle to achieve just that. Only one
army would leave Caravalis.

Cain and Cate Gilson had led the reconstituted Corps into
the war, and there had been half a dozen battles on worlds all
along the enemy's line of advance. Gilson had been the Marine
Commandant, but the prewar Corps had shrunken almost to
nothing. When they'd formed the Army of Man, and absorbed
dozens of different contingents from worlds across Occupied
Space, they'd agreed to split command. But then Gilson had
been hit on Balzara. She had survived, at least—and that had
been anything but certain at the time—but she was out of
the fight for at least a year. And by then it would all be over.
Either the First Imperium forces would be defeated. Or man's
last line of defense would be destroyed, and on a thousand
planets, the last of humanity would wait silently, helplessly for
doom to reach their worlds.

Teller's command was the strongest in the hodge podge
army, consisting mostly of Marines and Janissaries called
back to the colors. They were coming in behind the enemy,
slamming the line shut like a trap door. Then it would be a
fight to the finish. The First Imperium had committed most
of its strength to the invasion of Caravalis. If Cain's army
could prevail there—and Garret's fleet could win the battle
raging in the space above the planet—the rest would just be
mopping up.

The past two years of war had been among the bloodiest
Cain had fought, and he had struggled to keep his army
together, to maintain their morale in the face of devastating
losses. He had precious few old veterans and too many
planetary levies and raw recruits. But every one of them
understood they were fighting an enemy that would not stop
until all humanity was dead. There was no possibility of

surrender, no chance for survival save to fight. And Erik Cain had been there, in the front lines of every battle, at each point where his soldiers wavered. He'd kept the army together and in the field, as much by force of will as anything. Now was the final contest. It would be victory or death here.

"We'll be engaged in ten minutes, Erik." Cain could hear the stress in Teller's voice. The stakes were as high as they could be, and even grizzled veterans like James Teller were on the verge of collapse. Cain knew he need a final battle now, and not just because it was the only way to defeat the enemy but because his people couldn't last much longer. He'd driven them harder than men could endure, and he coaxed greater strength from them than anyone had imagined possible. But they were near the end. This had to be the last battle.

"No more than that, old friend. These planetary troops have already held out longer than I'd dared to hope. We need your veterans now."

"We're on the way, Erik. After these battles, all the victories…and the defeats too. And all the losses. It comes down to this." Teller had driven the fatigue from his voice. Cain knew it was still there, as it was for him as well, but he also knew he could count on his friend. James Teller would fight—he would lead his soldiers to the bitter end.

Cain glanced up at his tactical display. The battle was degenerating into a confused, wild melee. His eyes flashed to the side, settling on the small column of red symbols. The First Imperium had not employed nuclear weapons. As in most of the earlier war, their doctrine seemed to regard the target worlds as their own, and their invasions as liberation efforts designed to destroy an invader. They refrained, therefore, from going nuclear. But Cain was under no such restriction. Caravalis was a human planet, with a population of just under a million—at least before the invasion. But the survival of mankind was at stake, and Erik Cain was prepared to sacrifice every man, woman, and child on the planet— including himself and all his soldiers—to destroy the First

Imperium forces. Before they moved through the heart of Occupied Space. Before they reached Atlantia.

"Hector, get me Colonel Cho." His voice was somber.

"Yes, General Cain." Cho had been an enemy at one time, a junior officer for the Central Asian Combine during the devastating battles late in the Third Frontier War. But he had been an ally more recently, during the initial war against the First Imperium. And now Erik Cain had entrusted him with his nuclear arsenal.

"I want your weapons ready in twenty minutes, Colonel."

"How many?"

"All of them."

The line was silent for a few seconds. "General, we have thousands of unarmored troops out there."

"I am aware of that, Colonel."

"But a full strike will be devastating, as much to our own people as to the enemy."

Cain's voice was like iron. "I am aware of that as well, Colonel." He paused. "But we are all expendable. There is only one absolute in this battle. The First Imperium must be stopped. Here. Now. I want you ready." Another pause. Even Cain's iron will was being put to its ultimate test. "Because if it appears we are losing this battle, you are to launch a full strike...and you are to do so without consideration for casualties caused to our own forces. Your only concern is the destruction of the enemy. You are to proceed no matter what. Even if you cannot reach me. Even if I am dead already. But the enemy does not leave here. Do you understand me, Colonel?"

There was a short pause then Cho's voice came through the com. "Yes, General. Understood."

Cain stared out over the field again. He could see Teller's people approaching. They were the cream of humanity's remaining warriors, the strongest and bravest remaining to the colors. *C'mon, James. Cut these bastards off. Blow 'em to hell...and don't make me nuke everyone down here.*

*   *   *   *   *

The cheers echoed through the corridors of the ship, momentarily drowning out the secondary explosions and the sounds of work crews frantically trying to fight the fires and stop the spread of the damage. Garret knew *Pershing* was dead. She would never fight another battle. Her spine was broken, and the thousands of kilometers of conduits spanning her 1,800 meter length were twisted wreckage. Her engines were destroyed, and her last surviving reactor was down to 20% output. But she was still there…and the last First Imperium warship was gone, blown into a floating pile of radioactive debris. His beloved flagship would give one last service, surviving long enough to get her crews home.

Garret sat in his command chair. The left side of his face was covered with blood, just beginning to dry into a crust. Half his bridge crew were casualties. Indeed, at least 50% of *Pershing's* complement had been killed or wounded. Garret and his fleet had put all they had left into this fight, and winning the victory had taken it all.

"It's time, sir." The voice of the tactical officer seemed remote, distant. "Admiral Garret, sir? Are you ready to transfer the flag?"

Garret rose slowly from the well-worn chair, realizing in his heart it would be the last time. It felt disloyal to abandon *Pershing*, at least while she had some level of functionality, but he still had work to do, and his longtime flagship could no longer take him where he had to go. The war against the First Imperium was almost won, but there were stragglers, robot-controlled warships of astonishing power, all of which would keep fighting until they were hunted down and destroyed. He had to get them. He had to get them all. And he had nothing but the shattered remnants of a once-great fleet to do it.

*   *   *   *   *

"You go back to Armstrong, James. I'll take half the Corps and Janissary survivors and flush out the last few remnants of the enemy." There were small detachments of First Imperium robots remaining on a number of worlds. They were too small to seriously threaten humanity, but they would kill any people they encountered. The war was won, but there was still mopping up to do.

"You sure, Erik? I can take care of it if you want to go back." Teller couldn't hide the exhaustion in his voice. He knew his friend had to be even more spent, but there had always been something about Erik Cain, an almost inexhaustible capacity to drive himself further. Teller knew even Cain had a limit—all men did. But he'd never seen it.

"I'm sure. You earned an early ride home, my friend. I was two minutes, maybe three from ordering Cho to launch everything we had. That would have been the end of all of us. But then your people broke through. I've never seen a deadlier killing ground than the one you managed to set up." He smiled at his friend. "Well done, General Teller. Well done." *And thank you for saving me from taking one more regret to my grave.*

Teller smiled. "Thank you, Erik." He paused. "Before I go, I want to tell you something. I won't be the last to say this, I am sure, but I'd like to be the first. "This victory is yours. Yours and Garret's. Without the two of you, none of the rest of us could have made it through." He paused. "I don't know where you get your strength from, but I thank whatever powers exist in the universe that you have it."

Cain reached out and shook Teller's hand. "Thank you, James." He took a breath. "Now go back to Armstrong, and tell Cate Gilson she'd better listen to her doctors and get the hell better. Fast. Because as soon as I hunt these last few units down, I'm headed for Atlantia. It's time for me to hang up these stars, for good this time."

*   *   *   *   *

Sarah walked into the large front room of the house. When the AI informed her that Augustus Garret was there to see her, she immediately suspected something was wrong. Why would Garret be here without warning, without sending a message? But it wasn't until she saw his face that she knew for sure.

"Sarah…I…" Garret spoke slowly, forcing out the choked words.

Her face went white. "Erik?"

"Sarah…I'm so sorry." Fleet Admiral Augustus Garret was mankind's greatest hero, a warrior idolized on a thousand planets. But it was an old man who stood in front of Sarah Cain, sad and broken. "I…" he tried to speak, but the words wouldn't come. He didn't know what to say. And as devastated as he was at the news of Erik Cain's loss, he couldn't imagine what it would do to her.

"How?" She barely managed to force out the single word.

"His ship was destroyed. He was on his way back, Sarah. He'd finished off the last enemy garrison, and he was on his way home." Garret hesitated, struggling to continue. Sarah could see he was wracked with pain, with guilt. "I don't know how it happened, Sarah. I thought we had gotten them all." He paused, his voice choked with emotion. "I must have let one slip through, it's the only answer." He was looking down at the floor, unable to face her. "I missed one, Sarah, and it killed Erik…and all the Marines with him."

Sarah felt the tears streaming down her face, but it was strangely detached. She had expected this news for fifty years, knew one day Erik's luck would fail him. But fifteen years of peace and happiness had stripped her of the strength she'd counted on to see her through. Decades of constant war had made loss easier to accept, at least in some ways. But now, after all they'd been through, he was gone. Their life along the Atlantia coast, the joys they had fought a lifetime to win—it was over. Gone forever.

"Are you sure?" she croaked miserably, knowing as she did

that Augustus Garret would not be there if he wasn't certain.

"His ship disappeared…no distress call, nothing. I took the fleet there, Sarah. All of it. We scoured the space around its last reported location. We blasted out one communique after another, burned out our scanners, all the while hoping beyond hope that his ship was just stranded, her com units down." He forced himself to look up, to meet her gaze. "Then we found a debris field, Sarah. We scanned it a hundred times. The reactor had blown, so there was nothing big enough to identify, but the total mass matched projections for a ship that size."

Sarah was trying to hang onto what little control she had left, but she could feel it slipping away. She lunged forward, wrapping her arms around Garret and plunging her face into his chest, crying inconsolably. She felt his arms around her, trying to provide what comfort he could. She could feel him shaking. The grim, invincible admiral was broken—by the loss of a friend, and the heartrending grief of another.

"We kept looking, Sarah. We explored every centimeter of space, anywhere a lifeboat could have gotten. If there had been anything, so much as a man in a suit of armor floating powerless through the void, we would have found it. But… there was nothing." She could hear the pain in his voice, the sense of guilt and failure. She knew his self-flagellation was undeserved, that Erik would be the last one to want his friend to carry more pain for his loss. But she knew Garret too well to imagine that he would ever feel differently.

Sarah tightened her grip. In many ways, Garret had been like a father to her, especially in the years after General Holm had died. She knew there was nothing that could console her, no comfort or support anyone could offer her. But she couldn't let go. She knew that when she did, she would have to begin the rest of her life…and she would have to go on without Erik. She realized she would, somehow. She was a Marine and the wife of a Marine, and she would accept nothing less from herself. She had two sons who needed her, teenaged boys

who idolized their father—and who would be devastated at
the news. But now, she clung to her old friend and put off the
future. Just for a few moments...

Chapter 20

Command Center – Spaceship Eagle One
Sol System – 1.2 AU Past the Orbit of Pluto
Earthdate: 2318 AD (17 Years After the Fall)

Darius Cain sat quietly in the command chair of *Eagle One*'s control center, deep in thought. The meeting on Mars had gone on for hours, each attendee reporting in turn on various events, none of them obviously linked, but all of them possibly connected nevertheless. There was much to consider.

First and foremost, at least as far as Darius was concerned, someone was after the Eagles. He believed that even more now than he had before. If a hidden enemy was attempting to frame his private army there had to be a reason behind it, a longer term plan to destroy the Black Eagles. And just making his people appear to be guilty of attacks they did not execute wouldn't be the end of it. People might hate the Eagles—indeed, most already feared them at least—but that didn't give them the courage or capability to attack and destroy his band of deadly fighters. Whatever people might say, whatever whispers might be exchanged in the dark, everyone in Occupied Space knew what fighting the Eagles meant. And they just got a reminder. News of the destruction of the Gold Spears had spread like wildfire. The complete obliteration of one of the other Great Companies sent a message, confirmation of what people had already suspected. The Black Eagles were in a class by themselves.

No, there is more to this than a PR war. Whoever is doing this will eventually make a more direct move. This is all just preliminary skirmishing. And I have to be ready when the shit hits the fan.

"Are your people set, Colonel Kuragina? I want them ready to hit the ground as soon as we reach Eris." He wondered why he'd chosen Cyn Kuragina's people to bring with him to the Sol system. They'd been the hardest hit on Lysandria, and they deserved a long rest and time to replace their losses. But he knew they were questioning themselves, feeling as though they should have swept aside the Spears' mysterious allies. Cain suspected those 3,000 troops had been a force far deadlier than Kuragina and her soldiers imagined, but his people felt they should have crushed any force they'd never even heard of. Cain had ordered them to join him as a way of showing that his confidence in them was undiminished. After all, he'd just been exerting some caution in bringing an escort to Sol; he hadn't really expected any fighting.

But now, that unexpected combat was looming. Vance's probes had revealed a concentration of structures on Eris, a base of some kind—something that didn't belong on the dwarf planet so far out in the depths of the Sol system, past the warp gates. The Martian Confederation claimed the entire system, but Mars had suffered enormous damage in the Fall, and its attempts to rebuild had required prioritizing its needs. Its outer system facilities were severely pruned, and those in the great depths beyond the two warp gates were abandoned completely. That had made sense at the time. Eris and the other trans-Neptunian objects of the Kuiper Belt and beyond were of little value, whatever resources they offered long eclipsed by richer sources in other systems. But now it was apparent that the Confederation's lax vigilance had allowed someone—and Cain couldn't imagine how it wasn't an enemy—to occupy that real estate, and fortify it strongly.

"We're ready, sir. The armor is checked out and ready,

and the troopers are on alert, waiting for the orders to suit up." Kuragina's voice was firm. He could hear the resolve, the determination to wipe away a disgrace that only she herself—and her warriors—recognized. Cain suddenly realized another reason he had brought the diminutive but tough-as-nails Kuragina, one he hadn't consciously considered before. Somewhere over the last year or so, the mysterious recruit turned senior officer had become his best regimental commander. Falstaff's Black Regiment was the Eagles' senior unit after the Teams, but Cain had seen Kuragina's Whites in action on Lysandria, and he had to admit, she'd forged them into a weapon as tempered and sharp as Falstaff's unit.

"Cyn, I want you to exercise extreme care on this drop. We know very little about the enemy—numbers, equipment... nothing. Even who they are." He knew the White Regiment would be at a fever pitch, ready to prove to their commander that they were as good as any of the other Eagles...something Darius Cain already believed with all his heart. He knew they could do the job, whatever that turned out to be, but he was worried about foolish heroics, about watching his veterans throw their lives away trying to prove their courage.

Such foolishness accompanies war, he thought. *Honor and duty and loyalty...they are noble concepts, yet they can be so destructive. How can Kuragina's people believe they have failed me? Yet nothing I say can purge them of this nonsense...and despite my best efforts, they will wash away the non-existent stain with blood. And too much of it will be their own...*

"Yes, General." There was a short pause. "We'll get the job done, sir. You can depend on us."

I do depend on you, Cyn. You and all your people, with every fiber of my being. But you won't believe that until you fight for me again... and more of you die. "Very well, Colonel." He closed the com line and sighed. He hadn't expected her to take his point, but he'd had to try.

He felt a rush of guilt about sending his people in at all. His initial thought had been to obliterate the base with a few nukes. Most contracts forbade the use of nuclear weapons except in an emergency. Those who paid the Eagles to conquer worlds for them wanted productive new populations, not radioactive graveyards. But his people were well-equipped with atomic ordnance nevertheless—and his vessels were some of the few in space that still packed even a small complement of the massive half-gigaton ship-to-ship weapons that had last been carried en masse by Admiral Garret's huge fleets.

Unfortunately, vaporizing the base would do little to provide the answers he needed. Who was targeting his people? And why? Was this enemy a danger to Occupied Space? He had to know. He needed prisoners…and intact facilities to investigate. And that meant sending his people in on the ground.

He turned toward Eagle One's tactical officer. "I want all weapons systems checked and double-checked. If we miss something and it costs us lives on the ground, by God, I will space whoever is at fault." Kuragina's people were going to drop onto Eris, but not before his ships did one hell of a softening up job.

"Yes, sir," came the prompt reply. "Projected entry into extreme weapons range, two hours, eleven minutes."

A little over two hours, Cain thought. *Then maybe we'll start to unravel this mystery.*

*   *   *   *   *

Roderick Vance stared at the data on his screen. *How the hell did someone build a base that big under my nose? You know how, you old fool. Your own weakness. For decades you knew the council's isolationism was destructive, that one day the Confederation would pay the price, but you were too exhausted, too spent to do what had to be done. Now, it appears the day is at last here. You will do what you have to do, but now more will die because of your failure to act earlier.*

He had no idea what was waiting on Eris. The base had effective shielding, and his limited probes had only been able to gather basic information. He had a rough idea of the facility's size—big!—but he had no real data on its weaponry and defenses. And even after he'd obtained proof that someone had built a massive base right in the Sol system, the council had refused to deploy any military assets, preferring to debate endlessly rather than act.

He felt the g forces as *Tarkus* decelerated. His personal yacht was an extraordinary vessel, the indulgence of a man who, despite the massive financial losses incurred in the Fall, was still one of the richest in Occupied Space. *Tarkus* was fast and maneuverable, and she had a weapons suite capable of mounting a credible defense if she was attacked. But she hadn't been built to assault fortified bases.

Thank God, Darius Cain came prepared. Though 'prepared,' he realized was a charitable term. He suspected the council would see it differently. No doubt they would be quite alarmed to know that four of Cain's ships and two battalions of his deadly fighters had been hiding in the outer system the entire time he'd been on Mars, awaiting his orders. Though what could they do about it? Attack the Black Eagles? Not likely. Try to take Darius Cain prisoner? Then they would know the wrath of his veteran warriors. Vance didn't know Erik Teller, but he'd heard enough of Cain's second-in-command to have a pretty good idea how he would react to Darius' arrest—or kidnapping, as he would see it.

Vance didn't know what was waiting on Eris, what he would discover there about recent events and how they were related to each other. But he had been through many crises in his life, and he didn't think there was much chance the news would be good—and if it was as bad as he expected, he knew he had to move quickly.

A coup. It is amazing how life leads us places we couldn't have imagined. For all of Roderick Vance's cold devotion to duty, the last thing he'd have expected was to lead a move to seize power. The Vance's were among the earliest colonists to set foot on the red planet. One of his ancestors had been an officer on the first colony ship. Preston Vance was Roderick's great-great grandfather, and the statue of the great man still stood proudly.

Though now it presides over the cold, abandoned ruins of the Ares Metroplex, while the people still live crowded together in underground shelters. That is because I underestimated Gavin Stark...because I didn't move quickly enough, forcefully enough. I will not make that mistake again. Not ever. If I must go down in Martian history as a tyrant, so be it. But I will not see another enemy inflict such grievous harm on humanity. No matter what I must do.

*   *   *   *   *

"Evasive maneuvers. Now!" Cain sat on *Eagle One's* bridge, watching as the crew sprang into action. He'd been about to get down to the bay and spend some time with Kuragina's people, but the attack from the enemy base had stopped him cold. There were missiles coming toward his ships. Not the small, close range weapons most ships used in the post-Fall era. No, these were massive 500 megaton ship killers, the kind Augustus Garret's deadly fleets had carried in the massive wars of the previous generation. And there were a lot of them.

"All personnel, secure for high-gee maneuvers." The pilot's warning blasted from every Speaker in Eagle One. A few seconds later, Cain felt the pressure as his ship blasted at eight gees, changing course radically, trying to fool the AIs in the approaching missiles.

He knew the ships of his father's day had been capable of much greater acceleration and deceleration, but the massive tanks needed to keep men alive during such maneuvers was beyond even the resources of the Black Eagles. The fleets that had fought the Frontier Wars and the struggles against the First

Imperium had been built in an age when the labor of billions could be poured into the tools of war. But after the Fall—and the subsequent Second Incursion—the best estimate was that something less than two hundred million human beings were still alive, and half of those were scraping by at sustenance level on Earth. Ships had become smaller, and maneuvering at 35g was an unaffordable luxury, at least outside of specialized courier and spy ships.

Cain struggled to draw breath into his straining lungs. "All defensive batteries, prepare to open fire." *Eagle One* and her sister ships had been carefully designed, and Cain had spared no expense to make them as formidable as possible. Since few ships still carried long-ranged nuclear armament, it had become rare to outfit vessels with extensive point defense suites, most shipbuilders opting instead to increase primary laser batteries. But Thomas Sparks had helped Cain design the Eagle-class, and he had developed an efficient weapon that served as both point defense and a highly accurate gun for close-in fighting. So the space the Eagle vessels deployed to anti-missile use also provided them with a way to target enemy vessels with pinpoint accuracy, disabling engines and knocking opponents out of the fight.

But now, Cain was just grateful he'd ignored the calls to eliminate the point defense entirely. His embrace of an unorthodox design was about to save his life—and those of 1,500 of his Eagles. At least he hoped it would.

"Defensive batteries live, sir. Targeting AI is engaged."

Cain could hear the strain in his tactical officer, but also the strength. He doubted there was another group of spacers anywhere who could match his people at eight gees. Eagles were Eagles, whether they landed on a planet clad in powered armor or operated the ships that got them there.

The door of the main lift opened, and a man in a powered chair slid out. "General Cain, if I may interrupt…" The voice was weak, the speaker out of breath as his lungs strained against the g forces. But few men were as used to combat conditions as Fleet Admiral Augustus Garret.

Darius turned his head, his gaze falling on the greatest living naval tactician in Occupied Space. "Of course, Admiral Garret."

Darius had suggested Garret come along because the old admiral had been one of his father's closest friends. It was a matter of respect…and if he was being truly honest with himself, he also did it to piss off his brother. Elias had suggested Garret remain behind on Mars where it was safe. That had rubbed Darius the wrong way. Augustus Garret was old and becoming increasingly infirm, but he was still one of the greatest warriors in human history. If Garret wanted to go into a battle, Darius Cain would carry him if need be.

"I have a few suggestions on how to deal with these missiles."

"Please, Admiral." Cain stared at the old officer. Whatever age was doing to Garret's body, it had left his magnificent mind untouched. Darius had realized that the moment he'd seen the admiral on Mars. "In fact, would you be willing to take command of the fleet? It would be a great honor. Not to mention, we all have a better chance of getting through this with you at the helm."

Garret nodded, at least as much as the crushing g forces allowed. "Yes, General Cain. I believe I can help get us through this." He paused for a second. "Thank you, General."

"The fleet is yours, Admiral." Cain forced a tiny smile. He knew whoever built the base his people were facing had clearly prepared it to face intruders. *But did you plan to deal with history's greatest admiral?*

*   *   *   *   *

Axe lay on the small bunk, struggling to breathe as the g forces pressed down hard on him. Unlike the others onboard, he was not an experienced spacer. The short trip to Mars had been his first venture outside Earth's atmosphere, and now he was on his second. He was far stronger than he had been, his gunshot wounds completely healed and the cancer that had been eating away at him reduced to a vague tenderness in his chest. But the overwhelming feeling of eight times his body weight pressing against him was almost unbearable. He couldn't imagine how Cain and his crews could actually function under such conditions.

Things had been bad enough before the missile attack. But the wild maneuvers the ship had made to avoid the nuclear explosions had almost turned him inside out. He'd vomited at least ten times. The ship's maintenance robots had cleaned most of it up, but he knew he stank from head to toe—and he felt like his insides had been ripped out and stuffed back down his throat.

He'd heard the alarm bells and felt the ship shake several times—damage from nearby detonations, he suspected. But everything appeared to be functioning normally, and the lights hadn't so much as blinked, so he figured they had gotten through with minimal damage.

None of it mattered, though. Axe knew he had to be here, no matter what danger or discomfort he faced. Vance had tried to convince him to stay behind. And Sarah Cain—and Elias. They had all told him he had no place on the mission, that if his people could be saved, the Black Eagles would see it done.

Only Darius had refrained from arguing with him. Axe had realized immediately. The commander of the Black Eagles understood him like no one else could.

Everything had been stolen from him—everyone he cared for had been kidnapped and taken to Eris. Axe suspected that nothing in Occupied Space—or beyond to the core of the galaxy—could have made Darius Cain stay behind if he'd been in Axe's shoes, and the mercenary commander hadn't even argued. Instead, he'd offered Axe a berth on Eagle One.

Axe realized Darius knew there were things worth fighting for, worth dying for—and he had not denied that right to his new acquaintance. He was grateful, and he began to understand why Cain had so many loyal followers.

Axe wondered about Ellie, about the others. And Jack. Of all of the captives from Jericho, Jack Lompoc had gone willingly, at enormous risk to himself. Indeed, they would know nothing at all about the base without Lompoc's efforts. The ex-Alliance Intelligence enforcer had redeemed himself, atoned for his old sins. Now it was time to rescue him, and the others.

Or was it all too late? Axe had to admit, even to himself, that the response of his new allies had been more than he'd dared hope for. When he'd first set eyes on the slavers' camp, he hadn't imagined it possible to assemble so much force to deal with the enemy. His initial thoughts about following the slavers and rescuing his people had been pipe dreams, fantasies with no chance of success. But now there was a real prospect of defeating the enemy and saving everyone. Saving Ellie.

But it's been almost a month now. They could all be dead. No, he thought. *No one would go to the trouble and expense of transporting them to the fringe of the solar system just to kill them. But are they still here? Or are they gone, shipped off somewhere else in the depths of space where I can never find them? Will we be able to get to them? Or will the enemy massacre them all as soon as Cain's people attack?*

*   *   *   *   *

"All batteries, cease fire." Cain stared at the screen, watching as the ship's AI reviewed the scanning data and updated the damage reports. His ships had been bombarding the surface for over an hour, targeting anything that looked remotely like a weapon. Eris was a planet about the size of Pluto, with no appreciable atmosphere—and that made surface targets highly vulnerable to lasers fired from orbit. The Eagle ships, built from the ground up to carry and support ground forces, had extensive surface bombardment batteries, and those had been put to good use.

The four Eagle ships had come through the enemy attack in far better shape than Darius had dared to hope. Eagle One had suffered minor damage from the missile barrage, and Eagle Four had taken one particularly bad hit, but overall, Garret's innovative combination of defensive fire and evasive maneuvers had brought the Eagle fleet through the missile attack with all ships fully functional. Casualties had been light—2 killed and four wounded—but Cain still felt each one.

"All batteries silent, General."

Cain had been worried the base would have orbital laser platforms and other close-in defenses, but that hadn't proven to be the case—the missiles had been its primary armament. *Whoever built it didn't imagine any ships of today could survive that kind of barrage. But they didn't plan for the Eagles...and certainly not for Augustus Garret.*

"Damage assessment?"

"Data coming in now, sir." A brief pause. "All identified weapons systems have been destroyed, General Cain."

"Very well. Bring the fleet to lower orbit, and prepare to commence the landing." Cain flipped the com switch on his chair. "Colonel Kuragina, is the White Regiment ready to launch?"

"Yes, General." Her voice was crisp and clear. "We are ready."

"Very well, start your final diagnostics, and prepare to begin landing operations in twenty minutes."

"Yes, sir!"

"And Cyn..."

"Yes, General?"

"Save a slot on the first wave. I'm going down with your people." *If that doesn't prove they have my confidence, I don't know what will.*

Chapter 21

Concourse A
Beneath the Ruins of the Ares Metroplex
Planet Mars, Sol IV
Earthdate: September, 2318 AD (33 Years
After the Fall)

Jackson Devane stood alongside one of the large structural supports, looking out over the bustling concourse. The large chamber was full of Martian civilians, going about the dreary tasks of their subterranean existence. The concourse was one of several in the underground vastness of the Ares Metroplex. It served a dual function, as a gathering place and also as a shopping pavilion. It wasn't an ideal location for his purposes, but he'd been stalking his prey for almost a week, and this was the most exposed he had been.

Devane moved slowly, cautiously, keeping his eyes fixed on his target as he worked his way closer. He needed a clean shot. There were Martian Security personnel everywhere. He'd only get off a couple rounds before they took him out.

He knew he was on a suicide mission, but he didn't care. It was an odd feeling. There were strange bursts of concern, tiny panic attacks, his psyche rebelling against the prospect of imminent death. But his conditioning countered those almost immediately. He had a purpose, and that was all that mattered. He was here to serve the Plan. And nothing else was a consideration.

Devane followed his program perfectly. He acted almost robotically, without emotion. Emotions were a waste of mental resources. He had felt them once, he knew, long ago, but the past was no longer part of him. He had memories other than his training, that was true, but they were fractured, without clear meaning. There were images too, strange scenes of other people—and of destruction, recollections of hardship, of hunger and pain. He was grateful to those who had saved him from whatever nightmare those images represented. They had rescued him from Hell, made him a part of something, and his loyalty was unshakable. He lived now only for the Plan, and dying in its service made him one with it. The small attacks of fear, they were vestiges of that terrible past, and he knew he must not allow them to deter him from his purpose.

He glanced over toward the nearest security detail. There were two of them. They were close, too close. But that was the best vantage point. He looked around the room, trying not to raise any suspicions. Mars had tight security everywhere. Indeed, he'd had a difficult time even gaining access to the colony.

No, there was nowhere else. At least he'd have surprise on his side. The small pistol wasn't an ideal assassination weapon, but it was all he had. And every meter closer he could get would improve his accuracy. He'd get a couple shots off before the guards reacted, maybe three or four at most. Then they'd take him down. The Martian Security personnel weren't just guards, they weren't police. They were military units, and well-trained ones at that. The Confederation's army had assumed all civilian security duties after the Fall, he remembered from the mission dossier, and they had never relinquished that responsibility.

He turned slowly, taking one last glance at the two guards.

One of them will kill me, he thought in passing. Then his gaze settled on a table outside a restaurant—and at the man sitting there alone. *It is time.*

*   *   *   *   *

Elias Cain sat quietly at a small table, watching the crowds go about their business. What a depressing place, he thought sadly as his eyes panned over the mostly gray walls of the large room. He was in a small café, sitting at what passed as an outdoor table, though "outside" was a relative term when you were over a kilometer underground.

It was hard for Cain to imagine people living this way, spending their entire lives scurrying through drab, colorless tunnels—no sky, no sun. He'd lived on Atlantia his entire life, a planet of magnificent coastlines, perfect blue skies, and temperatures so ideal they almost seemed artificial. But Atlantia had been spared the ravages of the Fall, most of them at least, and Mars had not.

The Red Planet wasn't a hospitable place, but before the final battles against Gavin Stark's Shadow Legions, its people had lived on the surface, under massive and beautiful domes built of pure hyper-polycarbonate. They didn't have Atlantia's windswept shorelines, but they did have the sun—and the stars. But now those domes were cracked, the perfectly-ordered little cities below now dust-covered and abandoned.

Mars isn't a poor world, even now. Why haven't they rebuilt the domes? Why do they live like this after thirty years?

He knew the answer, at least the one Roderick Vance had given him. Rebuilding the domes and rehabilitating the cities was an enormously expensive proposition—and the Martians had another priority. Since almost the day men had set foot on its red sands, their eyes had been focused on a single goal. Terraforming. One day, they had sworn, almost as one, men would walk on the planet's surface without special suits. Plants would grow and waves would crash onto rocky shores. And since the first colonies had planted themselves, the Martians had been united in this goal.

They sacrifice comfort, live their lives like rats in a maze…all so they can devote the resources to terraform the planet. Even knowing almost no one alive today will live to see the end results.

Cain hadn't believed it at first, at least not that the common people had made that choice. The wealthy, the leaders—even underground they lived in considerable luxury. Perhaps they had chosen their legacy over improved living conditions for the masses, but surely the people themselves seethed under the enforced penury. He'd imagined considerable efforts were required to suppress dissent and to keep the people in line. But then Vance had told him the Martian Council had held a plebiscite less than a year after the Fall. Eighty-four percent of the population voted to keep the terraforming program as the top priority, even at the cost of abandoning the surface cities.

Elias had never imagined that a whole population could be so farsighted…so selfless. They had sacrificed their own comforts, not for any future they would live to see, but for their grandchildren, for the generations of Martians to come.

Vance had tried to explain, telling him the quest to make Mars a habitable planet stretched back to very first colonists. Earth's close neighbor had been the only place with even the potential to become a hospitable planet. No one had doubted men would live underground and beneath domes on the other bodies of the solar system, but Mars was the true second chance, the place a forward-thinking group of people could imagine another home for mankind, a real alternative to the stifling and poverty-stricken world of Earth's Superpowers.

That had been before the warp gates were discovered, of course, before men found an entire universe full of habitable planets, but to the Martians, the dream remained, as ingrained as ever in their collective psyche. One day, their descendants would walk on the surface, feel the warmth of the sun as they breathed deeply of the oxygen-rich atmosphere. And they had remained true to that goal, through a century and a half of turmoil no one could have imagined.

Cain glanced across the room, his mind distracted from his thoughts. There was a man standing against a column. Elias wasn't sure, but he thought he'd seen him before... and now he had the feeling the man was watching him—and worse, perhaps, trying to look like he wasn't. *You're just being paranoid. Mars is one of the safest planets in space.* But still, there was something strange...

He saw the movement, even as the man made it. A wave of adrenalin surged through his body, and he pushed off with his legs, trying to dive to the side. *Fool...he's too close. You were too busy daydreaming to pay attention.* He pushed the table over, just as he saw the gun in the assailant's hand.

He twisted hard, doing what he could to move, to pull his body away from the attacker's targeting. He heard a crack, and he felt the bullet whiz by. Too close! But now he was in the air, his body moving toward the floor, unable to change direction. He felt the first impact in his leg, hard. Then another in the chest. And another.

He hit the ground hard, and his body came alive with pain. He was covered in blood and gasping for breath, his lungs struggling for air. He saw his attacker fall, shot multiple times by the guards. It was a hazy image, distant, dark. And then everything went black.

*   *   *   *   *

"How bad is it?" Sarah Cain burst into the operating room. Her stomach felt like it was clenched into a knot, but her mind was clear. When they'd told her Elias had been shot, she'd wanted to act like a mother, to burst into tears and fall to pieces. But she'd been a Marine trauma surgeon for far longer than she'd been a parent, and she reacted to this crisis as she had to all the others she'd faced.

"It's bad, Dr. Cain." The Martian surgeon didn't look up from table as he spoke. His hands were moving quickly, and his face was twisted into a frown of concentration. "He was hit in three times, and each shot is critical."

Sarah moved forward, sliding past two of the medical technicians, forcing her way to the table. She knew she had no surgical credentials on Mars, that what she was doing was technically illegal, but it was her son on that table, and anyone who tried to stop her was going to see the Marine side—up close and personal.

Her eyes looked down on his blood-covered form, lying motionless under the surgical lights. She felt a momentary wave of panic, of inconsolable distress. She'd seen thousands of grievously wounded men and women, but this was her son. But she forced it back. She wasn't a mother now, not a woman—she was the most experienced trauma surgeon in Occupied Space, the single person most able to save Elias. As long as she kept it together.

She realized immediately the Martian surgeon was right. All three wounds were critical. Indeed, there was no way to deal with them all, not in time to save Elias' life.

"Take off the leg," she barked after a few seconds.

"But we're trying to…"

"Take it off," she repeated, more forcefully. "The femoral artery is gone, and we don't have time to mess with it. Amputate, and we can focus on the two bullets in the chest… before they kill him." Sarah had served decades in the Corps' field hospitals, and she'd seen virtually every way a human body could be mangled. Surgery on the front lines was a different discipline than it was in civilian hospitals, and her mind had been honed into a razor, ready to make snap decisions. A few seconds could be the difference between life and death, and she wasn't about to waste any now. Especially when the leg was going to be a total loss anyway. "We'll just regenerate later. But first we have to save his life."

Save my son's life.

*   *   *   *   *

Elias Cain felt like a herd of Arcadian prairie cattle had stampeded over his body. *Still, feeling anything is better than feeling nothing*, he thought grimly. He'd been lost for the first minute or so after he awoke, woozy and distracted. But he quickly got his bearings. He remembered the attack in the concourse—the shooter, his own anger with himself for hesitating too long before acting, the shots impacting his body…

"I'm glad you're finally awake." The medical AI had alerted Sarah that her son had regained consciousness, and she walked into the room wearing a rumpled set of scrubs. "We put you under pretty deep. Your body needed the time to start to recover."

Elias looked up at his mother. "You operated?" He forced a smile. "I should have known. But aren't you a little rusty?"

Sarah smiled. Joking was a good sign. But… "Elias, we had to take your left leg. It was the only way to save you." Her eyes focused on the distressed look on his face as he reached down, feeling for the leg that was no longer there.

"We can regenerate it, Elias. It's a routine procedure." A pause then: "Your father regrew both of his legs, after all… and half his insides too."

Cain's face had momentarily turned into a mask of horror, but when she mentioned his father he almost laughed. He was distressed about the leg certainly, but he was well aware he'd be as good as new, despite the reputed…discomfort…of the regen procedure. And he'd always been amused by the story of how his parents had met. By all accounts, there had been no more than half of Erik Cain left when he'd found his way onto her operating table. Yet he'd walked out of that hospital and gone on to become the legendary Marine general. And Elias remembered his father's daily ten kilometer jogs down the beach each morning, proof enough that his regenerated legs served him well.

"What about the guy who attacked me?"

"The guards killed him, I'm afraid." She frowned.

Elias was well aware his mother had no pity for anyone who tried to harm her family, but he suspected she knew as well as he did that, with the assassin dead, it would be almost impossible to discover who had been behind the attempt. And whoever wanted him dead had come close the first time—and they would almost certainly try again.

Who could it be? He tried to think if he had any enemies back on Atlantia, criminals or other adversaries looking to settle a score. *No, no one with a reach that extends to Mars. Then who?*

He thought for a few minutes, and he suspected his mother's silence suggested she was doing the same. Finally, he moved his head, slowly, painfully, and looked up at her. "Is it possible this is related to the other incidents?" he asked, his tone doubtful. It didn't make any sense, not really. But it was all he could think of.

Chapter 22

Outside Unidentified Base
Planet Eris, Sol XIII
Earthdate: September, 2318 AD (33 Years
After the Fall)

"Companies C and D, form a skirmish line now. Squad weapons deployed every twenty-five meters." Cyn Kuragina was moving forward at a moderate walk, about as fast as she could maneuver safely on the frozen oxygen and methane that covered Eris' frigid surface. The Mark VIII combat armor had been designed for battle in any conditions, even in space itself, but it took a lot of extra care to operate in environments as hostile as Eris.

The two companies had been the first wave, and she'd had them formed up in a defensive cordon. But now the rest of 1st Battalion was down, and the first two companies of Second Battalion would hit ground in five minutes. She'd been afraid the enemy would attack and try to pinch out her LZ, but they hadn't made a move. If it hadn't been for the energy readings coming from inside the base—and of course the missile attack when the fleet was approaching—she'd have guessed the facility had been abandoned. There was no fire, no sign of any troops in defensive positions on the surface, no communications.

Now it was time to advance. Despite appearances, she knew there were enemies inside, and from the size of the base, she expected she'd have her hands full when they made their move. *Maybe they're trying to mess with my head, get me to drop my guard. They should live so long...*

"Companies A and B, occupy the defensive perimeter around the LZ until the first wave of 2nd Battalion is down. Then advance in support." She looked out over the eerie terrain, an endless plateau of nearly monochrome gray. She knew it was midday, but Eris was so far from Sol, visibility was poor, no better than dusk on Earth. Still, with the magnification turned up on her visor, she had a pretty good view of the base. There were damaged areas, sections where the fleet had destroyed weapons installations. She knew General Cain had ordered intensive scans, and that they had shown no remaining gun emplacements. But she was well-aware that orbital scans were far from perfect. If the enemy wanted to hide something badly enough, chances were they could.

She continued forward, moving a bit more quickly than she suspected she should. She wanted to get up to her forward positions and take a better look around. She had to decide where her people would hit the base and force their way in. The enemy shielding and jamming had prevented more than a cursory scan—enough to find obvious weapons, but not close to coming up with any reasonable guesses about the interior. Ideally, she'd break in as near the control center or vital engineering facilities as possible. But with the sketchy intel she had, she was just as likely to blast her way into the kitchens.

She stopped and stooped down behind a small rock outcropping. There wasn't much cover around the base, and it seemed as good a spot as any. She scanned the exterior of the facility, looking for something, anything that might be a good ingress point. But the enemy saved her the trouble. Suddenly, access ports opened all along the wall facing her people, and files of armored soldiers came pouring out.

"Eagles," she said calmly, grimly, "…open fire."

*   *   *   *   *

Darius Cain was lying flat on his belly, his assault rifle extending forward as he picked off the approaching enemy targets. It wasn't an easy position for a man in powered armor, but Cain and his Eagles had mastered it well. The ground surrounding the base was flat and open, with little natural cover. And, armored or not, a soldier was a much smaller target lying down.

The enemy troopers were proficient too, though their doctrine appeared to be more tolerant of casualties than Cain's was. They were advancing, pushing forward in fairly dense formations and raking his positions with concentrated fire. It was a good tactic for maximizing the intensity of the ordnance brought down on his people, but it was suicidal against soldiers as good as the Eagles. His people blazed away at the columns, their well-drilled marksmanship dropping hundreds of the enemy in just a few minutes.

But there were more coming, thousands, he guessed. The base was massive for a reason it seemed. For the second time in a few months, Kuragina's forces were fighting an enemy that vastly outnumbered them. But they were holding firm, using what little terrain there was to the fullest and coloring the gray surface of Eris with frozen sprays of blood.

He stared at the scanning reports coming in, the first close shots of the enemy soldiers. He had seen images like this before. On Lysandria. There had been no reason to suspect any relationship between Lysandria and Eris, but Cain found that he wasn't surprised to find one. Indeed, for no quantifiable reason beyond gut feeling, he'd expected a link. And now he had it. Whatever was going on was widespread, something massive in scope…and probably a threat to all of

Occupied Space.

Cain remembered the savage fighting on Lysandria, and he had no intention of allowing this to turn into another fight to the finish, not if there was anything he could do to prevent it. His people had endured a bloodbath on Lysandria, and he had no stomach for another one.

"Kuragina, hold your positions. Under no circumstance are you to advance without my express order."

"Yes, sir." He could hear the stress in her voice. She was dead center in the line, and that was where the heaviest enemy concentrations were headed.

"And Cyn, I want your people to get every drone ready to launch when I give the word. Every last one."

"Yes, General."

Cain flashed a thought to his AI, opening a com link to the flagship. "Eagle One, is Admiral Garret still on the bridge?"

"I'm here, Darius." Garret's voice was raw, hoarse, but there was a feral quality to it as well. Augustus Garret had a pleasant, easygoing personality—except on the bridge of a warship in battle, where he became the angel of death. "What can I do for you?"

"You think you could hit the area in front of this base without frying my people?"

There was a short pause, no doubt Garret checking the scanning data. "It's tight, Darius, but I think I can manage it. There's some risk, but probably less than you fighting without support."

"Do it." Darius Cain was many things, but indecisive wasn't one of them. "Give me thirty seconds, and then hit them as hard as you can."

*   *   *   *   *

Cyn Kuragina crouched behind the small rock and watched as the Eagle fleet pulverized the enemy positions in front of her line. Eris had almost no atmosphere, nothing to disperse the laser energy of the massive projectors now blasting away from orbit. The near-vacuum was almost devoid of particulate matter, so the lasers were mostly invisible, apparent to onlookers only when they slammed into the ground, obliterating a cluster of enemy troops and vaporizing the frozen oxygen and methane.

She was impressed with the discipline of the enemy soldiers. They ignored the heavy bombardment, taking their losses and continuing to advance. There was no rout, no panic, just a grim movement forward, through the deadly assault. Their dense columns were ravaged by the fleet's heavy weapons, but it didn't slow them at all.

"All units, prepare to fire on my command." She gazed out with icy eyes, watching the survivors reform and continue their advance. *That's the smart move*, she thought. *Staying where they were—or even retreating—would only leave them in the target zone longer. Moving toward us shuts down the fleet's fire. This is about as pinpoint as orbital barrages get, but once they get within 500 meters, Garret's going to have to silence the guns…or risk hitting us too.*

She glanced up at her display. The enemy line was 800 meters away, well within range of her fire. Normally, she'd wait until they were closer, hit them with a morale-crushing blast of fire at 500 meters. But that was a strategy for fighting planetary militias and other mercenary companies, troops whose morale could be broken by massive sudden casualties. She doubted that would work here, and the sooner her people started firing, the more casualties they would inflict.

They are coming through Garret's barrage in good order, as sharp and resilient as we could have managed. We're not going to break their will easily. Or at all. We're going to have to kill every one of them. Just like on Lysandria.

"All units…fire!"

*   *   *   *   *

"Let's go, Eagles! Into the breach!" Cain leapt forward, racing toward the shattered wall of the base. Garret's barrage had blown a 50 meter opening, and Darius Cain was the first man through, his assault rifle in hand, spewing death in front of him as he ran.

The sight of their commander charging alone into danger worked the rest of the Eagles into a wild frenzy. They chased after him, pouring into the facility, pushing ahead and forcing Darius behind them, interposing themselves between him and whatever waited in the unknown depths of the station.

The battle on the surface had been short but extremely bloody. Garret's bombardment savaged the enemy formations, inflicting casualties as high as 50% in some sections of the line. But the survivors continued their advance, ignoring losses and moving straight toward the Eagle positions.

The relentless enemy advance would have shaken many forces, Cain knew. Planetary militias, half-hearted mercenary companies, even veteran armies. But they weren't facing any of those. The force arrayed against them consisted of Black Eagles, and Cain's deadly soldiers had stood firm, unwavering, firing mercilessly and ignoring their own losses.

The battle had raged for half an hour, and in the end it even came down to hand-to-hand combat in a few places. The Eagles had inflicted damage that would have broken any normal force, but still the enemy fought on. When their lines were severed, they continued the struggle in small units and groups. When those were gunned down they fought alone, and when their ammunition was exhausted they charged toward the nearest Eagles brandishing their molecular blades.

Cain was always rock solid in combat, but this was the closest he'd ever come to being shaken by an enemy's intensity. When it was all over, there were almost 3,000 dead in front of the Eagles' battered lines—and a third of Kuragina's people had been killed or wounded.

He ran forward as his Eagles streamed around him, spreading out through the facility. The enemy soldiers were determined to fight to the death, and that's exactly what Cain's people were going to give them.

*   *   *   *   *

"We have to contact whoever is attacking the station and surrender." Barkley's voice was raw and filled with fear. "Before they blast through the door and kill us all."

Grax nodded. "I'm with you, Pete." Grax turned and looked out over the 150 or so others in the room. "Is everybody with us?" he shouted.

A chorus of yesses answered him.

"We need to get out of here." The Buyers had directed all the slaving crews on Eris to the bunker when the attack began, over a hundred others besides Grax's crew. They'd all obeyed without a second thought. They were used to rounding up helpless survivors, not facing armored soldiers, and to a man they'd rushed to the safety of the bunker. It was only after they'd gotten there that Grax realized they were locked in. It was a refuge certainly—but a prison too.

"Let's see if we can break out." Barkley was looking at Grax, but he turned to stare out across the room. "Grab this table." He gestured to his right. "Let's try to break down the door."

There was a general movement forward, and a dozen men, about half of them from Grax's and Barkley's crew, crowded around, lifting the heavy metal table.

"To the door," Barkley shouted, his voice strained from the exertion. Even with twelve men holding it, the long table was extremely heavy.

They ran toward the door, slamming into it with the table.

There was a loud crash, but the hatch held firm. "Turn it onto its side," Barkley said. The table was wider than the door, and the walls around the hatch itself had absorbed much of the force.

"Now...again." The crowd surged forward again, slamming into the door harder, bringing all of the force to bear. The hatch was dented, but still it held.

"Again," Barkley yelled, and the mass surged forward once more, pushing hard with all their strength.

*   *   *   *   *

Cyn Kuragina swung around, squeezing the trigger on her assault rifle as she did. Two enemy soldiers dropped, each with a pair of holes in the visors of their armor. Even without AI-assisted fire control, Kuragina was a crack shot. But in her armor, with the computerized presence assisting her, she almost never missed.

Her people had been moving through the facility, sweeping for the last of the enemy troopers and searching for the control room or some other vital facility. She knew General Cain wanted prisoners, but the enemy soldiers didn't surrender—indeed, they didn't stop fighting for an instant. Not until they were dead or incapacitated.

Dan Sullivan's voice blasted out of her com. "Colonel, I think we found the main engineering section."

Her eyes snapped up to her display. Sullivan was fairly close to her location. "Have you secured the position?"

"Most of it, Colonel. There's a group of enemy soldiers barricaded in what looks like the central core. They've got a heavy autocannon in there, and they're really fortified. I wanted to check with you before I did anything. I don't have any heavy ordnance here, just three squads, and they're pretty shot up."

She looked again at the display. Sullivan had 24 troops, including himself. An autocannon with a good crew could drop them all in a confined space like that.

"Set a cordon around the enemy position, Captain, but do not assault…" He eyes were scanning the OB scrolling across her display. "…I'll send down some heavier backup."

"Yes, Colonel."

"I want to know immediately if they do anything but sit where they are. Understood?"

"Understood."

"Kuragina out."

She turned around and walked back ten meters to the last intersection. She turned right, heading for Sullivan's position, activating her com as she did. She didn't have much heavy ordnance in the base itself—and no time to bring anything in from farther away.

Should I just send Sullivan's people in? At least half of them will die if I do.

She flipped on her com. "General Cain, I think we found the engineering section, sir. But there's a problem…"

*   *   *   *   *

Barkley was leaning over, gasping for breath. He felt like he was going to vomit, but he managed to hold it back. He and his dozen companions had slammed at the door with the table until they dropped it from sheer exhaustion. The hatch was dented and scratched, but it was still in place. And they were still prisoners.

"Maybe they just don't want us wandering out of here and getting in the way." The voice came from the center of the room. Barkley turned and looked. It was Steve Weld, the leader of one of the other teams. His crew was smaller than the one Grax and Barkley led, but he'd been in the game just as long.

"Maybe." Barkley was still panting as he tried to speak. "But what if they lose that fight going on out there? Then what?"

Weld didn't answer. Barkley took another deep breath and then yelled, "We need another group up here." He waved his arms. "Grab the table...let's go."

He stepped aside, allowing those who responded to go past him. He almost reached down and grabbed the table himself, but he knew he was spent. And the job required every bit of strength they could muster. That meant someone fresh had to take his place.

He turned and looked toward the door, but he froze halfway. There was a sound. It was barely audible but he caught in anyway, some kind of hissing noise from the ceiling. Then he saw people start dropping.

He spun around. "Gas!" he shouted. But it was too late. Most of the others had already fallen, and he felt the strange odor enter his nostrils. He felt panic seize him, but that only lasted a second or two. Then everything went black.

$$* \quad * \quad * \quad * \quad *$$

Axe moved through the corridor, stepping over debris and the occasional enemy body. He'd been begging for Cain's permission to follow his people into the station, and the Eagles' commander had finally relented. Cain's hesitancy had been understandable. Axe wore only a survival suit, enough to keep him alive on Eris, but not much protection in a fight. But now, the station was mostly secured.

His stomach was twisted into a knot, and he could hear his heart beat pounding in his ears. Against all odds, he had managed to follow his people. Were they here? Was Ellie here?

He tried to control his expectations. The battle had been an enormously savage one, and there were thousands dead. Perhaps he had come all this way only to find his people dead, killed in the struggle or executed by their panicked captors.

Still, his excitement drove him on. Even this chance had seemed an impossibility a few weeks before. And maybe, just maybe…

Roderick Vance was walking next to him. The Martian spy had insisted on coming along. Axe knew that Vance was just as anxious to get a look at the mysterious facility that had operated for so long undiscovered right under the nose of the Confederation, though his reasons were different.

Vance stepped ahead, and he motioned for Axe to follow him around the corner. The Earther assumed Vance was getting instructions on his com unit, perhaps even from General Cain. He felt a flush of excitement. Maybe Cain's soldiers had found the captives!

Vance stopped abruptly. He hesitated for a few seconds then he turned around. "Axe…" he said, his tone grim.

Axe felt his heart sink. "The captives?"

Vance stared through the clear visor of his helmet, and his expression was one of sympathy. "The Eagles found a room with several thousand prisoners." He paused again, then croaked, "They're all dead, Axe. They were gassed."

Axe felt all the strength drain from his body. His legs went weak, and he reached out to grab the wall so he didn't fall down. *No. No, please…not after all this…*

"Axe, we have to go down there." Vance put a gloved hand on Axe's shoulder. "We need to see if you can identify any of your people.

*   *   *   *   *

"Be careful, Bull." Cain was standing in the hallway

outside the engineering section. Sullivan's people had held the room inside, but he'd pulled them back. "Just blast the door, and get the hell out. No heroics. You understand me?"

"Yes, General." Bull Trent was standing next to Cain holding a heavy rocket launcher. It was a two person weapon for anyone else.

When Cain had asked for volunteers, he wasn't surprised when Bull Trent had been the first to step forward. The massive non-com was on his short list as one of the best of the Eagles. He'd considered making Trent an officer several times, but the man was the perfect sergeant. He was at his best working closely with his men, and Cain had worried he'd take the best non-com he had and turn him into a mediocre lieutenant. It didn't make a lot of sense at first glance, but he'd seen it happen before, too many times.

Darius Cain wanted his soldiers operating at peak efficiency, and at whatever rank they performed best. He didn't like to cheat his people, and he'd long ago awarded the veteran sergeant a triple share of the pay and spoils. But he kept him where he was, in command of a crack platoon...and ready to respond when Cain needed someone for a special job. Like this one.

"The rest of you, we charge the second the rocket goes in."

"We?"

It was Teller on the com. Cain turned around to see his second in command standing a few meters away.

"Please tell me you're not seriously thinking about going along?" he asked, with a fatigue in his voice that suggested he already knew the answer.

"Yes, I'm going, Colonel. Whoever built this base, they are the same pieces of shit who hit us on Lysandria...and wiped out one of our platoons on Karelia. I want to see what they've got firsthand."

Teller sighed. "Well, I know better than to argue." He reached around and pulled the assault rifle from his back. "So,

I'm going with you."

*   *   *   *   *

Vance had seen his share of horrors, and he'd long before realized there were some things so terrible, you simply never became desensitized to them. The hold stretching out before him was one of them. There were bodies everywhere, two thousand at least. They'd been crammed together in the room, and it looked like they'd fallen in place.

That's how nerve gas works, Vance thought grimly. He imagined a life where he wasn't so familiar with the tools of mass killing, but he knew it was far too late for that. Vance wasn't a soldier, but he'd seen just about every way men could devise to slaughter each other. And he knew soldiers, some of the very best, and he'd seen firsthand what the years of war did to them. Courage and devotion to duty were all well and good, but no man could witness unspeakable horror day after day, watch friends die in the fires of battle, and not be changed by it…damaged.

Axe was trying to make his way across the room. There was nowhere to step without climbing over the grotesquely intertwined bodies, but he worked his way across the room, pulling aside the corpses, staring into cold dead eyes.

"Anyone?" Vance's voice was soft, sympathetic.

"No," came the reply. "Not one." There was hope in Axe's voice. "I've been around the room twice, and I haven't seen anyone I recognize." He stared across the room at Vance. "They're not here," he said, trying to stand up amid the heaps of bodies. "They're not here! They must have been sent somewhere else." It was news that would have crushed him an hour before. He had no idea where his people were…where Ellie was. But right now, anyplace was better than this horrible execution chamber.

"They're not here," he repeated loudly.

*   *   *   *   *

Cain stood in the room, surrounded by the bodies of the enemy. Trent had managed to score a bullseye with the rocket launcher, and he'd done it without getting hit. The rocket exploded in the room, giving Cain's people a chance to rush the door before the enemy could recover and blow them away as they entered.

It had worked, after a fashion, at least. The Eagles had six dead and another ten wounded, including Cain himself, who had taken a shot to the arm. But he knew it could have been worse, much worse.

"You should get to the infirmary, sir." It was Ernesto Alcabedo, the commander of Cain's bodyguard. There was a pall of guilt hanging over his voice. There wasn't much the veteran could have done to prevent his commander from charging headlong at the enemy, but it was apparent he still viewed Cain's wound as a symbol of his own dishonor.

"I'm fine, Ernesto. It's just a scratch." He slapped the captain on his back with an armored hand. "And stop acting like you did something wrong. I'm fine."

He turned and looked out over the room. It was huge, probably 40 meters square, filled with equipment and machinery. His people were moving around, checking the enemy wounded. Cain's mind drifted back to Lysandria, to the booby-trapped armor.

"Be careful with those wounded," he said into the com. "Remember Lysandria." *Yes*, he thought. *Remember Lysandria...*

He felt a cold pit in his stomach. He flashed a thought to the AI, opening the general com line. "Eagles, this is General Cain. All personnel are to move to the surface at once and prepare to evacuate to the fleet. I repeat, all personnel are to evacuate immediately."

"What is it, Darius?" It was Teller, on their private line.

"Just a hunch, Erik, but an enemy who would booby-trap its soldiers' armor…"

"Would do the same to a base…" Teller finished his friend's thought. "You're right. Let's get everybody out of here. Now!"

*   *   *   *   *

The battle was over, the slaving ring that had brought unimaginable misery to thousands of Earth survivors had been destroyed. But there was a heaviness in the air, not just because of the casualties, but because the victory was so incomplete, at least in terms of providing answers. Whoever was behind the operation—and the attacks on the Eagles and the other unexplained incidents—was still out there, still a deadly threat. And virtually a complete mystery.

Cain's intuition had saved his Eagles once again…most of them, at least. The base had indeed been booby-trapped, but most of his people were on their way back to orbit—or at least in cover at a safe distance—when the 500 megaton warhead detonated. The base was obliterated…and another 47 of Cain's people, the only ones who hadn't gotten out in time, were killed. Their deaths tore at him. If he'd paid more attention, if he'd only realized the danger sooner… But the evacuation had saved almost a thousand Eagles—including Teller and himself. Not to mention Roderick Vance and Axe.

"I'm sorry we were too late to rescue your people, Axe." Darius Cain put his other thoughts aside and rested his heavy gloved hand gently on the Earther. Axe didn't have armor, and Cain knew he could break his new friend's shoulder if he wasn't careful. "But don't give up hope. I am going to put all my resources to tracking down whoever is behind all of this." He paused, trying to make his voice as convincing as possible.

"We may yet find them."

Axe nodded. "Thank you, General. For everything." He hesitated. "If you don't mind, I'd like to go with you. There is nothing left for me on Earth, and whatever chance there is of finding my people, I'd like to be part of it."

There was a hint of hopefulness in Axe's voice, though Cain rather doubted its sincerity. The residents of Jericho, including Axe's wife, were lost now, somewhere among the thousand inhabited worlds of humanity. Finding them alive was an enormously unlikely proposition, and Axe struck Cain as a realist, not unlike himself. Still, he hoped his new friend could find some solace in self-deception, and in the well-meaning lies from those around him. Cain always faced everything head on in his life, cut through to the cold reality of each situation. It was an exhausting way to live, and if Axe could continue under the belief that he would find his people, Darius didn't see the harm in it.

"You are welcome, Axe. There is always room for another good man among the Eagles."

*   *   *   *   *

Cain was standing in Eagle One's cargo hold, facing away from Vance and staring at a pile of weapons his troops had collected from the enemy dead down on the surface. The hasty withdrawal had severely limited what they'd been able to bring back to the ship, and these few guns were just about all he had to go on in tracking down the enemy.

"I have faced fanatics before, but I have never battled an enemy that murdered their own wounded soldiers. Even to strike at an enemy." Darius' voice was soft, hollow. His Eagles gave him their loyalty, followed him into one incarnation of hell after another. He couldn't imagine using them in such a callous and calculating way.

"I have seen it." It was a woman's voice, and it came from behind him. There was a haunted sound to it, as if the speaker was recalling past horrors.

Darius turned to see Catherine Gilson standing just inside the door next to Roderick Vance. Her shuttle had just docked with Eagle One, and Cain had left orders for her to have the run of the ship.

"And your father did too, Darius." She paused, as if she didn't want even to utter the words in her mind. "The Shadow Legions. They killed all their wounded, just to keep them from falling into our hands."

Darius stared at her silently for a few seconds. "But the Shadow Legions were destroyed." Another pause. "And my father killed Gavin Stark."

"Yes, he did, Darius."

Cain took a deep, slow breath. He looked back at Gilson, then at Vance. "These forces can't have any connection to the Shadow Legions, can they? Or to Stark? How is that even possible?"

They both returned his gaze, but neither said a word.

"They don't look like clones," Darius said.

"No, I don't think they are clones," Vance said matter-of-factly. The Shadow Legions only had a few genetic strains, and within each they were virtually identical. The bodies here are all different. This is not the same thing we faced thirty years ago." Vance looked up at Darius. "I have no idea who they are."

"I don't either," Cain said grimly, staring back at his two companions. "But I'm damned sure going to find out."

Epilogue

The prisoner stood silently, staring up at the single, tiny skylight on the ceiling, ten meters above. It was covered most of the time, denying him even the faintest reminder that there was a universe outside his cell. But today it was unblocked, and a few faint rays of sunlight poked down to the hard stone floor, lighting his hellish little world. He wondered why it existed at all. Perhaps because one needed to be reminded of something from time to time to experience a true sense of loss from its absence.

He had been here a long time, though with no day, no night, he had lost touch with the passage of time. Years, he knew, must have passed, but he had no idea how many. For all that time he'd fought off the forces that had conspired to break him. The loneliness, the pain of constant beatings and torture, the boredom. The boredom…in some ways that was the worst of it. He had been an active man, and the countless days and nights—weeks and months—sitting in the endless darkness with nothing to do had come closer to destroying him than anything else his captors had done.

He heard the familiar sounds, the room's only door opening slowly. It was one of the few regular routines, and he'd come to depend on it in ways…even though it often signaled another beating. But it also meant food—on the days they chose to feed him. And a glimpse of a guard delivering a bowl of gruel, or even an enforcer come to administer another unexplained beating, was a form of contact, a connection to the world outside.

"How are you today, my friend?" The tone was pleasant, but the prisoner knew it was just mockery. This visitor was his favorite, the man he suspected was responsible for his captivity...the focus of his seething anger and craving for vengeance. Visits from the Tyrant were rare. Indeed, though he had no true frame of reference, he'd have guessed the last one had been more than a year before.

He glared at his adversary but said nothing. The prisoner did not speak to his captors. He would not give them the satisfaction. They could beat grunts and howls of pain from him, but he would not answer their questions, nor converse with them in any way.

"Still silent after all these years?" Every word from the Tyrant's mouth was a mockery. Years before, the prisoner would have lunged at his nemesis, willing to risk death for a chance to kill the man he blamed for his misfortune. But his body had been so battered over the years, it no longer had the strength to fight. Indeed, his legs had been broken and haphazardly mended so many times, he could barely stand. So silence was his last line of resistance, and he'd sworn to himself he would maintain it, no matter what. He knew it was all that held him together, that if he relented it would destroy him.

"I just wanted to pay you a visit, to let you know that after all the years of housing and feeding you, the time has come for you to serve a purpose." The Tyrant leaned down, staring into the prisoner's eyes but still maintained his distance. This had been a dangerous man, and even now he still remembered the fiery madness the captive had shown when they'd first brought him here.

"Don't worry, though. It will not be too strenuous on you. Indeed, you will not even know it is happening." The Tyrant smiled mockingly. "But don't worry...you will be a great help to my plans."

He turned and walked back the way he had come, pausing at the door and looking back. "I almost forgot the best news." His eyes glared at the prisoner, revealing a hatred his voice did not convey. "Once this matter is over, you will no longer be useful. We can finally put you out of your misery." He looked around. "Though I don't know how we'll get this cell cleaned after so many years of your rotting carcass befouling it."

The Tyrant laughed, a brutal, mocking sound, as he walked out slowly, and the heavy door slammed behind him, leaving the prisoner again in his endless solitude. A few seconds later, the cover slammed over the skylight, and the captive was again plunged into total darkness.

But for all his suffering, for the torture and the endless, agonizing passage of so many years of brutal captivity, the prisoner was not broken yet. He'd ceased to struggle, curbed the urges to fight back, to lash out at his tormentors, accepting that physical resistance was something his broken body could no longer sustain. But deep inside, in the place in his mind that made him who he was, the flame of defiance still burned. It was less fiery, perhaps—colder than it had been. But it was still there. And it was fed by memories—recollections of another life, one taken from him. One he silently swore he would one day reclaim.

He stared at the closed door, still seeing the Tyrant's hated face, and in that place where the part of him that was still himself dwelled, he clung to a tenuous existence…and a single thought burned.

One day I will kill you. And I will laugh as I spit on your corpse.

Coming May 25, 2015

The Prisoner of Eldaron
Crimson Worlds Successors Book 2

Crimson Worlds Series

Marines (Crimson Worlds I)
The Cost of Victory (Crimson Worlds II)
A Little Rebellion (Crimson Worlds III)
The First Imperium (Crimson Worlds IV)
The Line Must Hold (Crimson Worlds V)
To Hell's Heart (Crimson Worlds VI)
The Shadow Legions(Crimson Worlds VII)
Even Legends Die (Crimson Worlds VIII)
The Fall (Crimson Worlds IX)

War Stories (Crimson World Prequels)

Also By Jay Allan

The Dragon's Banner

Gehenna Dawn (Portal Worlds I)
The Ten Thousand (Portal Worlds II)

www.crimsonworlds.com

26498624R00167

Printed in Great Britain
by Amazon